OUR TRESPASSES

Michael Cordell

TCK PUBLISHING.COM

ISBN:
978-1-63161-153-7

Sign up for Michael Cordell's newsletter at
www.michaeljcordell.com/newsletter

Published by TCK Publishing
www.TCKpublishing.com

Get discounts and special deals on our best selling books at
www.TCKpublishing.com/bookdeals

Check out additional discounts for bulk orders at
www.TCKpublishing.com/bulk-book-orders

To my mother, Harlene.

You mean the world to me. Always have. Always will.

"The gates of hell are open night and day;
Smooth the descent, and easy is the way:
But, to return, and view the cheerful skies,
In this the task and mighty labor lies." —Virgil (The Aeneid)

"From there we came outside and saw the stars." —Dante Alighieri
(Inferno)

1998

Ruth stood at her ironing board, working her way through a pile of clothes in the bottomless laundry basket at her feet, mindlessly sweeping the iron back and forth across a blue denim work shirt, breaking her rhythm only to fire shots of steam at particularly stubborn wrinkles. It was the same routine she began fourteen years ago, when a very practical aunt gave her the iron as a wedding gift.

The farmhouse kitchen where she toiled was small and worn, like her. At thirty-eight, she was nowhere close to being old, but her spirit was threadbare. The life of a farm wife—nothing seemed likely to improve down the road, but then again, she didn't expect it to.

She glanced over at her five-year-old son sitting on the floor with his back against the refrigerator, either for support or to cool himself in the sweltering kitchen. Wearing a tiny pair of blue overalls, he diligently rolled his toy tractor back and forth in front of him—not going anywhere, just sitting there with his thoughts, like his dad, except he was humming softly. Ed, his father, never hummed. In fact, Ed often went long stretches without making any sound at all, except the occasional clearing of his throat or a monotone request to pass the ketchup. But he definitely never hummed.

Ruth envied her son's carefree days, although she knew well enough that in a couple more years, farm chores would claim much of his free time. She also feared that as he grew older, he would have to deal with unique challenges that nobody else faced, so she didn't begrudge him his chance to sit and play while he could.

She checked the kitty-cat clock on the wall above the stove, its curled, pink pendulum tail clicking back and forth, in sync with the eyes stealing furtive glances from side to side. It was four o'clock, which meant she had two hours to finish up her ironing and get dinner on the table. As always, she would be on time.

She noticed a ripped shirt sleeve, assessing it as she ironed to see if it was salvageable with needle and thread when, without warning, her son screamed as if he were being mauled by a coyote. Startled, she jerked the iron off the shirt and muffled a yelp after burning her index finger on the hot metal.

"Good lord! What on earth's the matter with you?"

She walked over and knelt in front of him as he continued screeching at full throttle. She couldn't figure out what could be wrong.

"Boy, what in the world are you crying about? You were just sitting there. Did you—" Concern swept across her face. "Where's Jake? Where's your brother?"

When the young boy didn't answer, Ruth abandoned him as she ran to the foot of the steps leading upstairs. She listened but could only hear her wailing son in the kitchen. "Jake?" she hollered. "Jake, where are you?"

She returned to the kitchen. "Matthew, where's your brother? What's happened to him?" she asked, trying to convey calm, but all she got was another plaintive shriek. "Tell me what hurts. What are you feeling? You've got to help me, boy. What hurts? Please. Hurry!"

The child took a halting breath and pointed at his right foot. Ruth quickly examined it to make sure she hadn't missed anything, then looked out the kitchen window but saw nothing out of the ordinary. "You stay right there," she commanded. "Don't move!"

The screen door banged behind her as she stepped onto the porch of the old but well-maintained farmhouse. She scanned the property, but didn't see anything. She wheeled around and shut the front door to muffle the crying from the kitchen. Then she listened again.

They lived a mile from their nearest neighbor, but the loud grinding of Ed's tractor in the cornfield made it difficult for Ruth to hear anything else until the piercing blast of a car horn and the sound of tires skidding on gravel seized her attention. She froze, then raced down the dirt driveway toward the narrow country road.

It was a good thirty yards from the front porch to the road, and running wasn't something she had done in many years. Sweat poured down her forehead before she was halfway to the road, but adrenaline kept her moving. When she finally reached the gravel road, winded, she saw a beat-up white pickup that had stopped, its driver trying to get a stray cow to move out of the way.

She wheeled around and walked as quickly as she could toward the blood-red barn with a broken-down '68 Ford sitting on blocks next to it. Her pace slowed as this sudden exertion got the best of her. The door to the barn was open, but that didn't necessarily mean anything.

"Jake?" she said. "Jake!" The rattle of the tractor faded as her husband drove farther into the field. Finally, she heard the cries of a young boy. She trotted into the barn and found her five-year-old son, Jake, a perfect replica of the boy in the kitchen, sitting on the ground barefoot and crying as he cupped his right foot in his hands. A few drops of blood dripped from the sole of his foot through his tiny fingers, where the hay absorbed it. The culprit—a board with a protruding rusty nail—lay next to him.

He looked up at his mother plaintively and wailed, "The nail sticked my foot!"

She examined his foot after managing to pull his hands away. The nail had broken the skin, but it was more of a deep scratch than anything serious.

"What'd I tell you about wearing shoes when you go outside?" she said. "I swear you have the sense of a tadpole. I suppose now we're going to have to get you a tetanus shot. Your daddy isn't going to be happy about this."

Jake sobbed even harder as his mother pulled a couple of wadded-up tissues from her pocket and wiped his foot. She picked him up and carried him to the house, caressing the back of his head as he burrowed it into her shoulder.

"Stop your crying," she said gently. "You're going to be all right. I just wish you could figure out a way to stay out of trouble. Is that too much to ask?"

By the time Ruth pulled open the door and entered the kitchen, Jake's outburst had reduced to sniffling. As they headed toward the bathroom, Jake glanced at his brother, who was once again playing with his tractor, pushing it back and forth and humming a new tune.

ONE

Grease snapped and popped off the diner grill as Matt flipped a couple of burgers, causing them to hiss like a bucket of snakes when their uncooked sides hit the hot metal. He glanced at the fries in the deep-fat fryer, even though he already knew they were about two minutes from golden perfection.

His movements were rote, the result of having spent several years behind the blazing grill. He didn't even have to think, which was one thing he liked most about his job. He wiped the sweat from his forehead with a once-white bar rag, then took a deep swig from a bottle of Budweiser sitting on an adjacent counter.

In his late twenties, Matt avoided wearing a hair net while working, choosing instead to cover his hair with a discolored New York Yankees ball cap. He wasn't delusional enough to wear a traditional chef's hat; the small, no-star Brooklyn diner where he worked didn't merit anything that pretentious, nor did he. People assumed he must be a Yankees fan, which he didn't understand: why would he wear a ball cap from a team he liked where it was guaranteed to be ruined with grease and grime? Thus, the Yankees cap.

The door that separated the kitchen from the bustling dining area swung open and Sheri swayed in, the sharp clicks from her heels sounding like a metronome. Blond and hazel-eyed, she looked like a stunning, soon-to-be Hollywood starlet who was only waiting tables until her big break finally came. She leaned back against a table next to the grill, looking disgusted.

"Didn't I tell you? I told you!" Sheri exclaimed, her Brooklyn accent further highlighting her outrage. "The guy at table three always asks for a second refill of coffee, then never even touches it. *Ever!* What the hell?"

Matt grabbed an eight-inch butcher knife and scowled. "That son of a bitch. I'm going out there and cutting the bastard. This ends now."

"Fine," she said, holding back a grin. "I'm not saying it's a crime against humanity, but would it kill him to drink at least a little of it one time? Just once? Why get a refill if you're never going to drink it, and

4

believe me, he doesn't even take a sip. I've watched him."

"You know they have medication for your type of OCD, right?" Matt said. Sheri finally gave up a killer smile as Matt set the knife back on the counter.

A plump, balding man in his late fifties sporting a JCPenney short-sleeve dress shirt, clashing tie, and a scowl plowed through the kitchen door as if he had very important business to tackle and knew time was money. His aftershave overpowered the smell of cooking grease, which was no small feat, and possibly even combustible. His nametag said "Manager," but his demeanor said "Prick."

"Ms. Evans," he said, as if calling her by her last name sounded like something an executive would do. "Instead of standing around flirting with Matt, how about you go do some actual work?" The man puffed out his chest as though he'd made quite the astute managerial observation.

Sheri glanced over at Matt, rolling her eyes as she pushed away from the table.

"Lighten up, Stu," Matt said. "A customer changed his order. How am I supposed to know if someone now wants fries instead of coleslaw if she doesn't tell me? Don't you care anymore about giving our customers a superior dining experience?"

"Well, now she's told you, so she should get her butt back out there." Stu started turning toward the dining area door but then stopped and did a double take at Matt, pointing to the bottle. "Is that a beer?"

Matt picked up the bottle and held it toward Stu so that he could see it. "Yes, that's what it's called. Beer. Have you never had one before?"

"There's no drinking on the job, buddy." Apparently, Matt didn't merit a last name, let alone a first.

Matt took a drink, then looked at the bottle, pretending to study it. "Apparently that's not correct, Stu. There does, in fact, appear to be drinking going on."

Stu stared at Matt as if mentally sifting through all the possible managerial responses to that level of insubordination before finally settling on the easiest. "You like having a job, wiseass?"

Matt surveyed the kitchen, taking a quick visual inventory as Sheri leaned back against the table, looking intrigued to see how all of this would play out.

"You mean this minimum wage shit job where I go home every

day smelling like a human french fry? Yeah, Stu, even as a little kid I always dreamed of being a short-order cook at a crappy, low-rent diner. Please don't fire me. I'd hate to have to apply at any of the other twelve thousand Brooklyn diners that would kill to find a cook who will stay with them for years."

Stu started to respond but appeared to be at a loss for words. He looked Matt over and finally shook his head, as if this loser standing before him wasn't worth his time. "Yeah, sad to say, but this probably *is* the best job you're ever going to have."

"Says the middle-aged man with the clip-on tie," Matt said as he took another long drink of beer.

Stu glanced down at his tie, then directed his wrath back toward the waitress. "What the hell are you still doing here? Get back to work." He stomped out of the kitchen.

Sheri grinned. "Is it really a clip-on?"

Matt shrugged nonchalantly. "I look like I've ever worn a tie? I was just playing the odds."

As Sheri headed back to work, she paused at the door. "Thanks for covering for me. Don't suppose you'd let me buy you a drink after work, would you? As a thank you?"

Matt turned to the basket of fries and lifted it out of the bubbling grease. "I'd like to," he said, not making eye contact with her. "But I'm afraid I'm meeting friends for dinner later. Sorry."

Sheri looked at him skeptically, but apparently not surprised. "You and your friends sure do get together a lot. Maybe another time." She shrugged, as if she wasn't quite used to her offers being turned down, then returned to the clattering dining area.

Matt sometimes surprised himself when he did things like that. Sheri was not only beautiful, but she also seemed like a genuinely nice person, which was one of the reasons he evaded her occasional invitation to get together. A woman like that deserved someone better than him.

He tried one of the french fries from the basket, but as he already figured, they had overcooked while he was sparring with Stu. He dumped the fallen soldiers into a nearby trash can and filled the basket with a new clump of frozen fries, lowering them into the hot grease before finishing off his beer.

The burger displayed the perfect shade of blood-red after Matt's first bite. Buzz's Brooklyn Bar and Grill had little going for it in terms of ambiance, but the cook grilled a pretty decent hamburger, and the serving portion of fries was respectable.

Even though Brooklyn, his home of ten years, offered an endless array of restaurant options, he often found himself at Buzz's, where the burgers were not only cheap (an important consideration), they also satisfied some sort of primal need. Something about the place calmed him. Of course, the bourbon and Coke didn't hurt.

He usually just grabbed something from the diner to save money, but he had committed to his story of meeting friends for dinner without thinking through his lie, so here he was, pretending he had friends. Maybe it just depended on one's definition of the word "friend." Buzz's bartender, after all, knew him by drink, if not by name, so perhaps that counted for something.

Matt sat at the dimly lit bar, staring at his phone between bites as he rapidly swiped through profiles of women on a popular dating app, rarely spending more than a second or two on each photo. He told himself he was taking action by at least opening the app, although he knew he wouldn't be doing anything with it, at least not now. He thought of it more like window shopping for something he likely could never attain. Women entered from the right side of his phone's screen, then just as quickly exited through the left side, as if just passing through.

One picture, though, caused him to pause: an attractive woman with dark hair and piercing gray eyes that looked like they had seen pain. He studied her face, not looking at her profile or anything else other than her eyes.

"Finally," said a young woman sitting a couple of bar stools down from him. "I was starting to think you were being far too picky with your machine gun swiping."

She offered a sincere smile, letting him know she came in peace. She slid over to the bar stool next to Matt to look at the photo, but Matt swiped left before she could see.

"Darn," she said. "I thought we had a winner. You ever swipe right?"

"I'm just cutting out the middleman," Matt said.

"Who's the middleman?"

"Disappointment."

"Men." She shook her head and sighed. "Maybe you're not giving the women you meet a chance."

"Maybe I'm not the one disappointed."

She raised her eyebrows in surprise, perhaps not accustomed to hearing men take responsibility for relationships that went bad. She continued watching him in a way that conveyed her interest in the rest of his story, but Matt didn't feel ready for story time just yet, so she simply nodded at his response.

She exuded a sense of self-confidence that Matt felt lacking in himself. And she obviously resided much higher on the extrovert scale than him. He decided maybe a drink and a conversation with a woman didn't have to be a major production.

"But what do I know?" he offered as a way of letting her know he was open to a conversation.

"How about I take a look?" she asked brightly, holding out her hand for his phone, a genuine smile on her face. "I can give you expert feedback on your profile, which might lead to better matches. I've had more than my share of online dates. Trust me."

When Matt didn't immediately hand over his phone, she gently took it from him. Not in a pushy way, but like someone who already knew she'd end up with it anyway, so why waste her time? She clicked over to his profile and without looking at him said, "Hello, Matthew. I'm Esther."

Matt raised his shot glass and gave her a nonverbal toast before kicking back his bourbon, then watched as she scrolled through his profile, reading the information he had written about himself when he first signed up on the app. It had taken him far longer than it should have to answer the various questions, but he wanted to get it right.

She stopped scrolling and smiled.

"I like this line. 'While everyone has emotional baggage, I like to think mine is compact and would fit under the seat or in the overhead compartment.'"

"Thanks. It's not true, but thanks."

"What in the world does truth have to do with a dating profile? Tip number one: your line is clever, and that's what counts. Do you by chance work in advertising?" She held up her hand before he could answer. "Oops. Hold that thought: I think I see the problem. You say you're a short-order cook."

"Yes, but in my defense, I only did that because I'm a short-order cook."

"There you go again with that truthiness obsession of yours," she said, shaking her head. "Seriously, dude, we need to talk." She reached over and took a fry from his plate without looking for permission. "Things like that can come up after you meet. Be vague. Maybe say you're in the culinary arts."

"So women don't think I'm a loser?"

"I didn't say that." Esther looked up at the ceiling as if replaying the audiotape through her mind. "Well, okay, maybe I did."

"But what if I am a loser?"

"Then keep swiping left, but I have to be honest, you don't strike me as a loser. Believe me, I wouldn't say that unless I meant it."

"Because you're all about 'truthiness.'"

Esther offered a strong laugh, then leaned over to where she had been sitting and dragged her purse and her martini in front of her, apparently having decided their conversation was far from over.

Matt felt encouraged, which wasn't an emotion he knew well. He decided maybe it was once again time to be open to meeting someone new. Besides, she'd asked if he worked in advertising. That meant a lot to him, even if it also stirred up the disappointment that always hovered close beneath the surface. He signaled for another shot of bourbon to the bartender, who almost looked surprised to see Matt talking to another person.

"So, do I get to read your profile?" Matt asked.

Esther grabbed her bag. "Of course. Fair is fair."

As she dug into her oversized purse in search of her phone, Matt began to hear a soft buzzing in his head, a presence louder than the barely audible white noise that was usually there. He froze, staring at his empty shot glass, wanting to write it off as a case of indigestion, or perhaps too much bourbon, but he knew exactly what it was.

He just didn't want to believe it.

Esther pulled out her billfold and a small umbrella from her purse as she continued searching. "What is it about phones that makes them burrow to the bottom of bags every time? They're like little electronic gophers." She leaned closer to the bag's opening. "Don't be shy, little one," she said gently into the bag. "He seems like a nice man."

The buzzing in Matt's head continued to build as he sat up straight and alert, detecting an alarm no one else could hear. Sweat appeared on his forehead as he focused on his breathing and tried to take deep breaths, but even his lungs felt paralyzed.

A ripple of fear washed over him, a sneak preview of a larger wave that nearly pulled him off his bar stool. It had been a decade since the last severe attack, and it felt as though years of emotions would soon be crashing over him like a tsunami. He desperately wanted to get up and bolt from the restaurant, but he knew that wouldn't do any good.

He closed his eyes and tried visualizing a brick wall being put up around his brain, an exercise that had rarely failed in the past, but this wall might as well have been made of tissue paper. This attack was not going to be turned down one decibel, let alone stopped.

He tried silently reciting the internal mantra he used to know so well, but the ever-growing pressure inside his head neither subsided nor made it possible for him to keep from shifting into total panic mode. He was about to get hit with the mother of all connections, and there was nothing he could do to stop it, like being chained to railroad tracks and seeing the blinding light of a train barreling toward him.

The static in his head intensified until it sounded like a chainsaw, drowning out the background noise. His mouth felt so dry he thought he would cough dust. Nausea swept over him.

Esther finally pulled out her phone. "Ta-da! I knew I'd find it eventually. Now you can . . . Hey, you okay? Christ, you look like hell!"

The bartender appeared out of nowhere, setting a glass of water in front of Matt and joining Esther to watch him with concern. Matt looked at the water but remained focused on trying to block the noise, until deciding he needed to get away from there. Finally, he slid off his bar stool, unsteadily, and took another deep breath.

"Excuse me," he stammered in a mangled voice. "I just need to use the restroom."

Matt power-walked down a narrow hallway at the back of the bar toward the bathroom. Desperate to get somewhere private, he made a beeline to the single, unisex restroom, but encountered a locked door. He couldn't understand what was happening to him, or more accurately, he couldn't understand why it was happening.

Matt tried the door again, as if expecting a different result. A gruff voice on the other side of the door hollered for him to hold on a damn minute, but Matt didn't think he had a damn minute.

He turned and pressed his forehead forcefully against the wall, pulling the collar of his T-shirt up into his mouth and biting down hard as he closed his eyes, once again focusing on his breathing.

Deep breath in, hold it, exhale slowly. And again.

The raging emotions continued crescendoing to something stronger than he'd ever experienced before. It wasn't pain, and it wasn't anxiety; it was an all-consuming terror flooding over him.

He whipped around and pressed his back against the wall, wishing he could disappear into the paneling. His eyes shot open wide as panic coursed through his body like an open fire hydrant. He didn't know how anyone could experience something this intense and not pass out, but he was apparently not being offered that opportunity to escape.

At its peak, he clamped his hands tightly over his mouth, but they only partially muffled his guttural cry, "Nooooooo!"

Turning and then flinging himself backwards, he slammed against the opposite wall, slowly sliding down until he was sitting on the floor in a small puddle of beer. He remained paralyzed, staring at the wall in front of him. He didn't move for at least another minute, as the all-consuming fear slowly dissipated.

Esther rushed over to him.

"Oh my God, are you okay?"

He sat for another moment as he processed what he'd just experienced, panting heavily, as though he'd just run a sprint.

"Matthew, talk to me. What's going on? Are you on something? Do you need a Xanax?"

He finally spoke, more to himself than to Esther, as if he needed to hear himself say it out loud before he could believe it. "My brother's dead."

"Your brother? What do you mean your brother's dead?"

Matt shook his head, stunned by the realization of what he now knew to be true. He looked back up at a puzzled Esther.

"My brother, Jake. Someone just killed him."

TWO

Within half an hour, Matt was in his apartment, hastily hauling a suitcase out from under his bed. The lone, anemic lightbulb in his bedroom helped disguise the state of the battered, twenty-two-inch piece of brown leather luggage he had taken from his grandfather's basement after the old man's funeral. When he'd first called dibs on it ten years ago, he didn't realize he'd be needing it just a few months later. Now, after a decade, he was once again bringing it back out into the light.

The suitcase wasn't the only thing looking the worse for wear; his apartment had also seen far better days, if not decades. Frayed red curtains did nothing to complement the peeling, blue and yellow floral wallpaper that looked like something found in the bedroom of someone's great-grandmother. He guessed the college kids who lived in the building would call it vintage; he knew it was just old.

He noticed a cockroach scurrying along the baseboard, which surprised him—not that a cockroach was in the room, but that he noticed it. He would have thought he'd be used to them by now, like just another feature of the apartment, albeit exceptionally small. And moving.

He'd lived on Meeker Avenue for ten years now, six blocks from a Whole Foods he couldn't afford, and a hundred feet from the Brooklyn-Queens Expressway, which ensured his apartment, with its slipshod windows, was filled with a never-ending flow of noise, like living on the bank of a mechanical river.

The Williamsburg section of Brooklyn had cultivated the brand of being the place for hipsters, trendy shops, and avant-garde events, but that wasn't the Williamsburg Matt knew. His consisted of decrepit apartments, twelve-hour workdays, and the occasional use of the neighborhood food bank.

Not that he was complaining. He had settled into this existence willingly and wasn't trying for anything better right now. From time to time, he told himself that at some point he would make an effort to move toward the type of life he wanted. He believed he still had it within himself to get his act together, but the time never seemed right. Or he simply didn't feel he merited it yet.

He riffled through a limited option of shirts and pants in his chest of drawers, pulling out the few that looked at least halfway presentable and tossing them into the suitcase. He didn't know how long he'd be away, but he assumed it would just be a couple of days. It could be longer, though, given the circumstances.

He wished he'd had one more shot of bourbon before leaving the bar, something to help him calm down after his attack, but he had to start making plans. Plus, there would have been an endless barrage of questions from Esther. Even the bartender had looked concerned, which was no small feat given the crazy things the guy likely encountered on the job.

As he stood surveying the contents of his suitcase, conducting a mental inventory of what he would need, his cellphone rang, the caller ID displaying "Hatchett Sheriff's Dept." He waited for the ringing to stop and let the call go to voicemail.

"I already know," he said.

Matt stared out the airplane window at the green, brown, and gold patchwork quilt of land far below—a giant jigsaw puzzle comprised of nothing but large, square pieces. He was getting closer to home. Property lines and roads in Middle America were like the people who lived there—straightforward, direct, uncomplicated.

City streets extended as straight as a yardstick and had names like "First" or "A." When towns grew too large to stay within that nomenclature, the street names expanded into the arboreal or presidential series—Oak or Chestnut, Washington or Jefferson. Simply gazing down upon the square grids reminded Matt of the expectation to follow the rules and do what you're supposed to do.

He'd finally listened to his voicemail message from a Hatchett deputy sheriff. The hesitant voice was awkward but to the point: *Please give me a call; I have news about your brother.* Matt had called back just so they could check that off their to-do list.

He'd waited until early that morning before returning his mom's voicemail message and letting her know he was getting ready to board his plane. She'd almost sounded surprised to hear he was coming home for the funeral. His own brother, and she didn't think he'd come back? That made him feel terrible, a good reminder that he'd better get used to feeling like the bad son for the next couple of days.

In fairness to her, he couldn't remember the last time he'd been home. Six years at least, and that was only for a day, for his aunt's funeral. Apparently, the best way to get him to come home was to organize a funeral. There were no other draws for him in Nebraska anymore.

The roar of the jet engines comforted him, soothing his head like the waves of the ocean. It replaced the soft, white noise he'd known all his life, but had never noticed until Jake died and the sound had abruptly been silenced. He thought everyone heard something like that, but now he realized it was likely part of their connection.

The flight attendant announced the plane's impending descent into Omaha, and expressed her sincerely scripted hope that those passengers whose final destination was Omaha enjoyed a pleasant stay. He saw the chances of that happening for him as slim, although possible if he didn't leave the city.

Matt closed his tray and stuffed the book he had yet to open into his backpack under the seat. His seatmate—a personable guy who looked like some company's salesman of the month—took this opportunity to once again try to strike up a conversation, something Matt had successfully evaded most of the trip.

"You connecting in Omaha or is Nebraska your final stop?" the man asked, as if the answer greatly interested him.

Matt glanced over at him, tired, and not looking to make a friend. "Final stop."

"Business or pleasure?"

"Family," Matt said. "So I guess neither."

His seatmate thought about it for a second, then let loose a booming guffaw. "Neither! That's funny. I'll have to remember that one." The salesman put up his tray table and shifted toward Matt, not yet ready to step away from his new friend. "You get home often?"

"It's been a while," Matt said, turning and looking back out the window, abruptly ending their conversation as the plane continued its descent.

Inside the airport terminal, he stepped onto a moving sidewalk and glided past enormous images of sandhill cranes in flight, the Omaha skyline, and an aerial shot of the Henry Doorly Zoo, known for its indoor rainforest. The color red dominated the crowd of bustling travelers, people proclaiming their unwavering commitment to the University of Nebraska Cornhusker football team.

Matt worked his way to the rental car booth. A skinny young man sporting a discount suit, a home-cut hairstyle, and a great-to-see-you smile stood ready to assist in any way he could. That was one thing you could count on in Nebraska: most everyone was nice and more than happy to help.

It was already starting to put him on edge.

After a couple of hours driving down Interstate 80 in the blazing August sun, Matt exited onto Highway 28. The further he drove, the smaller the towns got and the greater the distance between them. Each town had an obligatory silver grain elevator abutting the highway, reflecting the sun like a giant, shiny thimble. The road had shrunk to a two-lane highway by mid-morning and cars were few and far between. It appeared most everyone was already at work.

On more than one occasion, Matt found himself behind a tractor chugging along at the pace of a wheelchair. The straight Nebraska roads made it easy to spot the rare oncoming car from half a mile away, so pulling into the other lane to pass the green behemoths wasn't a problem. He probably could have gotten out and pushed his car past the farmer and not been at risk of being hit by oncoming traffic.

It had been ten years since Matt left Nebraska, and none of the cornfields or lonesome windmills or herds of cattle could make him wax nostalgic. The one thing that did strike a chord, though, was the endless sky. It rose from one horizon and stretched to the other like a snow globe, the landscape uninterrupted. He could detect the curvature of the Earth at the end of the horizon.

He suddenly found himself looking forward to seeing the stars. When he left for New York, he never imagined the only thing he would truly miss was the expansive Nebraska night sky. This was especially the case after having spent time in the city; it was hard enough to spot a large patch of sky, let alone stars. But back here, he knew the stars would put on a show.

Twenty miles from Hatchett, faded billboards popped up with slogans like, "You'll Save A Lot of Dimes at Dollar Central," and "Catch Yourself the Best Customer Service at Hatchett Bait and Tackle!" He remembered a lot of the same billboards growing up; not just the businesses, but the exact same advertisements, many of them now rotting and peeling, like promotions for stores in a ghost town.

Hatchett was made up of around 1,800 people, yet it was still the largest town in any direction for over a hundred miles. Hatchett was where the country people came to do their shopping.

He used to think of his time growing up in Hatchett as just one chapter of his life. Now that he was back, he realized it was a totally different book—one that had been read, then put up on the shelf, never to be pulled down again. Yet here he was. Home.

The radio tower in the distance, with its blinking red light at the top, was the tallest structure in a seven-county radius and meant there were only a couple of miles between him and Hatchett. His gas gauge warning light flashed on about fifteen miles back. Having forgotten how few and far between gas stations were, Matt hadn't paid much attention to how much gas the car had. He felt fortunate that he was at least close to home now.

He wondered what the odds were of him feeling fortunate to be in Hatchett a second time during this trip. He felt sure Vegas would list him as a long shot.

THREE

Matt pulled into the Gas and Go on the outskirts of Hatchett. He'd have thought it abandoned if not for the lone customer at one of the pumps. Weeds the size of small shrubbery emerged from the cracks in the concrete, and it appeared the station's last paint job took place during the Nixon administration. Clearly, the place didn't feel the need to compete on anything except the price of gas.

As Matt stepped out of his car, the stench from the largest cattle feedlot in the state punched him in the nose, nearly causing him to retch. Approximately 125,000 head of cattle were corralled fifteen miles north of town, but depending on which way the wind blew, residents of Hatchett either enjoyed the fresh country air, or felt like they lived next to a factory that manufactured cow shit. When he was younger, Matt had asked his mother if she thought the feedlot owner ever felt bad inflicting that sort of odor on the town, but she just shook her head and said that to him, it probably just smelled like money.

A cherry red Chevy pickup with a shiny silver horse trailer sat at the adjacent gas pump, with two long horse tails hanging over the trailer's back half-door. A rotund man wearing dirty cowboy boots and a spotless straw cowboy hat nodded to Matt.

"How's it going?" the man said as he pulled a round can of chewing tobacco from his shirt pocket.

"Good," Matt said.

Stuffing a small wad of tobacco under his lip, the man checked out Matt's car. "Where 'bouts in Colorado you from?"

"It's a rental. I'm visiting from New York."

"No kidding," the man said, as if Matt had just told him he was a member of the royal family. "Long way from home."

"I'm originally from Hatchett. Back for a visit."

The cowboy tipped his hat after he put the gas nozzle back and secured his gas cap. "You picked a hot time to come a callin', but I hope it's a good one."

Matt watched the man aim a shot of brown spit into a trashcan, then heave himself up into his pickup and drive away, lifting his index finger as he passed. Midwesterners could ask questions of a total stranger and not sound intrusive. In New York, the immediate response to those questions would have been "Who the hell wants to know?" He needed to get used to total strangers striking up conversations now that he was back home.

While the numbers on the gas pump clicked upward, Matt looked out at Highway 28 cutting through Hatchett. It was the major road connecting the small town to the rest of the world, but there was hardly any traffic on it. All it needed was a tumbleweed tumbling down the middle of the road.

Across the street, the time and temperature sign at the Hatchett City Bank—a building the size of a 7-Eleven—claimed it was 103 degrees outside, but that seemed far too optimistic. Sweat trickled off him like a soaker hose, even though he was just standing next to his rental. He couldn't imagine working out in the fields on a day like this.

Staring mindlessly at the alternating time and temperature displays, Matt heard work boots striding quickly toward him from behind. He turned with only enough time to see the red-stitched name "Teddy" on the station attendant's oily blue coveralls before the man's fist plunged into Matt's stomach, doubling him over.

He staggered backward against the side of his car, raising his hands in a bewildered, feeble plea for a truce as he tried straightening up, but Teddy shoved him hard in the chest.

"Hey! What the hell?" Matt gasped, trying to find a breath. Teddy stood at least six-and-a-half feet tall but couldn't have weighed more than 180 pounds. He had the frame of Shaggy from Scooby Doo and the crew cut of a cowboy. His hair was the color of a sparrow.

Matt pushed himself away from the car, but froze when Teddy pulled a foot-long crescent wrench from his coveralls and raised it like a club.

"Whoa, whoa!" Matt said, raising his hands as if they had any chance of preventing his skull from being crushed.

"I told you if I ever heard you was sniffing around my sister again, I'd bust you up good, and I meant it." Teddy cocked back the wrench, his jaw clenched tight as a vice, his narrowed eyes leaving no doubt about his intention.

"I don't even know your sister."

Teddy shook his head like a horse and muttered, "You're a real shitty piece of work, Jake. I should have cracked your head open the first time you hurt her, you son of a bitch."

Matt waved his hands in front of his face. "I'm not Jake! I'm his brother!"

"Yeah, right. I'm going to make sure that next time you remember to steer clear of Lorraine. You don't give a damn about anyone but yourself. You know you got this coming."

Teddy swung the wrench toward Matt, who narrowly evaded the strike by sliding down the car to the ground. The wrench put an impressive dent in the car's roof.

"I'm sorry, but I swear, I'm not Jake! I'm sorry!"

Teddy paused, perplexed, then stepped back before holstering the wrench in his deep pocket.

"You really aren't Jake, are you? I never heard he had a twin."

Matt cautiously pulled himself up off the ground and leaned back against his car, relieved to finally draw a full breath again. "Well, he does."

"How about that? You're like the only person I ever met who can honestly say it was your evil twin who did something. My bad." He turned and started moseying on back toward the station as if he'd just finished pumping Matt's gas.

Matt wiped the gravel from his hands. He had barely made it across the Hatchett city limits, and already he just about got busted up. He called out to Teddy, "Hey, how come you suddenly believed me?"

Teddy turned back. "Cause you said you was sorry. Don't matter how cruel Jake is, he'd rather be hung by his balls and beaten like a piñata than say he's sorry about nothing. That word don't come out of him, no how. Doubt he even knows what it means."

Teddy continued toward the station, hollering out to Matt as he walked away, "Tell that piece of shit brother of yours to keep the hell away from my sister. Next time I may not care which brother I break."

"Jake's dead."

Teddy stopped and looked back as if Matt was conning him.

"That's why I came home," Matt said. "To go to the funeral."

Teddy thought about it, then heehawed a shrill laugh. "Someone tried telling me that yesterday, but I thought they was kidding, just trying to cheer me up." He headed toward the station again, this time with more bounce in his step. "Tell you what, if you grab me a copy of the funeral program and bring your car by sometime, I'll see if I can't get that dent out for you. No charge."

The pump nozzle clicked off when the car's tank hit full. If Matt wanted, he now had enough gas to turn around and hightail it straight back to the airport. Tempting as that was, he brushed the dirt off his jeans, gingerly lowered himself back into his car, his ribs throbbing, and turned onto the highway that led into town.

FOUR

Upon seeing the turnoff to his mother's house down the country road, Matt slowed his car until he could have been overtaken by an old dog, as if a couple extra minutes by himself would make a difference. Dust from the gravel road rose like a storm cloud stalking him, which he feared might be a harbinger of the day to come. If he hadn't already rolled up the windows in a futile attempt to keep the feedlot's noxious smell at bay and to give the car's air conditioning at least a fighting chance, he would have had to close them by now to keep out the dirt.

Sections of the barbed wire fence that ran alongside the road leaned over as if exhausted, and more than a couple of fence posts had rotted and broken in two, but there wasn't any livestock around anymore, so it didn't really matter. His mother had tried keeping a few head of cattle and an old horse, but once Matt and his brother left, she sold the cattle and the horse died, most likely of boredom.

Matt maneuvered his car between two mammoth azalea bushes flanking the long driveway that looked like they'd been fertilized with steroids. The house looked smaller than he remembered; he'd be surprised if it was more than 1,100 square feet.

Everything looked dirty—the porch, the paint, the barn next to the pasture, even the trees—as though a century of dirt had settled onto every structure. He'd arrived at a place the world had forgotten, where everything had surrendered to the elements.

Matt turned off his car but didn't get out right away. He looked around and saw the rusted swing set across the yard. He doubted anyone had played on it for decades, but it was easier to leave the metal monstrosity where it sat than have it carted away. It wasn't as though it was a blight on the property; the entire property was a blight.

He finally willed himself out of the car, knowing his mom would have heard him arrive the second he pulled into the driveway, and started toward the house. The porch swing the family once gathered around was gone, its useless hooks in the ceiling the only evidence of its existence.

The front door opened, and his mom appeared behind the screen door. She wore a black dress that extended a couple of inches below her knees and a single pearl necklace. Matt recognized the combination from when he was in high school. Anytime there was a formal event, she wore the same outfit, mostly because those were the only nice things she owned. She didn't worry about being seen in the same outfit because formal occasions were rare, so who would even remember?

Like the house, she looked smaller than he'd remembered. And older. Her hair was the color of ash, and her skin lacked vibrancy. She opened the screen door and nodded at him while scrutinizing his outfit.

"You made it," she said.

"Hi, Mom."

Matt walked up the steps, set his suitcase down, and gave her a hug. She put her arms on his side, barely touching him, as if hugging a wisp of smoke. It felt like they were both going through the expected protocol.

"Don't worry," he said. "This isn't what I'm wearing to the funeral."

"I didn't think it was," she lied. "Come on in out of the heat. You hungry? Funeral's in an hour and a half, but I can make you a sandwich or something."

"No, I'm good."

She stepped to the side as he entered. The place smelled like his childhood: a familiar aroma of food, cleaning supplies, and disappointment.

She followed him in. "Come sit down in the kitchen. I'm finishing up the dishes."

"I can help."

"How would you know where anything goes? Just sit."

Matt leaned against the counter next to the sink while his mom picked up a dish from the soapy water and rubbed it with an old red rag.

"Your flight okay? It's already been a long day for you."

"It was fine. But how are you doing?" Matt asked. "You holding up okay?"

"I'm doing. Not sure what one is supposed to say when something like this happens. Not sure there's anything to say. This isn't the way things are supposed to be. There's a natural order to things, and this isn't it." She paused, staring at the plate in her hand before putting it in the plastic drainer. She fished out a pale blue glass from the suds and ran the rag around it. "I'm glad you came. Wasn't sure you'd make it."

"Of course I came."

"Well, I wasn't sure. I don't know how things work back there, and I know how important your job is to you. Around here, nothing comes ahead of family, but how would I know how big companies view things like this?"

Matt started to respond but caught himself. He took a deep breath and put his hand on his mom's shoulder. "Well, I'm here."

"Go on and sit. You're making me nervous hovering over me."

Matt pulled back his hand and straddled one of the metal chairs at the chipped Formica kitchen table where he'd eaten most every meal growing up. It sat four people: he and Jake were always across from each other, with their mom on Matt's left and their dad on his right. Nobody would have dreamed of sitting in a different chair. Even now, he sat in his assigned spot.

"We should leave in an hour," his mom said. "You can use your old room to change. Don't know if I told you or not, probably not, but I turned Jake's and your room into a sewing space. Jake took the beds apart and stored them in the barn so I could set up my things."

"Oh, I assumed I'd be staying here, but I'm sure the hotel's got some vacancies. Never could figure out who stayed there anyway."

"I thought maybe you could stay at Jake's. He got himself an old place a couple miles south of town. It'd help me a lot if you could go through his stuff and see what's worth keeping. I can't bring myself to go over there. Lord knows what I'd find; probably some things it's best I don't know about. Think you could do that?"

"Sure, Mom. I can do that. I'll go change now."

"Can I ride with you to the funeral?"

It hurt how his mother seemed to question his ability to do the right thing, asking as if she didn't want to impose on a stranger. He hadn't done a stellar job of keeping in touch the past several years—actually, he'd been horrible—but even so, she acted like he couldn't meet the minimum standards of a decent son.

"Of course you can ride with me, Mom. Whatever you need, let me know. If there's anything I can do around the house, or anywhere on the property, just tell me. Whatever you need."

She nodded unconvincingly.

Matt made his way down the hall toward his old room. The layout of the one-story house could have been designed on the back of a grocery sack by a six-year-old: living room and kitchen at the front, two bedrooms down the hall across from one another, and a tiny bathroom at the end shared by everyone.

He paused and looked in his mother's bedroom. One nightstand held a lamp, a clock, and a bible; the nightstand on the other side of the bed had nothing on it. On one wall hung an old black-and-white picture of his dad sitting on a tractor when he was in his early forties, just a few years before he died. There was no smile, more like tolerating the person with the camera until they snapped the photo so he could get back to plowing. Whoever took the picture probably didn't even bother trying to get him to smile. Everyone had always said what a hard worker his dad was, but Matt believed the man just felt more comfortable out in the fields by himself than in the house with his family.

His dad suffered a massive coronary when Matt and Jake were fifteen. He couldn't speak for three days, although Jake had joked that it had taken a couple of days before anyone noticed a difference. Their father managed to force out a few words the morning he died. Matt and Jake had been sitting on the other side of his hospital room when he waved them over. Matt thought maybe he was going to tell them he loved them, or impart some words of encouragement, but instead he said neither he nor Jake were cut out for farm life and that they should sell the land. Matt understood the gesture, but Jake took offense, even though he'd rarely done more than an hour's worth of chores on any given day, and even then, under protest. Nevertheless, he took it as an affront to his abilities.

Matt and Jake's senior class pictures hung on the wall next to his dad's photo. If it weren't for their clothes and expressions, his mom could have gotten by paying for just one picture. She could tell them apart, but no one else could, and they hadn't made it easy. It never occurred to them that they might cut their hair differently or do anything to differentiate themselves. They didn't dress identically, but they did dress similarly, pulling from a communal pile of T-shirts and jeans each morning.

Matt turned and entered his old bedroom, shutting the door behind him. How two brothers coexisted in a room this tiny without killing each other was surprising, but then again, they were closer than most siblings. Whether it was because they were twins, or shared a connection no one else had, they were a team. For most of their school years, every kid knew that if they took on one of the Davis boys, they'd be taking on the other as well.

As his mother had warned, most everything he remembered had been removed from the room, as if another family had moved in. The space now looked like a third-world sweatshop. An old sewing machine sat on plywood held up by cinder blocks, with a dirt-stained, white plastic chair positioned in front of it. The brothers' posters of Metallica and Foo Fighters, however, still hung on the wall, the band members looking defiant.

Matt placed his suitcase on the stained plywood top and unpacked the sport coat he had picked up a couple of years ago from the Salvation Army, and the closest thing he had to a dress shirt. As he changed clothes, he thought about all the conversations he and Jake had shared over the years after the lights went off, from their debates about which teacher was meanest in grade school, to the long lamentations they exchanged as teenagers while trying to navigate high school. There were very few dreams or fears they didn't talk about. They were as close as brothers could be.

Being in that space, even with all their possessions gone, Matt became so lost in childhood memories that he stopped for a moment and stood in the middle of the room, staring at nothing, as if watching old family movies in his head. For an instant, he thought he heard Jake just barely calling out to him in a melancholy whisper, a sound distinct enough to make him spin around and look behind him.

But of course, no one was there.

FIVE

Matt drove toward town well below the speed limit, as though the reason for their journey required a solemn pace. Once they reached town, he passed a house with small children running through the sprinkler in a yard so flawless it looked like Astroturf. They screamed each time they hopped through the cold water like it was the most fun they'd ever had. A couple of the kids stopped and watched Matt's car pass, in case it was someone they knew.

His mother sat in the passenger seat staring at her hands in her lap, looking like a life-sized, mechanical doll that needed to be wound. If he hadn't been able to see her eyes, he would have thought she'd fallen asleep.

"The church is on Twelfth Street, right?" he said.

"It's where it always was."

"I didn't figure it had moved. I just wasn't sure what street it was on."

"Can't believe you forgot where everything is."

"I haven't forgotten everything," he said, battling to keep the irritation out of his tone. "I just wasn't sure about the church. We didn't exactly spend a lot of time there growing up."

His mother shrugged. "Your father wasn't much of a churchgoer, so I stopped going after a while, too. But I tried getting you boys to church more when you were little." She glanced at Matt. "We're not having a full service, but I wanted there to be something said at the gravesite. Jake wouldn't have wanted even that, but I don't care, I'm doing it. Funerals are for the living anyway."

"Have you been told anything about why someone would kill him?"

"Because there's a meanness in this world. That's all I know. But nobody's told me anything about why it happened. They'll catch whoever did this, I'm sure about that, but that won't bring him back."

"Still, I'd like to know if the sheriff . . ."

"No. Don't bother yourself with it. Let the authorities handle it."

He let it rest. The day of the funeral wasn't the best time to be talking about murder and motives, at least not with the mother of the victim. Matt wanted to turn on the radio to beat back the oppressive silence, but figured that would be seen as a sign of disrespect.

"I knew when it happened," Matt finally said, surprising himself with the admission. "With Jake. I felt it."

His mother's expression softened. "I wondered. I didn't want to ask, but I did wonder." She paused. "Were you okay?"

"I'd never experienced anything like it before. The connection hadn't been there for a long time, probably because of the distance, but nothing was stopping that one."

She shook her head and gazed at the road. "I'm so sorry you had to experience that."

"When did you and Dad realize? About Jake and me. I don't think I ever heard how you figured it out. We never talked much about it."

"Your father never did get too comfortable with it. Bothered him something fierce sometimes, which is why he didn't want to talk about it."

She didn't mention her own discomfort, which Matt seemed to recall.

"But as far as *when* we realized, it was early on, at least for me. Took a while longer for your dad. You two were just babies, probably seven or eight months. I was changing your diaper on the kitchen table and I started tickling you. I heard Jake giggling in the next room even before you started laughing." She chuckled softly before the sound dissolved into a wistful sigh.

"I picked you up and went to the living room where Jake was in the playpen. He wasn't laughing anymore, so I started tickling you again and immediately Jake's face lit up, and he started guffawing like he'd plumb lost his mind. When I stopped tickling you, the both of you stopped laughing. That was the first time. Now I'm not saying I totally understood it right then, but I knew something was different. I also felt certain that whatever it was you shared, it would be something that kept you closer than other siblings, and I was right. The two of you used to be inseparable."

She nodded and refocused her attention out the passenger side window. They drove the rest of the way in silence.

Matt drove to the other end of town until he saw the unique yellow brick of St. Luke's Catholic Church up ahead. Its spires and tall, stained-glass windows made it one of the most ornate buildings in Hatchett, although the competition in that category was thin. A

27

good-sized cemetery behind the church gave way to corn fields that stretched as far as the eye could see. He pulled into the entryway and drove toward the main door to let his mother out, but she said she could walk from the parking lot with him.

Matt parked on the side of the building, facing the cemetery. A quarter of the way down the rows of headstones, a couple of sweaty delinquents in dirty coveralls stood next to an open grave, leaning on their shovels, smoking and laughing at something. One of them checked his watch, then flicked his cigarette into the grave and threw a shovelful of dirt on it. Matt wanted to punch him.

There weren't many cars in the parking lot, perhaps because he and his mom had arrived ten minutes early. It was a graveside service and, given the blistering heat, people would likely arrive just before it started. Those who had already shown up were waiting inside the church until it was time for the service to start.

"We might as well sit in the car where there's air conditioning," Matt suggested.

His mother said nothing at first. She just sat there looking at the church. "Matthew," she finally said, then paused. "You might hear some things about your brother," she continued, resentment betraying her voice. "But don't pay any attention to it. None. Jake got into some trouble now and then like most every boy in Hatchett, but he wasn't a bad kid."

"What kind of trouble?"

"I'm just saying in a small town like this, people don't have anything better to do than spread gossip without caring if there's a lick of truth to it. Your brother always did right by me. So just remember that if you hear anybody trying to fill your head with untruths. He had a good heart. In the end, that's what matters."

"Okay, Mom."

They sat quietly in the car until five minutes before the service. A few more cars had pulled into the parking lot, and a small group congregated at the front of the church. She slowly gathered her purse. "I suppose we can head on over to the graveside. Andy said once we're settled, he'll lead everyone else from the church."

"Andy?"

"Andy Pearman. Father Pearman."

Matt was stunned. "Andy Pearman is doing the service?"

"He called me after it happened and offered. Besides, this is my church now, and he's my priest. I've been going a lot more lately."

Matt laughed. "So he really is a priest? He sent me a card three or four years ago saying something about that, but I just assumed he was pulling my leg."

"I'm guessing you didn't write back to him. Andy does good work here. The town is lucky to have him."

"Yes, but . . . Andy? I honestly thought one day he'd end up in Hollywood."

Andy had been Matt's best friend from kindergarten through high school. He always got the lead in the school plays, having first been bitten by the acting bug while playing a shrub to Matt's cornstalk in their second-grade Christmas pageant. He used to talk incessantly about being a famous actor, and the best birthday present he ever got was tickets to see *Les Misérables* in Omaha. The drive from Hatchett was twice as long as the play itself.

He'd invited Matt to go with him and while they both enjoyed the play, Andy appreciated it on a whole other level. He'd gone on for days about the nuances of the lead actor's performance and the lighting tricks the director had pulled off. In college he majored in theater to the surprise of no one. Matt lost touch with him—and everyone else—after high school graduation, but Andy remained one of only two people Matt was tempted to contact, and the only one he felt he had the right to.

But Andy, a priest? Hard to imagine. Andy's parents had been more likely to pick up a cocktail on Sunday mornings than a hymnal. If Matt had to guess the top one hundred most likely professions for Andy, becoming a priest wouldn't have made the list. He'd sooner imagine a rodeo clown or snake wrangler before anything related to the church. People changed, he supposed, but becoming a priest was a curveball.

Matt went around to his mother's side of the car to open her door, the searing heat striking him like he had stepped directly into a bonfire, but his mother was already climbing out by the time he got to her. Once out of the car and standing, she paused, then took a deep breath, looking more worn down than Matt had ever seen her. She hadn't cried since he'd been home—at least not in front of him—and he didn't expect her to. She'd always been tough, her hide impenetrable, and he never quite knew for sure what went on under the surface. He took her arm and they slowly headed down a gravel path toward the freshly dug grave.

As they walked, Matt's mother checked out his frayed sport coat and scuffed loafers. "Did you think wearing one of your nicer work suits would have looked out of place here?"

"Sorry, mom. My office is business casual, and my nicer dress clothes are all at the cleaners. I didn't have time to pick them up before coming."

"I don't know anything about 'business casual.' I just thought maybe you assumed we don't dress up here."

As Matt and his mother neared the gravesite, Andy, in his clerical dress cassock, emerged from the church through a side door, leading close to sixteen people who had come to pay their respects.

Twenty-four metal chairs flanked the gravesite in two rows of six on each side of the open grave. Matt sat at the end of one front row next to his mother, while the chair next to her remained empty, as if no one wanted to impose. Ten middle-aged and elderly people, most likely friends of his mother, filled some of the other chairs and gave her sympathetic nods as they took their seats. Most fanned themselves with their programs as sweat dripped down their faces. One woman's mascara was already running, and it wasn't because she was crying.

A tribe of four twenty-something guys and one woman stood behind the seats across from Matt, all dressed like they were heading out to get wings and beer rather than attending a funeral. A couple of them kept staring agape at Matt, his resemblance to his brother clearly too much for them to comprehend at once. Fortunately, they had the attention span of squirrels and before long, one of the guys began nudging the woman during the eulogy, forcing her to muzzle her laughter. Another had trouble keeping his right arm from twitching, while the tallest kept rubbing his nose with his index finger. All of them looked like they had come straight from filming a public service announcement about the dangers of doing drugs.

A pot-bellied man in a sheriff's uniform stood across the way in the parking lot, watching the proceedings closely enough to observe, but from enough distance to be respectful. Matt didn't know if he was there for Jake or because Jake had been murdered. Maybe both, although he assumed any law enforcement officer wouldn't have known Jake socially. After a few minutes, the man climbed into his patrol car and drove away.

Other than Andy, the only attendee Matt knew was Claire. The joy he felt at seeing her was equaled only by his discomfort. She sat at the end of the second row of chairs across from him, wearing a flattering dark gray dress and sunglasses, either because of the sun or to keep from making eye contact. Probably the latter. Her tall, slender body looked the same as it did when she captained the girls' volleyball team, and her hair was still the color of coal.

His immediate inclination was to go over and tell the five tweakers to step back so they wouldn't be standing in her general vicinity, although he had no doubt about her ability to handle them. Given her home life growing up, she could deal with most anything. But she seemed oblivious to the whispering and giggling of the socially inept idiots.

"Jake Davis was taken from us far too young," Andy said in a heartfelt voice from the end of the open grave. "Twenty-eight years old and entering the prime of his life. A beloved and devoted son to his mother Ruth, helping her however he could. And I always envied the relationship that Jake and his brother Matt had. Growing up, they were as close as two siblings could be."

Matt gave Andy a small smile at this understatement, but Andy's focused expression of sorrow did not change. His face had become rounder over the years, perhaps trying to keep pace with his waistline, which had also expanded noticeably since Matt last saw him ten years ago.

"Jake lived his entire life in Hatchett," Andy continued. "He said he could never imagine moving away from where he grew up, in part because of the friends he had made here in our humble little town."

Matt wondered if Andy was taking a subtle jab at him, but then noticed the ragtag group fist-bumping each other at the mention of friendship. If these were the friends Jake couldn't leave, that didn't say much about Jake. Matt immediately regretted being so judgmental, especially given his cowardice when it came to his own friends once he left Hatchett.

"So Lord, we ask you to watch over Ruth and Matt as they say goodbye for now to their son and brother. Help them in the weeks and months to come to hold on to their treasured memories of Jacob Davis. Help them retain in their hearts the affection they have for him, and show them the beauty of Your mercy, the strength of Your support, and the glory of Your unconditional love, forever and ever. Amen."

Andy made the sign of the cross, bowed his head for a silent prayer, then closed his bible. "Please remember Jake, Ruth, and Matt in your prayers this evening. Go with God." And with that, the service concluded.

Jake's five friends started scampering back to the parking lot before Andy even finished, not bothering to give condolences to Ruth or Matt. The twitchy guy shoved one of his friends playfully to the side as they walked down the path, a gesture that wasn't appreciated. It looked like a wrestling match could break out any minute.

An elderly couple and another woman approached Ruth and said a few words. They glanced at Matt expectantly, but his mother didn't introduce them.

Matt stood and laid his hand on his mother's shoulder as more people approached, then he stepped to the side and walked over to Claire, who held back from the others.

She removed her sunglasses as Matt approached and offered a half-smile, as if unsure how to acknowledge him after all these years. Her eyes resembled the color of a heavy fog, the eyes of a ghost, even more beautiful than he remembered, and he had thought about them often. She bore a strong resemblance to the woman on Matt's dating app that had caused him to pause when sitting at the bar. As he neared, she extended her hand, but then drew it back and put it over her chest, as if feeling his pain.

"I'm sorry for your loss, Matt."

"Thanks, Claire. And thank you for coming."

"I wanted to be here for your mom. Jake and I, well, let's just say we weren't close, but your mom's always been so kind to me."

Matt looked down at the ground, then mustered the strength to meet her eyes again. "How've you been?"

A small laugh slipped out of Claire's mouth, but she reeled it back in. "Guess the same. I don't know. Sort of hard to sum up the last ten years. Still at the Dirty Creek. Don't know if you heard, but it's mine now. Dad passed away a couple years ago and left it to me. Can't say as I've done all that much to it, but around here, people don't much care about that, as long as the bar is stocked."

Matt tried not to be overcome by yet another in the endless litany of strikes against him. "I heard about your dad passing. I'm sorry. I meant to send a note."

"That's okay, I understand. Anyway, I didn't exactly grieve the loss. Besides, I've seen pictures of New York City. Looks like you all are always on the go, doing fancy things and going to big places with bright flashing lights."

Matt started to respond, to tell her his life wasn't like that, but then realized from her smirk that she was giving him a hard time.

"You've seen pictures, huh? Sorry, but I'm not sure the role of rube fits you."

"You should see me working behind the bar. You might change your mind."

Matt jumped on the opening without thinking it through. "I'd like to. Would it be all right for me to stop by one evening? Maybe we could talk a bit?"

Claire stiffened slightly before nodding, but no words followed, as if her head had answered before the rest of her could come up with an excuse. "You're welcome to stop by," she finally said. "Not a lot of other choices for nightlife around here. I'll even buy you a beer, unless of course you only drink martinis now. I once saw a picture of some fancy New York City fellers and they were all drinking martinis."

Matt couldn't help but grin. "I reckon I can handle a beer. I'd like to catch up with you. Very much."

They looked at each other a beat too long without speaking. Claire broke away first to check her watch. "I have to go. I'm expecting a delivery at the Creek." She turned but looked back. "It's nice to see you again, Matt. You're looking well. And I'm sorry about Jake. I really am." She raised her hand in a half wave and departed.

Matt watched her float away, the sun illuminating her hair. She stepped off the path leading back to the church, kicked off her uncomfortable-looking dress shoes, and walked barefoot through the grass until she reached the parking lot. Matt had to smile: he'd never

33

seen her wear high heels before, so it didn't surprise him that they didn't last long on her.

"Looks good, doesn't she?"

Matt turned and found Andy standing next to him, the sweat streaming down his face like he'd just stepped out of a sauna. He looked his friend over from head to toe, taking in his black cassock, stole, and the white collar. He could only imagine how hot he must be. Then he turned his attention back to Claire.

"How's she doing?" he asked.

"Good, as always. She's not seeing anybody, at least not to my knowledge."

"I didn't ask about that," Matt said.

"Sure you did." Andy nodded toward the rest of the people walking into the church as he wiped the sweat from his cheeks with a handkerchief. Two older women had flanked Ruth, each taking one of her arms in theirs as they escorted her to the church. Ruth probably hated the assistance, but other than that, Matt had no idea what she was feeling. Given how rarely he visited, perhaps she worried she had now lost both of her sons.

"Shall we follow them to the land of air conditioning?" Andy asked. "This outfit isn't exactly moisture-wicking."

"Give me a sec," Matt said. "Then you need to tell me more about that 'outfit' of yours."

Matt walked over to Jake's coffin, which would be lowered into the ground after everyone left. The two young men he had seen preparing the grave waited several yards away, standing under a tree. One of them lit another cigarette. The other checked his watch, eager to finish up this final chore and find some place cooler once Matt left. But this was his brother. They could wait.

He thought about Jake, about growing up together, about the last ten years. He had often imagined their futures, but one of them burying the other at twenty-eight wasn't one of the scenarios he'd come up with.

He tried thinking of one last thing to say to Jake, even if silently, even if only a prayer, but nothing came. How did one sum up a life together? Were there even words that could describe what they shared, including those things they shouldn't have shared? He felt conflicted and found that all he could do was put his hand on the coffin, bow his head, and think of his brother.

As he stepped back from the coffin, he suddenly became disoriented, radio static filling his head. He staggered sideways, wavering as he tried to regain his balance. A blast of nausea punched him so hard it almost brought him to the ground. He doubled over, gripping his head. Darkness crept into the edge of his vision, but then the dizziness disappeared as quickly as a cloud floating past the sun.

Andy walked over and put his arm around Matt's shoulder. "Hey, you okay, Matty?"

Matt immediately went through his meditative mantra to quiet his mind. He remained motionless for a few seconds, then slowly straightened up. "Yeah, I'm good. I just didn't have time to grab anything to eat today."

"Come on, there's food inside, and by food, of course, I mean five kinds of Jell-O salad. After all, you're back home."

They took a few steps before Matt glanced back over his shoulder one last time at the coffin. He thought once again about the barely audible white noise that had been silenced the night Jake died. But now, after trying to figure out what he could offer as last words to his brother, he hoped he had just imagined the brief snippet of connection flitting through his head once again.

But he knew he hadn't.

SIX

Matt leaned against the basement wall of St. Luke's Fellowship Hall, a vast expanse of cheap linoleum flooring, water-stained ceiling tiles, and harsh fluorescent lighting offering all the ambiance of a bus station. A half-circle of folding metal chairs claimed one side of the room, while tables littered with unhealthy food lined the other side.

Across the room, Matt's mother and her acquaintances sat close together, speaking quietly, sometimes not at all, as if waiting for an A.A. meeting to begin. Occasionally one of the women sitting next to his mother reached out and placed a hand over hers, a gesture acknowledged with the merest of nods.

Andy appeared next to Matt, offering a pie-sized wedge of green Jell-O salad, a stack of communion wafers, and a bottle of warm water. "Nothing but the best for you, my friend. Here, eat this," he said. "You need to get something in you."

"Thanks." Matt looked at the wafers, then glanced at Andy with raised eyebrows. As Matt stuffed a couple of the wafers into his mouth, he once again assessed the priest's vestment on his friend. "There's something different about you I can't quite place. You doing something new with your hair?"

"It's probably that I used to wear shorts when it was this hot out."

"Maybe. I certainly don't seem to recall the robe. And just out of curiosity, what am I supposed to call you?"

"What you always did."

"Dickhead?"

Andy laughed. "Oh, yeah. I guess maybe 'Andy' is the better way to go now."

Matt leaned over to set his bottle of water on the floor and winced in pain.

"You're just a damn train wreck, aren't you?" Andy said.

"This morning at the gas station some guy mistook me for Jake and sucker punched me."

"I'm not surprised. Jake became kind of a royal asshole around here."

"I know I haven't spent much time in church, but you don't sound like most priests."

Andy glanced around, then whispered conspiratorially, "If it makes you feel any better, I'm not really a priest."

Matt looked at Andy in disbelief, but his friend just shrugged.

"Excuse me?" Matt said.

"Keep this between us, although the church leaders know, so it's not like I'm running a scam. After college, I held my Theater Studies degree for a minute and a half before I was confronted with the fact that there was next to nothing I could do with it. Most people with my degree don't make a living with it, unless they want to teach, which I didn't. I wanted to act."

"So you figured the obvious alternative was to impersonate a priest?"

"Surprisingly, it wasn't as obvious as you might think," Andy laughed. "I worked in restaurants and bars while auditioning for parts in local theater groups. I know, I know, total cliché, right? I moved back to Hatchett when my mom had a cancer scare a few years ago. There was absolutely nothing I could do here jobwise. But then Father Francis passed away, and it became obvious to the laity that they weren't going to find anyone to take his place. There's a serious shortage of Catholic priests in the Midwest, and the odds of getting one to come to Hatchett, Nebraska are somewhere between slim and you're-out-of-your-frigging-mind."

"So you applied?"

"I inquired. At first, the response was understandably lukewarm, to say the least, but after far too many months of congregation diehards driving ninety minutes to go to Mass with a real priest, the conversation took on more momentum. I'd started going to church in college, so it wasn't like I was just looking for any job opening: I was already a good Catholic boy. Eventually, I auditioned and got the gig, and it's been perfect. It's a killer role, and I perform on stage several times a week. I'm always memorizing new lines—some may call it a sermon—and I have people who follow all my performances. Groupies, if you will. I barely make enough to get by, just like acting, but I get free housing and health insurance, not to mention people are always bringing me pies, which you might have already guessed." Andy patted his bulging stomach.

"And you don't worry about being struck by lightning?"

37

He leaned toward Matt, his eyes shining. "That's the most amazing thing: I believe in this. Call it method acting or inhabiting a role, but I'm sincere about all of it. I'm helping people. My main goal in every role I ever played was to connect with the audience, and I'm doing that in spades here. Weddings, baptisms, funerals . . . I'm making a difference."

Matt couldn't help but smile. "I'm sure I've heard stranger things, but I can't think of any off the top of my head."

"If it didn't take a lot of time and sacrifice to become a real priest, I'd consider it. Maybe one day, but it doesn't matter right now because everybody in the church seems happy. Plus, I don't have to worry about makeup, and the costume changes are easy. It's the role of a lifetime."

"Any friends from high school feel awkward confessing to a guy who used to moon City Hall?"

"That's the incredible thing about Catholicism. Once you put on the robe, you're someone totally different. People are no longer speaking to Andy Pearman; they're speaking to God, through me. Or at least that's the case with a real priest, but everyone seems willing to go along with the show."

Matt used a wafer to shovel in the last sizable chunk of Jell-O salad, then tossed his empty plate in the plastic trash can and retrieved his bottle of water. He and Andy walked over to the stage at the far end of the room and hopped up on it, away from the others. They sat with their legs dangling over the edge.

Matt looked across the room to see how his mother was doing. She made eye contact with him, but her expression remained lifeless. He couldn't tell if she wanted to leave or if she was just looking at him, perhaps trying to figure him out. Then someone in her group spoke to her, and she turned to listen.

"So, what was going on with Jake, anyway?" Matt said. "It'd been a while since we spoke."

"Yeah, you big city ad execs aren't especially good at keeping in touch with us little people, are you? But I can beat you up about that later. I always thought, though, that you'd at least stay in touch with your brother, but apparently not. As far as what was going on with Jake, he got himself pretty deep into the meth business around here."

"Meth? Hatchett has meth?"

"You really have been off the radar, haven't you? Hatchett has a shitload of meth. It's not uncommon in these small Midwest towns, but Hatchett's one of the worst. It's like musk thistle; you try to control it, but it keeps popping up and taking over the pasture. People can't find work, so they start doing drugs to kill the depression, but they soon discover that as hard as it was finding a job before, it's even harder when you can't sit still during an interview and you look like you're hooked up to an electric current. Nobody wants to hire a tweaker, but there's a lot of money in it for the dealers. A lot of money."

"What about Jake? I can't believe he got involved in that."

"Jake was smart. Never used the product so far as I could tell, but he definitely worked the business side of it."

"Is that what got him killed? Some angry customer?"

"The sheriff doesn't think so."

"Do you know if he has any suspects?"

"I don't know if your mom told you, but I'm actually the one who found him."

"Seriously? What were you doing at his house?"

"I had some business with him. It's not important now, but I found him on his front porch, shot in the head. I spotted a large bag of meth vials through his living room window. Don't tell anyone, but I took the meth and threw it in the dumpster behind the church. I'm sure that's some sort of felony, but I figured your mom didn't need to deal with that."

"Thanks. I appreciate that."

"Anyway, I'm not claiming to be Sherlock Holmes, but if someone in the drug circle took Jake out, there's no way that bag would have been there. Also, when the sheriff got to Jake's, I overheard him tell one of the deputies he thought the killer was female. Don't know why he thinks that, but apparently he saw something. Does your mom know anything?"

"I tried getting some information from her," Matt said, "but she either doesn't know anything, or else she's not looking to share it. She even told me to leave it to the sheriff's department and to not bother myself with it. Those were her exact words: 'don't bother yourself.' He was my brother, for Christ's sake."

"Yeah, I know. And I'm sorry for talking smack about him, especially today," Andy said. "As much as he could be an asshole, there are others who are a lot worse. A couple of dealers around here are total psychos."

"No need to apologize. I knew Jake better than anyone. I have no illusions about his ability to be a jerk."

"Speaking of jerks, you owe me an explanation as to why you just cut everybody off and disappeared. Now that was a real jerk move."

Matt knew he'd need to face this conversation with his friend at some point, even if he just made something up, but he wasn't looking to go down that road right then. "I know, and I really am sorry."

"Well, you're lucky you caught me when you did. I pretty much have to forgive everything nowadays."

Matt looked over at his mother once more, then gingerly lowered himself off the stage, wincing again. He took Andy's hand, clasping it in both of his. "We'll talk again before I leave, preferably over a beer next time, but right now I've got to see how Mom's doing."

"All right, but if you disappear on me again, Matty, I'm hunting you down."

"Fair enough."

Matt's mother saw him approaching and stood. When he reached her, he offered his arm, but she turned and headed toward the door on her own. He didn't know why he had expected anything different.

"I thought the service was nice," Matt offered as they drove home, finally breaking the awkward silence.

"Yes, Andy did a nice job."

"I still can't believe he's a priest," Matt said, laughing.

"I would have thought you'd be more surprised by him moving back to Hatchett."

And with that, Matt realized that riding in silence wasn't so bad after all.

He pulled up to his mother's house and shut off the car. She didn't move until he reached to open his door, at which point she put her hand on his arm. "Matthew, if it's not too rude, I wouldn't mind having a little time alone."

The request blindsided Matt. He thought he could be a source of support and strength for his mother, but she wanted nothing to do with him. Then he immediately felt guilty for making this about him. She'd just lost a son, and he wasn't really sure there was anything he could do or say to make her feel better.

"Sure," he said. "Of course. I understand. It's been a hard day for everyone."

"I feel bad because you're finally back home, but I just need to lie down a bit."

"That's okay. I just wish I could do something to help."

"I know you do, but right now, I just want to rest. You've got the key to Jake's place?"

"Yeah, I've got it."

She opened her door and swung her feet out of the car. "Again," she said, "if you could go through his stuff, that would be a big help. Anything you think I'd like to have—or anything you want—put it in a box. If there are things someone else might be able to use, I'll donate them to the community center, although I don't reckon he'll have much of that. Get rid of everything else, or burn it if you have to. Do you understand what I'm saying, Matt?"

He understood perfectly. She must have had a sense of what he might find at Jake's that no one else needed to know about. "I'll take care of it. Should I come over sometime tomorrow?"

"Of course. It's your home."

She got out and made her way to the house. Matt watched as she walked toward the front door, dragging herself forward as if the weight of the day was draped across her shoulders.

She looked beaten. She looked old. She looked like someone who had just buried her son.

SEVEN

Matt got lost a couple of times trying to find Jake's place. It was two miles south of town off an old washboard dirt road that looked like it hadn't hosted a speck of gravel for a decade. The deep ruts kept lurching his car toward the side of the road, forcing him to overcorrect. He knew he must be close, but he couldn't find the driveway, even though he'd driven up and down this poor excuse of a road twice already. He finally spotted a rusted-out mailbox that looked like it had been used for batting practice, hidden by a renegade gooseberry bush.

He turned onto something that more closely resembled an overgrown cow path than a driveway. A row of cedar trees hid the house from the road; it was a foreboding two-story white clapboard farmhouse with black shutters around the windows, large enough to accommodate a family of eight.

A bright red classic 1979 Pontiac Firebird with black pinstripes, spoiler, and snowflake alloy wheels reigned proudly at the end of the driveway. Matt didn't know much about cars, but he knew the Firebird had "a kickass 220 horsepower V-8 engine and awesome power disc brakes," at least according to Jake when they were growing up.

Jake had been obsessed with buying this muscle dream car before he could legally drive. Around their seventeenth birthday, a well-off spinster aunt had passed away, leaving each of the boys a few thousand dollars from her estate. Matt deposited most of his into a college savings fund, but Jake went right out and bought his car as soon as the money was available. From that point on, given the choice between buying gas or buying anything else that most teenage boys usually wanted, Jake was more than willing to miss out on a new pair of tennis shoes or an Xbox if it kept the tank full. Matt smiled at the car, as it represented everything the house wasn't: clean, cared for, and worth something.

Matt stepped out of his rental and surveyed his surroundings. Diseased Dutch Elm trees loomed near the house: three of them looked completely dead, and seemed to suggest impending disaster for the house's roof. He heard several birds cawing loudly, as though he represented a threat. He scanned the trees until he saw at least six black crows dotting the branches, one of them considerably larger than the others. Most of them stared into the distance, but the huge one appeared to stare at Matt with malice.

No neighbors in sight—the perfect place for someone who didn't want his business known. The other building on the property was a two-story green barn that sat forty yards away.

Matt pulled his suitcase from the car and hoped he'd packed enough. When he left New York, he'd brought enough for a two-day visit at most, but after seeing his mom, he realized he might not get away that soon. Plus, he really did owe it to Andy to catch up properly.

And there was also Claire.

Matt climbed the porch steps, pausing when he noticed a deep red stain on the front railing, and an even larger one on the porch. Jake's blood—the one part of the murder scene that couldn't be cleaned up. He stared at the stain as though it were an abstract painting that might show him Jake's final moments. He took the key his mother had given him, put it in the lock, and pushed open the door.

The pungent stench of rotting meat that assaulted him when he entered was so heavy it could have been weighed. He set down his suitcase and opened the living room windows. The scorching summer breeze did little to displace the odor, but at least it provided an escape for the stench. The windows had no screens, but Matt didn't worry about dirt or insects getting inside, as both were already duly represented. Fortunately, the breeze had shifted away from the feedlot, so he didn't have to worry about the aroma of cow manure wafting in. That, combined with the rotting meat, might have been lethal.

Jake's design motif appeared to be early American Depression. The sofa looked like something he might have found at the dump a couple of thunderstorms after its previous owners had discarded it. What Matt could only guess was a coffee table consisted of two gray cement cinder blocks on either end of an old piece of plywood, and the dirt-brown recliner appeared to be permanently stuck in recline. Matt imagined Jake climbing in and out of the chair, unable to lower it, but not really caring.

The only twenty-first century item was a seventy-inch flat-screen TV with surround-sound speakers haphazardly nailed around the room. Much like the Firebird, a large-screen television reigned supreme atop Jake's hierarchy of needs.

In the kitchen, the motor of the short refrigerator buzzed like a crop duster, but still failed to drown out the drone of the flies that had struck the mother lode. Two uncooked hamburger patties, each the size of a box turtle, rotted away on a dirty saucer. Jake had either forgotten about them or believed he'd be right back, but someone had other plans for him. Matt didn't understand why the cops didn't throw them out. Maybe they figured it wasn't in their job description.

An impressive tower of dirty dishes filled the sink, and the garbage can overflowed. Matt figured it might be easier to torch the place than clean it, but he sighed and got to work. In a way, he welcomed the physical distraction.

An hour and a half later, Matt had done what he could to at least make the kitchen non-toxic. He did a cursory check of the rest of the house but found nothing illicit beyond a baggie of marijuana and a bong next to Jake's recliner. He also, by accident, came across a loaded Colt .45 strapped underneath the kitchen tabletop. He decided to place it under a dishrag in a kitchen drawer for the time being, and told himself he'd figure out what to do with it later. If he was going to find anything criminal, it would most likely be in the barn, but after poking around the horse stalls and lofts, he found nothing of interest. Maybe he'd search for secret compartments beneath the floorboards tomorrow.

After making a peanut butter and jelly sandwich and opening a bottle of Bud, he sat at the kitchen table and started working his way through a pile of unopened mail. Mostly junk, renewal notices from *Guns and Ammo,* and catalogues from a variety of porn distributors.

He was on such a roll throwing things out that he almost discarded a typed letter to Jake before noticing something written on the other side of the page. Turning it over, he saw a written response signed by Jake.

The note read:

For what it's worth—and I know it probably isn't worth shit—I really am sorry about everything I've done to you. I don't expect you to believe it, and I wouldn't believe it either if I were you, but I do feel bad about what has gone down. I'd like to make it right but I know I can't, so the best I can do is say I'm sorry. I know last Tuesday you told me if I really wanted to make things right, I'd eat a bullet for breakfast, but girl, I think I'm going to go with an apology instead. I never was much of a breakfast person, even though they say it's the most important meal of the day. Jake.

Matt noted Jake referred to the person as "girl," so apparently somewhere out there was at least one woman who regretted having crossed paths with Jake. Matt leaned back in his chair and read the typed, unsigned letter that had elicited Jake's response. It talked about how Jake's actions had devastated her. How Jake had been told no, over and over, but acted like he couldn't care less. She accused him of having no shame and ruining everything that others had worked so long to achieve. It emphasized his total disregard for others' lives and said that no amount of time would ever heal the scar he had brought about: it would be inside of her forever.

He folded up the letter and set it to the side. Apparently, the police hadn't noticed it amongst the pile of bills and other paperwork, or else they didn't think it worthy of their investigation, to the degree that law enforcement was going to spend much time at all trying to solve the murder of a hometown drug dealer.

He remembered Teddy at the gas station saying Jake couldn't apologize for anything, but Jake's response to that letter sounded genuine; it was a good reminder not to turn his brother into a caricature based on someone else's perceptions. Jake wasn't some redneck drug dealer with no redeeming traits. He was bright, funny, and good to his mother.

Sandwich and beer still in hand, Matt headed upstairs to Jake's bedroom and peeked into the small walk-in closet. In one corner, two shotguns leaned against the wall, one of which Matt remembered using as a kid while pheasant hunting. He also discovered a bow and a full quiver, although none of the arrows looked like they'd ever used them. Matt imagined Jake thought it would be cool to be an expert archer, before realizing it would take actual effort.

He turned his attention back to the bedroom. On the nightstand next to Jake's bed, Matt saw three empty beer bottles, a *Hustler* magazine, and a hardback copy of *Anna Karenina* with a bookmark two-thirds of the way in. It had always been hard to pigeonhole Jake.

Matt put down his sandwich and beer and sat on the side of the bed, sighing. It was only 6:45, but he felt exhausted. He figured he'd done enough chores for one day.

He started pulling off his T-shirt, then paused and sat upright as he heard a very soft buzz making its presence known in his head. He instinctively closed his eyes and took some deep breaths at first, then stopped and looked around, now curious. He had to know what was going on, and he wouldn't accomplish that by trying to block it out. He walked into the center of the room, completely opening himself up to any possible connection.

"Jake?" he finally said when the buzzing started to subside. He stood perfectly still. Listening. Receptive. He felt silly calling out to his dead brother. Then he said his name again.

Hearing nothing more than soft, white noise, he gave up and once again started to remove his shirt, but before he could pull it completely off from over his head, Matt suddenly felt like someone had poured gasoline over every inch of his flesh and lit him like a human matchstick. The all-consuming pain and accompanying panic dropped him to the floor quicker than if someone had swung a baseball bat at his knees. Unable to get the T-shirt off from over his head, he couldn't see anything, which only amplified his terror and confusion.

The unfathomable torment struck even before he experienced what felt like a claw ripping into his right shoulder, the talons slicing into his flesh like meat hooks. He heard himself truly screaming for the first time in his adult life.

A second claw-like weapon sunk into and down the middle of his back. It had to have slashed his shirt to shreds, and all the while, he remained aflame. The terror consumed him; he opened his mouth wide, but nothing came out, as if his body finally realized no sound could convey his horror.

He frantically kicked his left leg out and back, thrashing at whatever was attacking him, but making no contact. He flailed inside his T-shirt, surprised it hadn't already burned off. Finally, he managed to jerk it over his head as he fell onto his back.

He flipped over onto his hands and knees and scrambled away from whatever creature was attacking him, but when he finally looked around, the room was empty. That didn't stop the razor-sharp pain across his legs and chest, or the throbbing third-degree burns that had to be there. As much as he hurt, nothing matched the sheer panic coursing through his body. His fight-or-flight instinct ramped to full throttle, but his body couldn't do either.

His head filled with roaring static like an untuned radio wired to a stadium speaker. He flung himself across the floor, still kicking and swinging, though he saw nothing there. He barreled into the side table next to the bed and rammed the crown of his skull against the bed frame; the pain didn't even register compared to the torture he felt in the rest of his body.

He'd take relief at any cost, even death. Anything to make this stop. If only he could reach Jake's shotgun, he'd put the barrel in his mouth and fire without hesitation, but he couldn't move in any deliberate direction.

He grabbed both sides of his head and forced himself to take deliberate breaths, to the degree he could manage, one after the other, to jump-start a mind control technique he learned in high school. As he began to regain control, he suddenly looked up, confused.

"Who else is there? What are you?" But whatever he was sensing suddenly dissipated, along with the horror, as if a switch had been flipped. He stayed on the floor, his hands gripping his head, his eyes closed, and his forehead pressed to the floor. He hesitated to move any part of his body, afraid of restarting the horror.

Finally, he rose slowly, gripping the bed frame for support. He staggered to the mirror on Jake's dresser, turned his back to it, and looked over his shoulder at the reflection. Not a mark. Other than his disheveled hair and frenzied eyes, there was no evidence of him having been sliced open, burned, or torn to shreds.

He turned to stare at his reflection, the torture still written on his face. He knew what had just happened and swore to never again open himself up to the connection with his brother, despite how absurd the possibility was. He refused to think about it anymore. How the hell could he?

He began crying uncontrollably, something he hadn't done since he left Hatchett ten years earlier.

EIGHT

After managing to compose himself, Matt slugged down a second beer and threw on a clean, light pink polo shirt before getting into the car. After the attack, he hadn't known what to do: at first he started to call Andy, then remembered Skiz, an old classmate from school, someone Matt never imagined he would ever seek out. He called his mother and learned that Skiz now owned a farm east of town, so rather than wait for the unfathomable pain to return, he headed over for an unannounced visit. He knew this was a conversation best held in person.

Matt arrived just after 7:30 p.m., but for a farmer in the middle of summer, that meant nothing. It was possible Skiz was still out in the field. If that was the case, Matt decided he would wait; it might give him enough time to remember Skiz's real name.

The nickname started off as Schizo, short for schizophrenic, but hardly anyone in sixth grade knew how to spell even the abbreviated version, let alone the whole word, so it got chopped down even further to Skiz. Matt couldn't remember whether the boy had accepted the nickname willingly or just knew there wasn't anything he could do about it. Either way, it stuck, but now that they were in their late twenties, a real name was probably the better way to go.

The siding on Skiz's house looked like it was recently painted a bright white, and the lawn surrounding the place was immaculate. Three plastic flamingos were the only evident stab at a lawn ornament. They definitely made a statement, although flamingos in Nebraska weren't exactly a statement that made any sense. There were no swing sets or toys indicating the presence of children. He knocked a couple of times on the front door. No answer. The only light he could see came from the kitchen.

A Ford F-150 sat next to a tractor that was parked outside the barn. Light spilled out from the open barn door, so he made his way over to check it out. As he walked past the pickup, he saw bales of hay in the cargo bed and a shotgun fastened to a rack in the cab's back window: a typical accoutrement for a rural Midwest pickup.

When he reached the barn, he heard muttering inside. Leaning in, he spotted Skiz on the other side of the barn, dressed in gray overalls and mud-caked boots. He had to weigh at least 350 pounds. At six-foot-six, Skiz could handle some extra weight, but not that much. Matt could easily tell, though, that a lot of the weight was muscle.

He watched Skiz carry a calf to a stall. It must have weighed over 200 pounds, but he carried it like a bag of groceries. Skiz spoke under his breath to the calf, a sort of unintelligible and uninterrupted commentary similar to those New York subway riders who hadn't held a coherent conversation with a living soul in years.

Skiz set the calf down in a stall, shut the door, and slid the bolt. Then he straightened up and stared at the calf as though he expected it to speak to him. Knowing Skiz, maybe it did.

"Hey," Matt said, trying to sound casual, like a neighbor who'd just stopped by.

Skiz looked over his shoulder and stared at Matt for a long moment before responding. "Hey."

"Catch you at a bad time?"

"Nah, this little fella's just got a hurt hoof, so I'm putting him in timeout for a while."

Matt walked over and extended his hand. "Do you remember me? Matt Davis. Jake's brother."

"Course I remember. Jeez, it ain't been that long." Shaking hands with Skiz was like getting your hand slammed in a car door. Matt knew he wasn't trying to make a statement with the firm handshake; he simply didn't do things any other way.

"My real name's Walter."

"Sure, I knew that, Walter."

"No you didn't, but that's okay. Can't imagine anybody from school remembering. Not like they ever used it, but names don't really mean nothing anyway, do they? Just the same, I go by Walter."

Matt looked around the barn, feeling awkward. "Your place is nice. Farming going all right for you?"

Skiz shrugged. "Going all right? I guess. It's just what I do. It's what I always knew I'd end up doing. What are you here for? I gotta assume you wasn't sitting around and suddenly started wondering what I was up to."

"I wanted to ask you something, if it's not an imposition. It'll sound strange as hell, but I don't know who else to ask."

"Because I'm strange as hell?"

"No, because you used to know things that others didn't. Do you still have that gift?"

A grunt forced its way out of Skiz's mouth. "People only call it a gift when they want me to tell 'em something. Otherwise, it's a good excuse to keep clear of me."

If the stakes weren't as high as Matt feared, he would have apologized and left Skiz alone. Instead, he walked over and leaned against a spotless workbench and tried to figure out the best way to explain the reason for his visit.

Back in eighth grade, Skiz displayed what could best be described as an ability to communicate with the dead. One time, he told a teacher he was sorry about her mother passing. The teacher looked puzzled at the left-field comment, saying her mother was fine, but Skiz just shook his head before pulling out the day's homework. The teacher soon got word that her mother had dropped dead earlier that morning of a heart attack.

Skiz was already considered an odd duck—mostly because of his awkward nature, and because he was often seen talking to people who weren't there—but that death call pretty much sealed his position outside any social clique. Even the teachers, who had tried being patient with Skiz's academic struggles, started giving him a wide berth after that.

Matt couldn't remember ever picking on Skiz, but he was also confident he'd done nothing to stick up for him either. That's how things played out in school. Few kids stepped up to do the honorable thing.

"Heard about Jake," Skiz said. "Suppose that's why you're here."

"I'm sorry if it's inappropriate to ask, but it's important. Really important."

"I always thought it'd be great to have a brother. Someone to be friends with, like you and Jake was. I remember hearing you guys had some sort of special connection back in the day. I sometimes thought maybe the three of us might end up being friends given that we all was a little different, but for whatever reason, you guys was popular while I just made people uncomfortable. Suppose it's 'cause people get nervous dealing with the dead."

"Probably," Matt said.

"Or 'cause I was weird. Suppose it could have been that."

"You weren't weird."

"Says the man looking for a favor." Skiz headed toward the barn door. Matt wasn't sure if he'd blown his chance until Skiz called out to him. "Come on in the house and tell me what it is you want. I gotta eat something before I fall over."

The farmhouse kitchen looked clean and functional. There wasn't much in the way of frills; the only object displayed on the wall was a 4-H plaque from high school acknowledging Skiz's blue ribbon hog. Matt didn't have to look around for more than a few seconds to know there likely wasn't a Mrs. Skiz.

Skiz grabbed a handful of cookies from a yellow teddy-bear cookie jar and stuffed three of them into his mouth at once. Then he poured a large glass of milk, holding it up to Matt to ask if he wanted any. Matt declined. They sat across from each other at the table.

"I don't do this much anymore," Skiz said as he inhaled another cookie. "Talking with the dead, I mean. Eating cookies, I do that a lot. I speak with mama from time to time, and sometimes granddaddy when I'm not sure about something on the farm, but I don't seek out other people's folks no more. There's no upside to it."

"I understand."

"Was it true you and Jake talked to each other telepathically?"

"No, we didn't talk to each other or anything like that. More like if either of us experienced a powerful emotion, the other would feel it. Strong fear, excitement, pain, things like that. Not all the time, only the really big things. We didn't even fully realize until kindergarten that other siblings didn't have the same connection we shared. We had no idea we were unique."

Their connection had often been fun when they were young, but as they grew older, the novelty wore thin. Neither of them told their friends about it—a demand from their father—although things obviously happened from time to time when classmates suspected something unusual, like during basketball practice when Matt got kneed in the groin and Jake dropped to the ground on the other side of town while talking with friends, but no one understood the extent of their connection.

Matt usually knew when the connection was about to kick in: his face grew hot, as if a fever was descending, and he struggled to take a normal breath. He learned to lessen the connection through breathing techniques and by tuning out the oncoming impact, but even in high school he knew if he stayed in Hatchett, he wouldn't be able to break the connections that stemmed from especially powerful experiences.

It didn't help that Jake would deliberately do things to mess with Matt, such as repeatedly diving into a nearby ice-cold pond when he knew Matt was meeting Claire's parents for the first time. Matt had to pretend to keep clearing his throat to cover up any sound that slipped each time Jake entered the frigid water, sending chills up Matt's spine. Matt never gave Jake the satisfaction of knowing he'd been successful.

Matt had hoped that moving across the country would diminish the connection—a wish that ended up being granted. Since he left Hatchett, he couldn't remember a time when he experienced anything other than a slight awareness of what was going on with his brother.

Three months after the move, Matt had sent a text saying he hoped Jake was enjoying the break as much as him. Of course, after that, Jake tried multiple crazy stunts to try to reestablish the connection, but Matt only felt slight twinges that could be blunted with minimal effort. The big exception, of course, came with Jake's murder, when Matt felt like the connection had been wired directly into his brain with a taser.

"I'd just heard rumors about the two of you is all," Skiz said. "Didn't know for sure."

"We kept it to ourselves as much as possible."

"Not like I ran an ad or nothing about what I could do." Skiz got up and poured himself a second glass of milk. "Wonder if there's something in the water around here. Twins talking without saying a word. Me communicating with the dead. We oughta be in a reality TV show." He finished off the second glass of milk. "Sure you don't want some? The only way to get it any fresher is drinking it straight from the udder."

"No thanks. I'm good."

"Suit yourself." Skiz sat back at the table across from Matt. "So, you looking to see if I can connect with Jake? Find out if he's got any messages for you from the great beyond?"

Matt leaned forward, figuring the best way to explain it was by just being totally open about it. If anyone could understand, it would be

Skiz. "My whole life, I had a soft buzzing in my head, sort of like radio static. A quiet crackling I never even noticed. I assumed everybody had it—like that was how hearing worked—but the second Jake died, it stopped for the first time. It's been eerie having total silence in my head."

Matt got up and grabbed a glass from the cupboard. "Think I'm going to have some water." He filled his glass and leaned against the counter. "At Jake's funeral today, I suddenly felt sick to my stomach. Nothing major, more like when you're really hungry."

"I know that feeling."

"I thought that's what it was, except I could hear the static again, a little softer than normal, but it was there. And then it disappeared just as fast, but I hadn't imagined it. And then tonight . . ." Matt shook his head and gulped down his water. "Look, do you think you can get any sense of what's going on with Jake? Any impressions or anything?"

Skiz eyeballed him as if his default reaction was to assume anyone from school was trying to make him look stupid, but he eventually nodded for Matt to come back to the table. "I can give it a try."

Matt sat across from him. "How does this work? Do we need to dim the lights?"

"Only if they're hurting your eyes. This isn't a séance. It's just me trying to tune in to the dead. I get what you're talking about when you say radio static. I don't actually hear it, but that's sort of what I do; I tune in to a different station that most people don't get." Skiz extended his arm across the table. "I need your hand."

Matt reached across the table and took hold of Skiz's hand. Skiz immediately pulled back. "I don't need to hold your hand, for Christ's sake. Set it palm-down on the table. Shit, man."

"Sorry."

Matt put his hand palm-up on the table and Skiz rolled his eyes. "You're determined to go steady with me, ain't you?" He motioned for him to flip it over. Once Matt's palm was laid flat against the table, Skiz placed his baseball-glove hand on top of it, his fingers thick as railroad stakes.

"This might take a minute or two, so just be quiet."

Skiz stared blankly at his own hand as if trying to see something invisible. They sat in silence for an endless five minutes, Skiz's only movement coming from his inhalations, and the only audible sound being the steady clicking of a lawn sprinkler outside. Skiz didn't even blink.

Matt glanced at the wall clock, ready to suggest maybe there wasn't anything there when Skiz's hand pressed harder on his. Not enough pressure to cause pain, but flattening Matt's hand a little more against the table.

Skiz's eyes suddenly doubled in size, as if he saw someone running at him with a chainsaw. His hand clamped down on Matt's like a hydraulic press, and Matt feared that every bone in his hand might shatter. He struggled to retrieve his hand. "Skiz! Skiz! Walter! Stop, man! You're hurting me!"

Matt reached over with his free hand, grabbed hold of Skiz's wrist and pulled, but Skiz didn't budge. Matt's eyes watered as Skiz started moaning.

"Oh my God, please, no, no, help me, oh my God, oh Jesus, please no." Skiz gasped for air like a fish.

Matt tried reaching over to slap him in the hopes of bringing him out of the trance, but he couldn't reach that far across the table. Matt banged his free hand on the tabletop, but Skiz's eyes only grew wider until it looked like his eyelids were being pulled back inside his head. Skiz's cries made it sound like his lungs were coming up his throat. He pressed down on Matt's hand even harder, something Matt hadn't thought possible.

"Please Jesus, please no, please no Mama, please, Mama help me!" Skiz pleaded, sounding like he might dissolve into tears. His mind had apparently locked onto something not in that room.

Matt shouted Skiz's name one more time, then kicked one of the wooden table legs. Nothing happened, so he kicked it again, this time a few inches higher. He heard the table leg crack. He kicked a third time, as hard as he could, finally breaking the leg and causing the table to topple. Matt retrieved his injured hand and leapt from the chair, putting distance between himself and Skiz.

Once their physical contact was broken, Skiz flung himself backward off his chair and onto the floor before crab-walking to the corner of the kitchen. He looked around, his eyes like fifty-cent pieces.

He finally looked up and scowled at Matt. "Get the hell out of here."

"What happened? What did you see?"

"Get out!" Skiz shouted before shakily pulling himself to his feet, his face as white as the refrigerator. He looked ready to hurl Matt headfirst out the door if he didn't start moving. Matt held his hands up and crept backward toward the door.

"I'll go, man. I'll go. But you have to tell me, Walter. I have to know. Earlier this evening, at Jake's, the static returned with a vengeance, and I felt whatever Jake was feeling. It was beyond words. So much pain and total, abject fear. It's the connection, Skiz. The connection is still there."

Skiz exhaled, looking like he'd just wrangled a Brahma bull. He staggered to a cabinet and grabbed a bottle of Jack Daniels, unscrewed the top, and took a hit. He winced as it went down, then took an even larger hit, the burn of the whiskey apparently calming him down and tempering his insistence that Matt leave, now that the threat seemed to have passed.

"You felt it too, didn't you?" Matt asked. "I understand what you felt, Walter. The connection hasn't been broken, has it?"

"It ain't broken," Skiz muttered. "And you're not the only one who knows about it." Skiz gazed at Matt, his anger dissolving into a look of pity. "It ain't good, man. Trust me, it ain't good."

Skiz took one last swig of whiskey before screwing the lid back on the bottle and looking at Matt matter-of-factly.

"You are so fucked."

NINE

Matt slouched on the bright blue sofa in Skiz's living room, his left hand still throbbing. Skiz sat on the edge of a faux leather recliner, his nervous trunk of a leg shaking the entire chair, like it was at the epicenter of an earthquake.

Once Skiz had calmed down, Matt pleaded for a few more minutes for Skiz to help him better understand his predicament. Skiz reluctantly agreed, although the pained expression on his face made it clear Matt was there on borrowed time.

Matt tried describing his experience at Jake's house, although he had trouble finding adequate words. It didn't seem to matter, because Skiz had felt something similar and knew exactly what Matt was trying to explain. At times Skiz looked like he might throw up just thinking about it.

"So when you and Jake used to share emotions, could you see what the other was doing? Or did you just feel it?"

"We could just feel the physical sensation that the emotion caused. Good, bad, whatever, but it had to be pretty strong. He was more into it than I was; he thought it was cool, whereas I kept trying to figure out ways to turn it off. When you're a teenager, you feel enough emotions without having somebody else's piled on top. I never could break it until I moved east."

"As I'm sure you already figured, the connection's still alive and ticking, even if Jake ain't."

"So what I felt is what it's like to be dead?"

Skiz screwed up his face, then shook his head. "No, that's what it's like to be dead . . . in Hell."

Matt did a double take, wondering if Skiz had just made a bad joke, but his grimace betrayed no hint of humor. "Hell? Are you serious?"

"Not many places more serious than Hell."

"You mean Hell, as in . . . *Hell?* An actual place?"

"Don't overestimate my expertise on the subject. I can't say it's an actual place, like some underground cavern with flames and pointy-

56

tipped hills or someplace you could MapQuest. Maybe it's another dimension, or maybe it's inside a person's head, but it's Hell, that much I'm sure about. Pain and torment and de—" Skiz cut himself off and shuddered, like he needed to expunge the memory from his brain.

"How do you know that's not what a person feels right after they die?" Matt asked. "What if the wiring in our brains is still active for a while after everything else shuts down? What if it takes a few days?"

"Jake is in Hell. He is."

"How could you tell?"

Skiz started to answer angrily. "Because I . . ." He caught himself and stopped. Whatever he had started to say, he apparently decided not to say it out loud. "Look man, you believe what you want, okay? I'm just telling you what I know. And trust me, I know."

Matt sank deeper into the sofa. He felt ashamed that his first concern was having a psychic connection to Hell; it wasn't until minutes later that he thought about what that meant for Jake. *His twin brother had been condemned to Hell.* Matt didn't know everything Jake had done in the last ten years, but he wondered what would merit a permanent placement in Hell.

Matt knew firsthand his brother could be a jerk, and sometimes "jerk" was too generous of a description. But he also knew Jake's rough demeanor occasionally acted as a shield for when he felt threatened. Jake could give you the shirt off his back, but he was also capable of coming at you like a sledgehammer.

Was it the meth? Had someone died because of Jake's illicit business? Had Jake killed someone in a drug deal gone bad, or was it something personal? If it was personal—if Jake had felt betrayed by someone—then God knows what he might have done. Matt understood that better than anyone. But for right now, all that really mattered was that his brother was in Hell, and he didn't know what to do about it.

Matt looked up and saw Skiz staring at him with one part compassion and nine parts "time for you to scram." But Matt needed guidance.

"What can I do?" Matt asked.

"You can't think of any way to break the connection?"

"I read a couple of books on meditation in high school that helped some. I learned to focus on my breathing and to build a mental wall around my mind that enabled me to tune out external stimuli, which usually worked. Putting miles between us, though, is what really broke the connection, at least until his murder."

"Yeah, well, it won't matter how far you run now. Seems like you got yourself a high-speed internet connection to Hell, so geography's no longer a factor. And I hate to tell you this, but your brick wall won't help you in the long run either. Eventually you'll have to let your guard down. If I were you, I wouldn't sleep for a while. I'm serious. You sleep, you lose."

"Sure. Who needs sleep?"

Skiz cracked his knuckles as he thought about Matt's dilemma, each crack sounding like a pencil snapping. "If you can't break the connection, then seems to me your only other option is to get Jake out of Hell."

"Okay, no problem. I'll get right on that."

"Hey, I'm not claiming it's likely, but it also may not be as crazy as it sounds."

"Care to tell me how?"

"I've communicated with spirits who've talked about being released from horrific torment, and it all came down to someone forgiving them. One spirit had killed a man, and as soon as the victim's wife forgave him, his spirit was set free."

"Forgiveness?"

"Look, it's not like there's an instruction manual to all this, but based on what I know, the common theme is forgiveness. So your best bet will be to find whoever it is Jake screwed over the most, and get that person to forgive him. It's more than likely there's one person he hurt far worse than anyone else. You're lucky, because with Jake, the odds are good it'll be the person who killed him, unless his murder was just business-related. If it wasn't, then murder is pretty much the ultimate response to the ultimate hurt. That's the person you need to find."

"I found an unsigned letter at Jake's from a woman who says he hurt her badly. He wrote back, apologizing, even though someone recently told me Jake never apologized for anything. Plus, the sheriff apparently thinks Jake's killer is a female."

"Then if I was you, I'd start with that."

Matt couldn't help his skepticism, but what option did he have? If he could have figured out all of this logically, he wouldn't have turned to Skiz.

He didn't know what else to do, and besides, it wasn't like Skiz was giving him advice he found on the internet. Matt really believed the man had conversations with the dead.

Skiz cleared his throat, his way of telling Matt to get lost. Matt got up and extended his hand to thank Skiz, but Skiz leaned back like Matt was radioactive. "You crazy? You want to thank me, get the hell out of here."

"I'm sorry about what happened. I didn't know." He headed toward the front door, then stopped and paused. "When I asked how you knew Jake was in Hell, you started to say something. What aren't you telling me?"

Skiz hauled himself out of his recliner but didn't move any closer to Matt. His face tightened, then he relented. "When I connected with Jake's spirit and felt his pain, I could tell something else had become aware of what was going on."

"What do you mean? Like another spirit?"

"More like a demon." Skiz wiped his sweaty brow. "Aw hell, man, I'm not going to say his—its—name. But I don't have any doubt in the world. I could feel him figuring out the score."

"What do you mean, figuring it out?"

"He—it—knows of Jake's connection with you; figured out that someone in Hell has a direct line to the living, and if you ask me, it's interested. Real interested. If it can use you as a conduit to the living . . . well, I'm serious about you not wanting to sleep for a while. I get the feeling it ain't done with you."

"At Jake's, near the end of my struggle, I felt like something else had tapped into my connection with Jake, like an eavesdropper on a party line. Some other presence was lurking nearby. It took everything I could do to keep it out."

"The absolute most important thing you need to always remember," Skiz said firmly but quietly, as if someone else might be listening, "is that this thing feeds on hate. That's probably why forgiveness works against it, because forgiveness overcomes hate. The person you're looking for needs to move away from hatred, because the more Jake's offense eats at them, the more powerful this thing becomes. And if this demon ever gained control of your soul and had a living presence on Earth, do you realize what . . ."

Skiz paused and thought about something for a minute.

"Do I realize what?" Matt asked.

Skiz thought a moment longer, then motioned with his hand for Matt to sit back down on the sofa.

"Give me just a minute. I'm gonna get something from the kitchen that will help you. Don't move, okay? Do not leave," he said in a tone that was more of a command than a request. He waited for Matt to sit back down.

After Skiz left the room—glancing back at Matt before he walked out to make sure he wasn't moving—Matt heard what sounded like the soft squeak of the back screen door. After not hearing anything for another minute, Matt quietly got up and looked into the kitchen. Skiz had disappeared.

Matt walked over and looked out the kitchen window, thinking perhaps Skiz had gone to the barn to get whatever it was he was retrieving, in which case Matt could join him out there and save him a trip back to the house. Instead, he saw Skiz outside slowly opening the door to his pickup as if operating in stealth mode. The big man snatched the shotgun from the rack on the back pickup window, cocking a shell into place. Skiz then surreptitiously closed the pickup door, being careful not to shut it completely and make a noise.

As Skiz headed toward the house with a grim expression on his face, he looked up and made eye contact with Matt through the window. Skiz froze, as if trying to think of a good reason for the gun, then broke into a lumbering run, charging toward the house like a bull.

Matt turned and raced from the kitchen and through the living room, tripping over a footstool but scrambling back upright without totally hitting the ground. He pulled on the front door to make his escape, but it was locked. He yanked at it a couple more times before regaining his ability to think and turn the bolt, enabling him to scramble outside as Skiz barreled through the kitchen screen door, this time with no pretense of being quiet.

Matt sprinted toward his car full bore like someone running from a pack of wolves. He flung the door open and leapt inside, shutting the door just as Skiz appeared on the front porch, firing his shotgun. The car was far enough away to be peppered hard with shell shot, like the briefest of violent hailstorms, but its windows held. Matt started the car as Skiz cocked another shell in place, lifting the gun barrel, then lowering it without firing.

"He's coming for you!" Skiz bellowed. "You have to kill yourself before it's too late. For everybody's sake. You can't let him in. *DON'T LET HIM IN!*"

TEN

As Matt sped away from Skiz's house, the gravel ricocheted off the bottom of his car, making the sound of a snare drum played by someone on cocaine. His back tires fishtailed on the gravel road twice before he regained control. If only life were that simple.

He tried imagining how the conversation would go when he returned his rental, given the dent Teddy made in the roof, and the pellet indentations that were now scattered across the side of the car. He was definitely putting more than just miles on it, but he quickly reminded himself that this was the least of his concerns right now.

He needed a drink. Even more, he needed a friendly face. While Claire could provide him with the first, he had far less confidence she would offer the second. She'd been gracious that afternoon, but that had been at a funeral—not exactly the ideal setting to bring up past wrongs. Regardless, his immediate reflex had him running to her.

He turned onto Highway 28 and drove straight to the Dirty Creek Bar and Grill, a mile outside Hatchett. He pulled into the dirt parking lot where about a dozen cars and pickups were scattered haphazardly at all angles. At nine o'clock on a Monday night, it wouldn't be the madhouse it used to be on weekends when cars filled the parking lot and the cow pasture across the road served as overflow.

The place looked like an old log cabin, but without the charm. Claire was obviously trying to give the run-down fire trap a hint of civilization with baskets of impatiens hung near the entrance, but drunks had already stuck beer bottles in them.

One lone streetlamp in the parking lot coughed up a forlorn circle of light; the other two looked like they'd been shot out. Bright neon Budweiser and Pabst Blue Ribbon signs in the bar's windows helped illuminate the front of the dark building, a small oasis of bright reds and blues that had been there as long as Matt could remember. Claire's father had built the bar in 1964 and worked it until about two years ago when, according to Matt's mother, he collapsed while yelling at one of his customers for ordering a frozen strawberry daiquiri.

The Dirty Creek was the nicest of Hatchett's three bars, which was a sorry thing to have to say about the other two. Even though Claire's dad drank up half the profits himself every month, he never let the bar spiral into a sanctuary for derelicts, and never put up with anything beyond the usual trouble that comes when people drink too much.

Matt entered the bar, pausing as his senses took a stroll down memory lane. The smell of beer and fried food wafted through the place like a greasy breeze. Metal overhead fans with blades the size of car fenders did their best to at least keep the hot air circulating, but it was a losing proposition. An old-fashioned jukebox blasted "Don't Stop Believin'." Apparently, Claire had updated the song selection. When her father owned the bar, only classic country music made it into the place.

A few customers appeared to be having a good time, a couple of them looked despondent, and one old guy wearing overalls sat at the end of the bar by himself, probably just trying to get through the evening until it was time to go home to bed. There wasn't much to do in Hatchett, and for a certain group of people, the Dirty Creek offered a somewhat reasonable alternative to an empty house.

Most everyone there wore faded blue jeans and either T-shirts or western shirts, and more than a couple were wearing seed caps. Four cowboy hats were hung next to a full booth, while its occupants finished off a pitcher of beer, adding to the collection of three empty pitchers that already decorated their table. Matt wished he'd changed into another T-shirt instead of the one polo shirt he owned. In New York, he didn't think twice about wearing pink, but standing in the Dirty Creek, he felt self-conscious, and then angry at the town's ability to make him care.

Matt and Claire used to do their homework in one of the back booths, sipping Cokes and nibbling on burgers and fries. It felt like their own private refuge, where the rest of the world was kept at bay. Even though Claire's father was always working nearby, Matt never felt like he was watching them.

It was probably unfair to call Claire's father an ugly drunk, but at a minimum he'd been a damn unattractive one, constantly muttering under his breath about everything wrong in his life. He had been relatively civil to Matt—at least he'd never given him a hard time in that way fathers of high school girls often did. Claire claimed that was because her father didn't give a shit who she hung out with or how they treated her.

Matt also didn't have to deal with the man when he was shit-faced drunk, the way Claire did. He knew her mettle was strengthened in large part by life with her father, especially after her mother died when Claire was sixteen and her father basically started treating her more as a cook and housekeeper than a daughter. Matt always tightroped the fine line between being polite to the man, while at the same time remaining loyal to Claire, which meant respecting the righteous hostility she felt toward him.

Matt started toward his and Claire's booth simply out of habit, then caught himself and took a seat at the opposite end of the bar, across from the guy sitting alone. He hadn't been in the place since he turned old enough to legally drink. It felt odd sitting there on a bar stool, a place that, while growing up, had only been the domain of adults, but now he had reached that status. He didn't see anyone around who could get him a drink, so he just sat there, trying to blend in, pink shirt and all.

A few minutes later, Claire appeared from the back room, carrying a tray of clean glasses. She instinctively scanned the place, checking to see if anyone needed her attention, pausing when she spotted Matt, then lifting her chin as a way of acknowledging him. She placed the glasses on the counter, wiped a bar rag across her brow, and walked over.

"And so we meet again," she said.

"I'm in pretty dire need of a beer."

"We happen to sell those here." She lifted the lid to one of the coolers and pulled out a Budweiser, her left hand sliding a napkin underneath it right before she set the bottle down in front of him, a skill obviously honed over time. "If by chance you've turned into one of those people who need to see a beer list, it's probably best you don't tell me."

"Bud's great."

"I had a twerpy salesman stop in a couple weeks ago, lamenting the fact we didn't have any micro brews. Good thing it was me working that night, because Earl would have taken a frying pan to the guy's head."

Matt took a long draw of the ice-cold beer, struck by how much he needed it. "Bar looks good."

"No it doesn't, but thanks for saying so. I suppose for a place that by all rights ought to have been condemned a decade ago, it's not too bad."

"I seem to remember it as being far smokier back in the day."

"Proof that some things actually do change for the better. I don't go home at night smelling like an ashtray anymore. My weekend bartender, though, had to get hypnotized to beat the urge to smoke at work." Claire leaned back against the sink across from Matt. "Hey, tell your mom I'm sorry I didn't have a chance to speak with her at the funeral, but I'll stop by next week and see if she needs anything. How's she doing?"

It caught Matt off guard that Claire had any sort of relationship with his mother, although they did have his abandonment in common.

"She's all right," he said. "Hard to say for sure, since she never says how she's feeling, but I suppose a person can only be so good after what she had to do today."

Claire nodded and snagged a Bud for herself. She opened it and took a swig. "How long you in town for?"

"Probably a couple of days."

"That's not bad for you." Claire looked at her bottle of beer, then shook her head. "Sorry. That came out far bitchier than I meant it to. I'm sure your mother will love having you around."

"I'm actually staying at Jake's place. Mom turned my bedroom into a sewing room."

"Good for her. She probably enjoys having the extra space. It's not like she needed a guest room."

Was that another dig at him? Matt wished he could talk with Claire about what happened ten years earlier, but he still had trouble figuring out how to explain his actions. Either way, it wasn't a conversation he wanted to have at the Dirty Creek.

"Speaking of Jake—and I know this is a left-field question—but do you happen to know of anybody around here who he really screwed over?"

Claire barely choked down her mouthful of beer without spraying it across the bar. "Sorry," she said. "I didn't mean to do that, especially not the same day you buried him, but it would be quicker to give you a list of the people Jake didn't screw over."

Matt nodded sadly, but wasn't surprised. "Know of any women in particular he had problems with? Even more than normal?"

Claire looked at him, curious. "How do you mean?"

"I found something at his place that made me think he did something terrible to someone, enough to make him feel guilty about it."

"Now that's a side of him I never saw. You thinking that's who killed him?"

"I don't know. Maybe. But do me a favor, if anything comes to mind, let me know, would you?" He tried calming his racing heart as he decided to quit stalling. "In fact, I don't know if you're working every evening this week, or if you'd have any interest in getting together sometime to catch up, but—"

"Oh, shit," Claire muttered.

Matt's face flushed, and he started to apologize, angry at himself for even broaching the absurd possibility of getting together again, but then he noticed her attention had shifted. Her face tightened as a walking "Wanted" poster ambled toward the bar. He wore a black Metallica T-shirt with the sleeves ripped off, dirty jeans torn at both knees, and a cap that read "Fuck You," although his caustic expression made the message redundant.

He was shorter than Claire, and could have put on twenty pounds and still been underweight, but the pounds he carried were pure muscle. His arms looked like they had rebar inside. His left bicep boasted a crude tattoo of a skull with a bloody knife in its eye socket that looked like it was made by a kid with a wood-burning kit for five dollars.

The man offered a twisted grin at Claire, then did a double take at Matt. He stopped cold, as if an invisible leash had yanked his collar.

"Holy crap, the prodigal shithead returns. Goddamn you woke me up. Should have known at first glance you weren't Jake—no way he'd wear that shirt. You just get off the polo court or something? And would you look at that color? What is that? Salmon?"

"No, salmon is a fish. This is cotton."

"I know salmon is a fish, asshole. But it's also a color."

"Well, you obviously know a lot more about fashion than me." Matt turned his attention back to his beer.

"Jesus Christ, lighten up. I'm just having fun. Didn't mean to make you cry." He leaned against a stool. "You don't remember me, do you?"

"Sure I do," Matt said. "Bone Nelson. You were three years ahead of me."

"I hear you're a big city boy now."

"Who told you that?"

"Your brother. He couldn't understand how you could leave all this behind. It's got everything you need, don't it?" Bone chuckled and glanced at Claire, but she looked through him like he wasn't there.

"Looks like you've done well for yourself, Bone. I always knew you'd do big things."

Bone's malevolent grin disappeared. "Matter of fact, I have done well for myself, shithead. Speaking of which, I've got a little business to discuss with this lovely little piece here. Now, you be careful not to spill anything on your pretty shirt."

Bone slithered a few feet down the bar, putting space between him and Matt, then put his arms on the bar and glared at Claire until she sighed and walked over.

The music didn't allow Matt to hear their lowered voices, but he could tell it wasn't a social visit. Bone's mouth looked as though whatever he was saying crawled out in the form of a snarl.

Claire shook her head and started turning away. Bone gripped the edge of the bar with both hands as though ready to snap off a piece. Claire stopped and listened again before throwing her rag into the sink. She shook her head decisively and pointed her finger as she spoke. When she turned to walk away, Bone's hand shot out across the bar quick as a rattlesnake and grabbed her wrist, jerking her back toward the bar.

Matt hopped off his barstool. "Watch it, Bone. Let her go."

Bone stared at Claire for a moment, as if incredulous anyone would interrupt him. Claire looked more concerned about Matt than her own situation as Bone released her and turned toward him.

"What the hell did you say?"

"Bone, let it go," Claire said in a quiet voice.

"What do you mean 'let it go'? I'm not the one butting my mug in where it doesn't belong." Bone moved menacingly toward Matt. "I realize you haven't been around much lately, polo boy, and probably don't understand how things work around here, so let me explain it to you. There are people around this town you can tell what to do—and to be honest, that's most of 'em—but there are a few you can't. And I'm one of *them*. Understand?"

"I understand that threatening a woman isn't a sign of toughness."

"Then how about I threaten a man, instead? Granted, a man

wearing a prissy pink shirt, but theoretically a man just the same." As Bone came within a foot of Matt, a switchblade clicked open in his left hand. Matt didn't even see him bring it out, but that didn't matter once he saw light reflecting off the blade.

In Brooklyn, Matt lived a life where sometimes fists got thrown. That didn't happen often, and most of those skirmishes took place right after he first arrived there—usually when too much alcohol started to affect his decision-making process, or when he felt like he deserved a good beating. For the most part, he could hold his own. Those scuffles, however, had never involved a weapon-wielding wacko with a name like "Bone." Apparently, Matt had to return home to Hatchett to suddenly encounter the face of true violence.

"How about if I slice off an ear or carve out an eye?" Bone said. "Does that meet your definition of toughness?"

"You with a knife and me unarmed? Yeah, that's my definition of toughness."

"Aww, you all weepy because I don't play fair? Boo-fucking-hoo."

"I'm not looking for a fight, Bone."

"No, 'course you ain't. Not now. But what you can't seem to wrap your little bunny rabbit brain around is the fact that it don't really matter what you are or aren't looking for. What matters is what I'm looking for, and right now I'm thinking 'bout cutting off a piece of you. A little souvenir of our time together."

Bone moved even closer as he rested the knife's icy blade just under Matt's left eye. His breath smelled like motor oil. Matt continued staring at Bone, not flinching, but also definitely not comfortable.

"Back off, Bone," Claire said, holding up the receiver to the bar phone, "or I'm calling Sheriff Wilson."

Bone continued staring intently at Matt, his eyes dead as a shark's as he tilted his head from one side to the other, as if trying to decide which piece of Matt he wanted to cut.

"Look, Bone . . ."

Bone slid the switchblade down and pressed it hard against Matt's bottom lip.

"Shhh. Unless you want to lose one of them lips of yours, don't say another damn word. You ain't nothing but noise to me, boy. Nothing but noise."

Bone leaned closer, their faces inches apart, but Matt didn't look away. Bone lowered his knife.

"Probably not right for your mom to lose both sons the same week, although who knows? Maybe she wouldn't consider you a loss. From what Jake told me, she barely considers you a son."

Claire put down the phone and turned to Matt. "Go on and get out of here. I'll catch up with you another time."

Matt didn't want to abandon Claire. He finally had an opportunity to be there for her, something he had wanted for the past ten years. He remained silent, unmoving.

Bone started laughing. "Guess you ain't one hundred percent pussy. You're not scurrying out of here like a scared little rabbit yet." Bone raised the blade of his knife in front of Matt's face again as his smile evaporated. "But you should be."

"Matt, I'll be fine," Claire said matter-of-factly. "Seriously. This probably looks like a big deal to you, but this dance with Bone, I just call it Monday."

Matt looked over to make sure she was serious.

"Go on. It's okay. Bone just sometimes gets a little full of himself, which always surprises me, since I figure he's already too full of shit for anything else to fit."

Bone chuckled at Claire's comment, though his expression didn't reveal any sort of amusement.

"She'll be fine, soldier," Bone said. "Why don't you head on home and cry about your piece-of-shit brother? Somebody oughta feel bad about him getting himself killed. Sure as hell won't be anyone around here, will it, girl?"

Matt wanted to show Claire he was there for her, that he wasn't intimidated, but her eyes told him to leave. He took another drink of his beer.

"I hope we can talk more sometime," he said to Claire, then turned and took the bottle with him as he walked out of the Dirty Creek, feeling smaller with every step.

ELEVEN

Matt's stomach churned like a washing machine as he made his way down the nighttime road back to Jake's. His pulse worked at a manic pace as he replayed in his head what had just happened at the Creek. His physical reaction was no longer the result of his encounter with Bone, but because he had left Claire to deal with him on her own. He knew she could probably handle that asshole better than him, but that didn't lessen his agitation.

He resisted the urge to turn around, because he knew nothing good would come of that. He wouldn't suddenly be able to take on Bone and his switchblade any better than he had the first time. If anything, it would only end with his blood on Claire's barroom floor. If he thought that would in any way change her opinion of him for the better then it would probably be worth it, but more than likely she'd just be pissed at having one more thing to clean up.

His thoughts returned to what Skiz told him about finding the person Jake had hurt the most and getting that person to a place of forgiveness. But what if that person was someone like Bone? He couldn't imagine persuading Bone to forgive anybody, although he agreed with Skiz that whoever murdered Jake was likely the person most wronged.

If the sheriff was right and a woman had killed Jake, then the letter on Jake's table seemed like Matt's best lead. He had to find out who wrote it—whoever she was, he hoped he could show her that Jake felt remorse. He recognized that an awful long stretch of road ran between murder and forgiveness, but it still felt like his best bet, even if it remained a long shot.

As he considered all of this, he noted how easily he had bought into this whole scenario. Skiz had told him a story that sounded as reasonable as talking monkeys riding unicorns, and yet he'd latched onto it as if it were a scientific fact.

What if the terror he'd suffered through was the last remnant of his psychic connection to Jake? Who knew what happened after death?

Wasn't it possible there were final neurons firing that would soon dwindle to nothing? That sounded like a far more logical explanation than Jake being in Hell, with Satan aware of their connection. His mind yearned for that explanation. His gut believed otherwise.

Matt reached the driveway leading to Jake's, which was even harder to find in the dark. As he drove toward the house, the end of Jake's driveway and the lawn next to the house undulated wherever his car lights landed, looking like the rippling surface of a lake at night. It disoriented him for a moment until he realized the area was covered with crows. He slammed on the brakes.

At first, it looked like fifty or sixty birds were scattered about, but those were just the ones he could make out. The black shapes blended almost indistinguishably with the shadowy ground beyond the reach of the headlights, with only the occasional reflection of an eerie doll-like eye betraying their presence.

The birds moved out of his way, unconcerned as they hopped to one side of the car or the other. When he reached the railroad tie that marked the end of the driveway, he killed the engine and waited. He honked the horn and a few of the crows hopped away, but most held their ground, like they were part of a collective rather than independent agents.

The crows didn't scatter as he tentatively exited the car, but instead seemed indifferent to his movement as he slowly shuffled his way toward the porch. The birds directly in front of him fluttered their wings and moved just out of the way of his step, but didn't give him any more space than needed. More birds blanketed large portions of the lawn. Maybe an infestation of some insect had drawn the birds, but that didn't explain the ones lining the porch railing.

He made his way toward the house and tried not to kick the visitors, tempting though that was after his confrontation with Bone. The emotional toll of the day and the churning beer in his stomach were starting to fray his nerves, and the crows weren't helping. Something about the crows was off. Maybe the way they all seemed to be watching him.

All he wanted was to go to bed, but after his talk with Skiz, he had crossed that off his list of things to do, despite his exhaustion.

He heard a loud screech behind him. He looked back over his shoulder and saw an exceptionally large crow perched on the roof of his car, staring at him and cawing so loudly it could have had a bullhorn. Other crows started to echo the large crow's cries, the sound building in intensity as more and more joined in until their chorus consumed the night air. Matt feared they were going to attack, even though they gave no indication of any movement. All at once they stopped crying out, and the night was again silent.

Matt continued to watch the crow on his car for a moment longer, then turned toward the house. He paused again when he noticed nearly every room in Jake's house lit up. He figured Jake must have had several lights on a timer, because he knew he hadn't turned any of them on. Given Jake's profession, it probably made sense to make the house always look occupied.

When Matt got a few yards from the porch, something inside the house caught his attention and he froze. A shadow flitted past the closed curtain in the living room. It looked like an unusually tall, slender man, but then the same shadow swept past the kitchen curtains immediately after. A second after that, it whisked past each of the four windows on the second floor running the length of the house, an impossibility at that speed.

Matt scanned the sky for the full moon, but he could barely see its dim glow behind the clouds. It could have been the shadow of a crow flying between a light and the house, but he couldn't pinpoint a light source. Plus, the shadow looked more human than crow.

He stood for a couple of minutes, waiting to see if anything else appeared in the windows, but the glow from the lights inside continued unbroken. He walked onto the porch and paused at the front door for a moment, then decided the day had been long enough without overreacting.

Matt stepped inside, pausing in the doorway and listening to the quiet house. "Hello?" he called out. He got no response, nor did he expect one. He didn't even know for sure why he felt compelled to say anything in the first place. Then he called out a second time.

He went into the living room and saw one of the frayed window curtains gently fluttering in the room like a flag, even though he was sure he had shut the windows after having aired out the place. As he reached over to close it, he glanced outside and no longer saw any crows. He leaned out the window and scanned the area, but they had all disappeared.

He closed the window before heading toward the kitchen, then quietly cursed when he remembered he hadn't picked up any groceries. The thought of more potato chips and beer didn't appeal to him. What he wouldn't give right now to be sitting at Buzz's Brooklyn Bar and Grill with a burger in front of him. Or, even better, at the Creek. But he grabbed the mostly empty bag of chips and stuffed a handful into his mouth, figuring it had to be better than an empty stomach.

As he walked past the stairway to the second floor, he heard a sound coming from upstairs. He willed himself up the stairs and walked down the hall toward Jake's bedroom until he heard it again. He stopped under the pull-down steps that led to the attic and listened: something scratched the attic floor every ten or fifteen seconds. He reached for the pull-cord, then thought better of it. The most likely suspect was a rat, or even a possum that had gotten up there from outside, and what could he do about that now? Try to catch it? Not tonight.

He started down the hall when the sound changed into something more of a rapping, like someone knocking on the attic floor every fifteen to twenty seconds, a sharp, distinct sound. The noise was strange enough that he knew he'd be thinking about it all night if he didn't at least take a look and see if he could find the source. Hopefully, he'd see something reassuring, like a loose board over the attic fan, but if he saw some sort of varmint, he'd put up with it for the limited time he stayed there.

He grabbed the rope and reluctantly pulled down the squealing retractable steps to the attic, praying nothing with teeth would drop onto him, then stealthily climbed the steps toward the dark attic. He hoped there was some sort of light up there that would be of more help than his phone's flashlight. It probably made more sense to wait until daylight anyway, but he knew most things that make their home in an attic are nocturnal. Plus, it took his mind off wanting to sleep.

He cautiously stuck his head up into the sauna-like attic, as if peeking out of a wartime foxhole. He glanced around, but couldn't make anything out. Waving his arm around slowly above him, his fingers finally made contact with a cord that hung from the ceiling. He pulled it, and a bare 60-watt light bulb did the best it could to illuminate the darkness.

Matt didn't realize how tense he had been until he felt himself exhale an apprehensive breath upon seeing a completely empty attic: not a single box, tool, or piece of clothing. He couldn't see into the shadows at either end of the attic, but felt confident they were equally empty. He climbed one more step so that his shoulders now cleared the attic door and stood quietly, listening to the silence until a savage snarl arose from the far corner behind him. Something charged toward his head, its claws clicking hard against the wooden floor. He whipped around and almost tumbled off the steps. He didn't see anything, but felt too unnerved to look carefully. He scurried down the steps and quickly folded them before flinging them back into the ceiling with a bang.

He waited under the attic door, breathing hard, ready to race down the stairs and out to his car if necessary, but the sound had stopped. He told himself the accumulated stress of the day had caused him to overreact to noises that could be explained in the morning. Critters in the attic weren't at all uncommon in the house where he grew up, and the animal was probably on the roof anyway, which is why he couldn't see it. Just the same, it unnerved him.

After a few silent moments, he went into the bathroom to clean up, more than ready to see this day end. At least he wasn't feeling sleepy anymore after his foray into the attic. He stood brushing his teeth, keeping his ears open for the scratching sound, but he couldn't hear anything.

The toothpaste took the beer-and-chips taste out of his mouth, but it couldn't prevent his stomach from starting to turn. As if a breaker had been flipped, his forehead became flushed and beads of sweat started trickling down his face. He spit out a mouthful of toothpaste and stood leaning against the white, chipped bathroom sink, staring at his pale reflection in the cracked mirror.

He felt the nausea building like a fast-approaching storm and tried fighting it back. He took labored breaths as he fought for control of his stomach. It could be a case of not having enough food in him, or the combination of what he had put in his stomach. As he imagined the mixture of potato chips and beer inside him, his stomach flipped again, and his face was now drenched in sweat. He tried holding his stomach back from the tipping point as long as he could, but he knew what the outcome of this battle would be.

Within seconds he dropped to his knees in front of the toilet, now committed, with the final act only being a matter of time. He felt a sharp pain in his stomach, as if Bone's switchblade had been inserted, and tried taking even deeper breaths to calm his system. When he put his head closer to the toilet, the distinct smell of sewer water triggered the inevitable.

He couldn't hold it back any longer, nor did he want to, knowing he would feel relief if he just let go. He gagged once before the contents of his stomach exploded into the toilet. After expelling everything, he retched again with nothing left to show for it, sounding like a wounded animal.

His fever started to subside almost immediately until his face felt chilled, as if covered with frost. He panted over the toilet, a small ribbon of saliva dangling from his mouth as the heat dissipated. He wondered why he always fought back the urge to vomit, even though the subsequent relief from doing so was welcomed.

He reached up and flushed the toilet. As he pushed himself up off his knees, he glanced down and saw what appeared to be five or six dirty gray grubs, each about an inch and a half long, squirming blindly as they spun away in the whirlpool of water.

He dropped back onto his knees and watched in disbelief as the formless creatures swirled out of sight. He continued staring as the bowl started to refill, watching in case they resurfaced, but the water remained clear.

It had to have been bits of potato chips, or perhaps the worm-like creatures had been under the rim of the toilet from the start. No way they could have come from him.

He stretched out on the floor, resting his cheek on the cool tiles. He closed his eyes, the acidic burn of vomit lingering in his mouth.

Matt got up onto his knees, faced the bathroom door, and bowed his head to pray. He couldn't remember the last time he had truly prayed for help, for strength, for guidance. At first, he wondered if it was sacrilegious to pray next to a toilet, then he decided God would understand. His larger concern came from feeling like a hypocrite, turning to a power whose existence he might have denied a few hours earlier. He still didn't know if he believed, but if he put any credence in Skiz's intuition about Jake's current predicament, he was willing to be flexible in his beliefs.

He made a vow that first thing in the morning, he would hunt down the person Jake had wronged. Until then, he'd make a pot of strong coffee and do his best to stay awake.

Tomorrow was going to be a long day. He caught himself wondering how many of those he had left.

TWELVE

Matt stepped out of his air-conditioned car and into a Nebraska heat that seemed to hold a grudge against him. It was only a little past noon and already 102 degrees, although the humidity made it feel like 250.

He was exhausted from not having slept the previous night, and although he was grateful that the birds hadn't returned—and his stomach had settled down after having thrown up—that didn't make him any more alert this morning.

His destination was a nondescript building wedged between a livestock feed store and a dry cleaner. The shades were drawn over the lone window, which identified the space as Hatchett Sheriff's Department. If not for the stenciled sign on the glass, the building could have easily passed for pretty much any type of business, albeit a small one.

Matt wiped his forehead with his shirtsleeve and walked into the sheriff's office. Four empty desks were behind the reception desk, but nobody was in sight. Three pedestal fans were scattered around the room, their heads moseying side to side in a half-hearted effort to provide relief, but in reality, they were just killing time.

Matt was searching for a bell or something to announce his presence when he heard a toilet flush. Immediately after, a door opened and Sheriff Will Wilson stepped out, zipping up his pants and cinching his belt at the same time that he noticed Matt.

"You caught me," he said, turning his back to Matt in order to finish dressing himself, then turning back around when he was done. "Sorry about that. Drives my wife crazy that I emerge half-assembled from the bathroom. Doesn't seem like it'd be too hard to get the belt fastened before walking out, but there you go."

Sheriff Wilson was a substantial guy in his late fifties, slightly under six feet and well over 260 pounds, with a gut that dared the buttons of his shirt to stay on. His black hair resided one stop down the road from gray, and his free-range mustache offered a sneak preview of the shade his hair would soon be. His out-of-control eyebrows resembled tiny bales of hay, but his goofy grin and 'what-can-you-do' shrug gave him the mien of a friendly guy.

"Not trying to show off my highly trained detective skills or nothing," he said as he approached the counter, "but I'm betting you're Jake's brother." He reached out and shook Matt's hand, then turned solemn. "Sorry for your loss."

"I was wondering if we could talk," Matt said.

"Nothing I'd like more. Come on back to my office."

In his office, Wilson motioned for Matt to have a seat. "Glad you stopped by. I was hoping to have a chance to speak with you. You saved me a trip."

"I saw you at the funeral."

"Yeah, sorry about that. Wasn't trying to be insensitive. I'd hoped to blend into the background and not be rude, but that's hard to do in a setting like that, especially for someone my size. I gotta tell you, you threw me for a loop when I first saw you sitting next to your mom. Anybody ever tell you that you and your brother looked alike?" The sheriff grinned and leaned back in his chair.

"It's come up a couple of times."

"I'll bet. Kinda spooky, the resemblance. I asked one of the deputies who grew up around here about you. He said you weren't nothing like Jake. You're living . . . where now? Somewhere back East?"

"New York."

"That's right. New York City. The Big Apple. Why's it a Big Apple, anyway?"

Matt wondered if the sheriff was giving him a hard time, but he appeared to be sincerely asking.

"I have no idea."

"Don't matter, I suppose. Regardless of what it's called, there's a hell of a lot of people in that place. Bet it was a big adjustment for you, coming from a place like this."

"It was fine. But this was a good town to grow up in."

"Probably a better town when you were young. We work hard to keep it that way, but sometimes I think we're losing ground."

"Because of the drugs?"

Wilson studied Matt carefully. "Pretty much. You know about that?"

"Andy told me."

"Who?"

"Father Pearman. We were friends growing up."

"Yeah, to be perfectly candid, this town's at serious risk of being flushed down the crapper. Meth is a big business around Hatchett. You got all these young people—actually, they ain't all young people—getting strung out because they can't find a job. Used to be more than enough work on the farms, but everybody's selling their land to the big corporations, and most of what needs to be done is being done with them big machines." Wilson tossed his pen onto his desk in disgust.

"Andy said Jake might have been part of the meth problem."

"Ain't no 'might' about it. That boy was in the thick of it. Don't mean to spit on your brother's memory, but this town is better off with one less supplier. Or would be if there weren't some other snake ready to slither out of its hole to take his spot."

Wilson sighed and bit his lower lip.

"Sorry about that, Mr. Davis. That was uncalled for. I got a brother, too, so I don't know why I said that. Suppose I'm just getting a little beat down by all this."

Matt always felt conflicting emotions when talking about Jake. On the one hand, he knew his brother could blow past any boundaries of acceptable behavior—something that had caused even Matt pain in the past—but at the same time, he felt defensive. Given how they used to always have each other's backs growing up, he wanted to stick up for Jake his brother, but he didn't know how to defend Jake the drug dealer, who profited off others' weaknesses.

"I was wondering if you could tell me a bit more about Jake," Matt said.

Wilson looked surprised. "Hell, he's your brother. I was sort of hoping you could do the same thing for me, but I'm fine going first. What do you want to know?"

"It's been made abundantly clear since I returned home that Jake wasn't on anybody's most popular list, but do you know of anyone in particular he especially hurt? Someone he might have felt guilty about?"

Wilson blew a puff of air from his lips as if he were spitting out a watermelon seed.

"I'm going to be candid with you for a moment here: your brother was trouble, pure and simple. Well, definitely not pure, and truth be told, not simple, either. That's probably the thing that disappointed me most about your brother: most of these asshole dealers have the I.Q. of an empty refrigerator box, but your brother had brains. Unfortunately, he also wanted money and power. It was all about him. But to answer your question, we don't have enough time in the day to go through the list of people your brother pissed off, and I doubt he felt bad about any of them."

"But do you feel the murder was drug-related?"

"No, to be honest, I don't. I've got some fairly reliable ears in that world. If it was about drugs, I'm pretty sure I'd know. But I do think it was someone he knew."

"What makes you say that?"

"He was shot up close. That usually makes it personal. Plus, Jake didn't let his guard down around too many people."

"Andy also said you think the killer is female."

Wilson looked surprised and took a moment before starting to answer, then stopped again, as if trying to figure out what he should or shouldn't say.

"Well, that wasn't exactly for the good Father to overhear, but since we're swapping information here, sure, I'll tell you, although I gotta ask that you keep this one between us, because the investigation is obviously ongoing. But I found a couple of shoe prints in the blood, the kind high heels would make. So either a woman did the shooting, or at least one was there between Jake getting killed and us arriving. Or it was a guy wearing high heels, but you probably see that more in your Big Apple than we do here."

"I appreciate you trusting me with that. And it might be relevant for you to know I found an unsigned letter at Jake's house," Matt said. "It sounded like he was trying to apologize to a woman he'd hurt. Since that's out of character, I wondered who it might be. It's sounding like it could be the same person."

Wilson perked up upon hearing about the letter. "I've no idea, but bring it in and let me take a look at it. Internal scars cause more murders than physical scars, so this letter might be a clue. Doesn't matter that your brother was a—pardon my French—a prick, he still deserves justice. Actually, I'm not sure 'prick' is French, although I suppose if any word was, it would be that one. Regardless, you don't need to be getting involved looking for this person."

"He was my brother, Sheriff. Don't you think I want to see this solved?"

"I'm sure you do, and I can respect that." Wilson leaned forward with a stern expression. "But let me give you a piece of advice: don't go messing around with the boys who are dealing the meth. I'm serious. They don't play nice. Last thing I need is some junior wannabe detective stirring things up. You want to help, bring me anything you find about your brother, no matter how it makes him look. Maybe it'll help me put away these other nimrods. You understand?"

Matt picked up a tougher tone from the Sheriff than he'd been using before. Almost threatening.

"Whatever he did in the past, it's done," Matt said guardedly.

"Look here, let me be real clear about one thing. I'm busting my ass trying to solve his murder, so if I find you come across something that might be of help to me and you didn't bring it to my attention, you'll see another side of me you won't like."

Matt stood. "I promise to take that into consideration, but I'm not sure you're in a position to threaten me, Sheriff. I don't think there's a lot you could do to me."

"Not to you, I suppose, but your mom wouldn't be so fast to forgive you."

Matt got caught by that curve ball. Wilson looked uncomfortable having played that card but was apparently willing to up the ante.

"What do you mean by that?" Matt asked.

"Okay, look, I didn't mean for us to get all adversarial here, but since you asked, it's not going to be long before I tie Jake to the drug money. He was smart, but now that he's passed, I'll have more latitude to check bank accounts, and trust me, I'll find where it landed. He paid off your mom's mortgage. Did you know that? I may be a small-town sheriff, but I'll tie the mortgage to the drugs, and once I do that, I could legally seize your mom's house." He sat back. "And I will, if I need to."

Matt was stunned. One minute he's having an aw-shucks conversation with the local law about Jake, and the next, his mother is being threatened with eviction. His blood pressure skyrocketed.

"What's going on here, Sheriff?"

"I'm sorry, but understand this, boy. I'm responsible for this town. I was elected to keep the people of Hatchett safe and to make this town better for everyone, and right now, I'm watching it all slip away. I'm outmanned, I'm outspent, and, truth be told, I'm out of my league. Shit, four years ago I ran a hatchery and sold baby chicks, and now I'm trying to deal with all this. These scumbags win through intimidation and violence, so I guess I'm starting to feel like I've got to play rough. Don't get me wrong. I'm not saying I'm going to take your mom's house just to get the last piss on Jake. Your mom's a good person. I'm only saying that if you find something that can help me make a dent with these assholes, then you need to share it with me. That's all I'm asking. No reason we can't help each other, is there?"

Although Matt was angry, he understood the point Wilson was making.

"If I find something, I'll let you know, Sheriff. You have my word. But quid pro quo. If you hear of anyone who held a notable grudge against my brother—male or female, dealer or not—I'd sure appreciate a heads-up from you. Fair enough?"

"I suppose, but I'm telling you, if you start poking around the meth business on your own, be darn careful who you trust. There's a lot of money at stake. A hell of a lot of money, and that does things to people like you wouldn't believe, so you best not trust anybody. If you've got questions you need answered, ask me. I've been burned too many times confiding in people I thought were good, God-fearing citizens, only to have it come back and bite me in the butt. Too much money clouds some people's brains."

The sheriff lifted himself out of his chair and extended his hand. Matt looked him straight in the eye and shook his hand.

"Again, I'm real sorry for your loss. Please tell your mom my Maggie will be bringing by a casserole later this week."

Matt turned and started walking out of Wilson's office.

"And don't be saddling me with another murder to solve, you hear? You best be careful. This isn't the town you grew up in. It's turned mean. Real mean. Be careful, or you'll find that out soon enough."

THIRTEEN

The sheriff's office was only three blocks from Hatchett's central square. Matt felt the need to walk off the tense conversation with the sheriff, so he headed that way, despite the blast furnace trying to pass itself off as weather.

He stopped at a gas station along the way and bought a can of Coke from what appeared to be the same vending machine from his youth. He then sweated his way to the town square where he'd hung out as a kid, a Midwest town's attempt at a park. It filled an entire block, with a gazebo in the middle, large enough to accommodate the twenty-member community band. If Norman Rockwell had ever stopped in Hatchett, he would have been drawn to that site.

Matt climbed the six steps into the gazebo and sat on the bench that ran along the perimeter of the inside. Being out of the afternoon sun provided at least a hint of relief, but not much. He pressed the cold can of Coke against his forehead, then sat back and checked out downtown Hatchett from his slightly raised vantage point.

The four streets that bordered the town square were home to stores Matt had known all his life. These shops made up the heart of town, and would probably keep kicking as long as the town did—although by the looks of things, Matt couldn't guess how long that might be.

In the center of the block that ran along the northern side of the park sat the dime store where he and Jake had spent hours as young boys each Halloween, trying to decide which cheap plastic mask they wanted to get. They could never afford the expensive rubber ones, instead having to settle for the plastic kind with the rubber band that broke just by looking at it too hard. Jake had always opted for ghouls and monsters, while Matt went with superheroes or sports stars. On Halloween night, they'd fill up their plastic pumpkins with enough sweets to open their own candy store, then dump their loot into one pile and start dividing it based on their individual tastes. Like most everything else they had, it was shared equally.

The pharmacy continued to hold its place on the southern side of the city square, next to the sandstone-colored bank that was built in the late 1800s and showed each and every one of its years. The clothing store still proudly trumpeted its offerings of polyester sports coats in the store window with large "50% Off" signs that had been there since Matt was in high school.

On the eastern side of the park—which also fronted Highway 28—sat the Dairy Barn, a place known for its soft serve ice cream, cheap burgers, and indigestion. The Dairy Barn also served as a type of feeder system for kids cruising the Hatchett strip. Kids in early junior high rode their bikes to "The Barn" in the early evening hours to hang out with friends and sit on the outdoor picnic tables facing the highway. They would lean back and watch the cars drive back and forth, checking to see which high school kids were out and about and what they were driving.

A small number of those kids, once they reached upper junior high grades, were fortunate enough—and usually had to be cool enough—to be invited to ride along with a high school friend who had a driver's license. Eventually, everyone grew old enough to get their own driver's license and got their turn cruising the strip, honking at each other while ignoring the dweeby middle schoolers who had taken their place on the picnic tables.

On the surface, most of the stores looked pretty much the same as Matt remembered, although they hadn't aged well. The entire town seemed to have turned gray, like a once-vibrant person who had grown elderly and couldn't hide the decay anymore. Downtown Hatchett, with its smattering of cars around the city square, couldn't exactly be called vibrant.

Even though he had only walked a short distance from the sheriff's office, the front of his T-shirt was already darkened from sweat. The humidity, on top of the already soaring temperature, could be sued for cruel and unusual punishment. He was sure he could actually see the waves of heat, although whether it was the heat, the moisture, or simply his brain short-circuiting, he didn't know. He considered heading back to his car and going over to his mother's, but decided to spend a few minutes taking in the scene.

A young woman sat on one of the park benches, staring at her phone as her small son sat on a nearby swing. Even the child appeared to be too hot to make an effort on the swing; instead, he just sat there, staring at his shoes.

On the other side of the park, three young guys who looked like they should be in high school were slouched against a set of monkey bars, not talking to one another. They were all skinny as neglected saplings and clearly strung out; they could have been extras in a zombie movie. Two of them wore jeans with a wide collection of rips; not the strategically placed cuts that fashionable young people paid two or three hundred dollars for back in New York, but the kind that came from decay and a lack of money to replace them.

He thought again about Wilson's threat. He didn't really think the sheriff would take his mother's house; instead he saw Wilson as a drowning man grasping at anything that could be a life preserver. But if Matt did find something that made Jake look bad, he'd have to rethink his original plan to destroy the evidence. The stakes were higher than he originally thought.

He looked up and saw that one of the young tweakers had entered the gazebo, while his two friends watched from across the park. The young man emitted an odor that gave the stockyard a run for its money. "You gotta set me up, man," he said to Matt, hesitant to make eye contact, acting like a house dog encountering a wolf. "I'm hurting."

"I'm not giving you any money."

"Money? No, man, I've got some. Or I will. I'm seeing Tank later and he owes me. I need something now."

Matt sighed. "I'm not Jake."

"Come on, man. Don't do me like that. I'm hurting real—"

"I'm not Jake. I'm his brother."

The tweaker looked at Matt as if trying to decide whether to be angry or start crying, then he kicked the bench weakly. "Rose is right, man. You're a snake. And what you did to her? What an asshole."

"Who's Rose?"

"Yeah, funny man. Screw you." He turned to head back to his friends, but Matt stood and grabbed his shoulder. The kid was so emaciated, Matt worried he might dislocate his shoulder when he spun him around. The kid cowered when Matt made contact, as if expecting to get punched.

"Okay, look, I know what I did to Rose was bad and I want to make it right. Seriously. Where is she? I want to talk with her."

The kid eyed him suspiciously, then shook loose from Matt's grasp. He stared at Matt with a glazed expression before standing up straight and trying to muster up his best impersonation of a position of power.

"If it's that important, give me a hit," he said as he held out his hand.

"I don't have anything on me, but I can get you some later."

The kid frowned, so Matt took out his wallet and put a twenty in his palm, then added another one when the kid kept his hand out.

"Here. Now when I catch you with some stuff, you can buy it back with the money I gave you."

The tweaker smirked as he looked carefully at Matt. "You really aren't Jake, are you? Holy shit." He shoved the twenties into his front pocket like a wad of tissues.

"So, Rose?"

The kid looked like he'd already forgotten what they'd been talking about. "Oh, yeah. She kind of floats around, but there's a soup kitchen across the street from St. Luke's where she helps out to get some cash. Otherwise, she could be in any shithole."

"What did Jake do to her?"

"That's between her and Jake. She can tell you if she wants."

The kid wobbled down the steps and slumped his way back over to his buddies, pointing at Matt but not showing them his newfound fortune.

"Making new friends?"

Matt turned and saw Claire looking up at him from the grass on the other side of the gazebo.

"Nice young man," Matt said. "He's thinking of Harvard when he graduates."

"You're the one with the college experience."

He nodded toward the steps. "Come on up. Get out of the sun."

"Sure, what the heck, but it's going to cost you a sip of that Coke." She walked around and joined him, grabbing his soda as she lowered herself onto the bench. "You do know this town has air-conditioned places to hang out, right?"

"I just wanted to check out the town square. I was meeting with the sheriff about Jake earlier. Sounds like he has his hands full."

Claire looked at the other side of the gazebo, where a dozen empty plastic meth vials were scattered under the bench like cigarette butts. "He's a good man, but probably not for these times. Seems to be trying, though, so I'll give him that."

"It seems like things are different since you and I were growing up here."

"Things change. That's what they do."

"But will the town recover? It looks like it's falling apart."

"Really?" Claire looked at him, surprised, then surveyed the town. "That's interesting. Maybe living here, it's harder to pick up on the changes since they're gradual, but they're hitting you all at once. But yeah, I have no doubt Hatchett will be just fine. It's a great little town. You've probably just forgotten how to appreciate its charm."

As if on cue, one of the high school boys staggered over to a tree and bent over before throwing up. His two friends just watched him, then returned to staring at nothing, as if neither were in charge of their own bodies and were just awaiting further directions from elsewhere.

"Okay, maybe 'charming' was a bit optimistic," Claire said, shrugging, "but it's still a good place to live."

"I'm glad I ran into you," Matt said. "I feel terrible about bailing on you last night with Bone."

"You did the right thing. It would have caused more headaches if you stayed. I've been dealing with his crap for over a year. I suppose one day he'll ramp things up, but so far, it's all bluster."

"What's his problem?"

"He wants to sell meth out of the Creek. The place is packed on weekends, and he thinks he's the Warren Buffett of drugs, but I'll shut the place down before I let him sell there. Or else he'll shut it down for me. That wouldn't help him any, but he's not exactly a Rhodes Scholar."

"Have you told Wilson about your issues with Bone?"

"Sure, but the best he can do is tell Bone he's got his eye on him, which pretty much means nothing, or at least Bone doesn't seem to give it any weight."

Claire lifted Matt's soda to her lips, tipping it back and keeping it there until she'd finished it off. She handed back the empty can and shrugged. "Oops."

"Come on. Let me buy you your own cold drink."

"If it will get me out of this heat, then I'm game. Besides, it's the least you can do, seeing as how you forgot to leave a tip last night."

"In that case, I'll buy you a candy bar, too. Does the pharmacy still have a soda fountain?"

Claire stood. "Yes, it does."

They walked down the gazebo steps and headed toward Struthers's Pharmacy, crossing in the middle of the street—there was hardly a need to look for oncoming cars.

Matt had to fight every instinct to reach out and take her hand.

They both sighed as the air conditioning at Struthers's Pharmacy embraced them, the cool air washing over them like a salve. Matt noticed the hodgepodge of items for sale on the shelf next to the entrance: boxes of bath salts, hand lotion, an alarm clock that looked like it came from the eighties—and probably did—a stuffed puppy with ping-pong ball eyes, and an impressive selection of toothbrushes, all priced to sell.

They made their way to the back of the store, where six stools covered with cracked red Naugahyde were tucked away behind the magazine stand. They grabbed two stools and looked around for someone to help them. Finally, Pete Struthers shuffled out from behind the pharmacy counter. He had to be nearing eighty, and appeared to be wearing the same powder blue bow tie and thigh-length pharmacy jacket that Matt remembered from ten years ago.

"How you doing, Claire?" Struthers smiled at her, then looked at Matt as if trying to pull a name from a filing cabinet, his eyes finally brightening. "Well hey there, Matt. Nice to see you. Heard about your brother. Very sorry for your loss."

"Thanks, Mr. Struthers. How are you doing?"

"Me? I'm sittin' on a rainbow. What'll you two have?"

Matt traded a look with Claire. "For old time's sake?"

"It's barely one o'clock!"

"It's three-thirty in the afternoon somewhere."

"I'm not sure time zones come in half-hour increments."

"Work with me here," Matt said.

Claire shook her head but couldn't restrain a slight grin. "You New York City boys and your decadent ways."

Matt turned back to the pharmacist. "Two root beer floats, please, assuming you still make them."

"Course I still make 'em," Struthers said. "I'm sure as heck not going to mess with a good thing."

Matt and Claire watched the elderly man create what they used to consider the quintessential display of alchemy, taking vanilla ice cream and root beer and pouring that elixir of the gods into a tall, frosted glass, then adding a maraschino cherry on top.

"I remember you ordering these back when you were both just pups," Struthers said, pushing the floats toward them. The vanilla ice cream bounced on the surface like a fishing bobber on a pond. "The two of you sitting there, sharing one of these with two straws straight out of some Disney cartoon. About as cute a couple as I'd ever seen. I know you were just kids, but I always figured if any of the high school sweethearts around here ended up getting married, it would have been the two of you."

Matt flushed. Claire kept her attention on her float. "Well," she said, "now we each get our own float, so sometimes things work out for the best."

Struthers chuckled and headed back toward the pharmacy. "Let me know if you need anything else."

"So how is life in the big city?" Claire asked, after Struthers was out of earshot. "You like living there?"

"It's fine," Matt said. "There's always something going on."

"Just like Hatchett," Claire said, "except for the 'always something going on' part."

"Very similar."

"Your mom says you're working for a big ad agency, just like you always said you wanted to do."

"Well, it's not all that."

"I'm sure it's very stressful. We don't have stress here in Hatchett, in case you've forgotten."

"What do you have here? What do you do on your evenings off? Assuming, of course, you get evenings off."

"Not on weekends, but I usually take off Tuesdays—today—and sometimes Wednesdays."

"That probably puts a crimp in your dating life," Matt said, trying to sound casual, but feeling as though his words came out with a mega-watt spotlight shining on them. He looked at his drink when he said it, as though that would somehow make it sound less prying. He immediately felt too uncomfortable to wait for a response. "So what do people do around here for fun, anyway?"

"Softball games, bowling alley. Same old stuff as when you were here. The movie theater is open again."

"No kidding. You still have movies here?"

"Yep," Claire said. "Talkies and everything."

Hatchett's movie theater was constantly opening and closing during Matt's childhood. Someone would take a stab at it, keep it open for a year or two, then give up after losing money, at which point it would stay shuttered until someone else stepped up, convinced that people in Hatchett would show. It was the standing joke that before you asked *what* was showing, you first had to ask *if* anything was showing.

Matt took a long sip of his float to keep his throat from turning into sandpaper before he had a chance to ask his question.

"Any interest in catching a movie tonight?"

He didn't look up from his drink, partly out of fear of seeing Claire struggle to come up with a quick enough excuse. She did, in fact, take longer than one normally would before finally answering.

"I could do that, I suppose. 'Course, don't forget you won't be catching a movie, you'll be catching the movie. There's still only one screen. Do you want to find out what's playing first?"

"Not really. If the movie's bad, we can get some popcorn and hang out. Sit on the hood of my rental and watch out-of-state cars drive by."

"I usually try to save that sort of excitement for the weekend, but sure. I guess it's a . . ." Claire paused as she retreated from her first word choice. "It's a plan."

She grabbed a napkin and a pen from the counter and wrote down her address and phone number, handing it to Matt. "Unless you'd rather meet at the theater. I didn't mean to presume you'd pick me up or . . ."

"No, I'm happy to come get you. This will be fun. It'll be good to catch up."

Claire finished her float with gusto, making a loud gurgling sound as she sucked up the last small puddle of root beer with no remorse at the noise, then looked at her watch. "Thanks for the drink, but I've got to get to the bank. Guess I'll see you tonight."

Matt started to rise, but she waved and walked away before he could say anything. He sat back on the stool and stirred the maraschino cherry around the bottom of the glass with his straw.

He felt torn between wanting to spend more time with Claire, and running away and hiding to avoid facing what he had done when they were younger. He knew he owed her an apology, as well as an explanation, but he had no confidence that he'd have the courage to offer either. He guessed he would find out that evening.

FOURTEEN

Matt retrieved his car and drove to the far side of town, where he found the soup kitchen across from St. Luke's. A crumbling one-story house most likely built in the 1930s, it looked like it should have been torn down in the 1990s. At least half of its white paint had peeled off, while the other half seemed to hold on out of sheer stubbornness. The porch, however, sported a fresh coat of bright red paint, with 'Wet Paint' signs taped on the porch railing.

Three middle-aged men sat on the front steps, debating whether it was hotter yesterday or today, as if it actually mattered. Each had an empty, food-stained paper plate and a bright red plastic cup sitting on the steps next to them, the only items remaining from their free meal. Matt paused when he reached the porch, trying to figure out another way into the building.

"Paint's dry," one of the men said. "They just haven't taken down the signs."

"Thanks," Matt said.

"Serving time is over, though. They stop at 1:30."

It was after two o'clock and Matt hoped he'd still be able to find the mysterious Rose there. He stepped into what had likely been the living room when the building had been a home. Several round tables surrounded by metal folding chairs with 'St. Luke Catholic Church' stenciled on them comprised the only furniture in the living room. An elderly woman sat at one of the tables, staring vacantly ahead as if watching a play no one else could see.

"Excuse me," Matt said. "Do you know if Rose is around?"

The woman glanced up at Matt as if startled someone was speaking to her. "What's she look like?"

Matt realized he hadn't even asked for a description. "I don't know."

"Ain't nobody here matches that description." The woman nodded to herself, as if glad she could help, and went back to staring into space. Matt heard dishes clanking in the adjacent room and made his way to the kitchen where a teenage girl was emptying a dishwasher.

A bandana tied back blue hair as bright as an indigo bunting.

"Are you Rose?" Matt asked.

The young woman turned, and upon seeing Matt, dropped a plate back into the dishwasher and covered her mouth to stifle a cry. She took a step back.

"Jesus Christ, I heard you were dead," she finally said when she regained her composure. "Guess I should have known it's hard to kill a cockroach. What the hell do you want?"

"You heard right about Jake. I'm his brother, Matt."

Rose studied him hard for a moment, then nodded. "Yeah, okay, I see that."

"That's pretty good. Hardly anyone could ever tell us apart."

"It's the eyes. Yours have a hint of humanity in them." She fished the plate back out of the dishwasher and put it away. "So what do you want?" she asked warily. "I hope you're not as big of a dickwad as your brother, although that'd be hard to do."

Matt walked closer to Rose, who flinched when he approached. He saw her covertly grab the edge of a plate as if ready to swing it at his face if necessary, so he stepped a bit farther away to put her more at ease.

"I wanted to talk with you if I could. I understand Jake did something bad to you."

"Did something bad to me? You mean like steal all my money?"

"I didn't hear the specifics."

"Well now you have. He told me he didn't do it, but I saw him take it for Christ's sake. Whatever. What's done is done."

"Do you mind telling me exactly what happened?"

"What's it to you?"

"Please. Trust me."

Rose scoffed at that concept, keeping her eyes on him as she decided whether to tell him what he wanted to know.

"Given you're Jake's brother, no, I don't think I will trust you, but you want to know what kind of brother you had? Sure, happy to share. I'd been saving up for a year to finally get out of here and go stay with my mom and sister in Georgia, and he took all my money. He knew I kept it in my knapsack 'cause I don't exactly got a home. My mom had been sick and getting worse every day, and I just wanted to see her before it was too late. Is that too much to want?"

Matt shook his head.

"I aimed to start a new life, but Jake took everything I had so I couldn't leave. A couple weeks later, my mom passed away and I couldn't even get down there for her funeral."

Her defensive stance deflated a little as she wiped the dishrag across her eyes and turned away.

"I'm sorry," Matt said quietly. "And I'm sorry for what Jake did to you. I wanted to find you, though, to let you know Jake was sorry. He knew what he did was terrible, and he wanted to make things right by you."

Rose spun around and all but spit in Matt's face. "Yeah, right."

"I'm serious. He wanted to tell you he was sorry and to pay you back. How much did he take from you again?"

Rose looked at him skeptically. "Five hundred. Five hundred and thirty-five, to be exact."

Matt took out his wallet. He had withdrawn some cash before coming back home, but he only had so much. He pulled out one hundred and forty dollars and handed it to Rose.

"If you tell me where to send the rest, I'll get it to you. I promise. Before he died, Jake told me he was going through some challenges and was ashamed of what he'd done. He said it hurt him and he wanted to make amends."

Matt felt miserable lying, but rationalized it by telling himself that getting Rose to forgive his brother would be as good for her as for Jake.

"I hope you can find it in your heart to forgive him. He had his problems, but he wasn't so far gone that he didn't know right from wrong."

Rose leaned over and took the money from Matt. She looked at it and cried softly. "Thank you," she said. "I just want to go to my sister's."

"Where should I send the rest of the money? I'll give you double what he owed. That ought to help you get a fresh start."

She looked suspicious but appeared to see Matt was serious. "Give it to Father Pearman. He'll know how to get it to me."

"I'm sorry, Rose, for what Jake did to you, and I hope you can find it in your heart to forgive him."

Rose thought about it, then nodded slowly. "Let he who is without sin, you know? Lord knows, I've done things I'm not proud of." She looked at the money in her hand. "I appreciate this."

"It's the least I could do. For you and for Jake." Matt's manipulation embarrassed him, but he hoped Rose's forgiveness would still work to release Jake. Given her reaction when she first saw him, he didn't think she had been the one to murder Jake, unless she was an excellent actress. But that didn't mean she wasn't the one Jake had wronged.

As he turned to leave, Matt noticed Rose's white shoes with their short, spiked heels, one of which had a spot of red on the side of it. Rose noticed Matt looking and raised her shoe to examine it.

"Oh, great. I must have walked on the porch before the paint was dry."

Matt bowed his head just low enough for him to still glance up at his mother as she said grace before dinner with her head lowered and her eyes closed tight. She acted like no one else was at the table. Matt assumed she must start every meal this way.

"Bless us, O Lord, and these, Thy gifts, which we are about to receive from Thy bounty. Through Christ, our Lord. Amen."

She placed her napkin on her lap and surveyed the table. "We're not having much," she said as she put a chicken breast on her plate.

Matt looked at the platter of chicken, the plastic bowl of Jell-O, two ears of corn, and slices of tomato. It looked like home.

"Thank you for humoring me while I said grace," she said. "I'm sure I seem like a hick to you."

"No, you don't."

"I probably embarrass you."

"Mom, stop."

Matt filled his plate and began eating a silent dinner across from his mother, watching her pick at her food with the enthusiasm of a sick bird. Looking at her was like staring at a black-and-white photograph: she appeared to belong to a time in the past, and in a sense, she did. Her husband and son were dead, and Matt might as well have been, for all the good he was to her. He told himself he would make a point to visit more often, but saw no use to say this aloud. She wouldn't believe him. He didn't totally believe it himself, although things had obviously changed. It would now mainly be a question of being able to afford it.

He had nothing to say. He didn't know how to talk to her. The silence made him uncomfortable, but he didn't know how to break it. His mother wasn't one for small talk, and he was too tired to pursue anything of substance.

"I ran into Claire today," he finally said, immediately regretting that he did.

"Did she talk to you?" his mother asked, without looking up from her food.

"Yeah, she talked to me. We're getting together this evening. Going to see a movie."

"Really? Well, she's very kind. She deserves the best."

"You mean someone other than me." While his mother's words cut, he couldn't argue. Claire did deserve the best, and that wasn't him.

"Now Matthew, I didn't say that at all," she sighed. "I just mean she's gone through a lot and I want her to find happiness, that's all."

"I want her to be happy, too," Matt said defensively.

His mother looked up at him like she wanted to respond, but realized she didn't need to say anything more about it.

"Eat before it gets cold," she advised.

He served up a couple more volleys of small talk, but got nowhere. After dinner, as they took their plates to the sink, he realized his mother hadn't asked him a single question about his life or job. She listened to what he offered, and never pressed for more. But this wasn't the time to play the needy son. Of course, he knew that her not probing worked out better for him, because he would feel uncomfortable answering questions. Just the same, it hurt that she didn't ask. Maybe, somehow, she knew his answers would be lies. They almost always were.

Before he could think about it, he put his arm around her shoulder and gave her a quick side-hug. She stared at the sink, then glanced up at him as if trying to figure out what had just happened. As he stepped away, she turned on the water and began washing the dishes.

FIFTEEN

As Matt drove Claire to the movie theater, he kept the music on the radio soft enough that they could carry on a conversation, but loud enough to cover the awkward silences. He had picked her up at her one-story brick house, indistinguishable from the other houses on that block, where she was waiting for him on her front steps. There was no offer to show him around, or even let him through the front door, which Matt understood.

She looked beautiful in her faded jeans and white top; she had never been one to keep up with the latest fashion, but the simplicity of her style complemented her sense of confidence. She wore little makeup, which made the overall effect that much more attractive.

Seeing her in his passenger seat brought back memories of cruising Highway 28, honking at all the other cars filled with high school friends. His beat-up Buick was easily identifiable, with its back door a different color from the rest, and its front bumper held in place by bailing wire.

Before Jake got his muscle car, he and Matt used to spend their evenings in the Buick driving up and down the main drag, along with most of the other Hatchett High kids, alternating who got to drive each night. Matt and Claire started dating the summer before he was a junior and she was a sophomore, and eventually she started joining the two boys, sitting in the back seat and smiling at Matt in his rearview mirror.

It was when Jake finally got his own car that Claire started sitting in the front. Jake was excited for him and Matt to have "a bitchin' set of wheels," and he even said they could still take turns driving it, although perhaps not switching off as often as every other night. He also added, reluctantly, that Claire could still ride along, though she'd have to sit in the back. But Matt wasn't interested in that arrangement. Matt could tell Jake was surprised, and more than a little hurt, by his new allegiance.

The Buick became Matt and Claire's special refuge, while Jake rode alone, albeit in one of the coolest cars on the road. Whenever they passed each other, as they were bound to do about twenty times a night since there was only so much road to cruise in Hatchett, Matt would often wave or honk his horn at Jake, but his gestures were usually ignored.

And now, ten years later, Matt and Claire were once again driving down the same road. They parked right in front of the Hatchett Bijou, whose marquee listed a vigilante action movie now on its second run. Since it was seven o'clock, there were only a couple of other cars parked on the street. Stores downtown usually closed at six, and the kids hadn't yet left home to see who was out and about, so the streets were fairly empty.

As she got out of the car, Claire looked closely at the rental, noting its dented roof and tiny indentations from the shotgun pellets.

"Do you save money by renting your cars from demolition derby companies?"

"Long story. Actually, stories."

The high school kid perched behind the concession stand also sold the tickets. He sat on a tall stool in the corner, his attention so focused on his cell phone that it took him a while to notice Matt and Claire when they appeared.

"Yeah, I don't know. I guess," the kid said, obviously bored. "You going to Jeb's party this weekend? I can't decide . . . I don't know . . . I guess." The kid jolted when he finally noticed them, almost toppling off the stool, probably wondering why in the heck anyone would be there on a Tuesday night. "Hold on a minute, there's someone here . . . No, I'm serious." He put down his phone. "You here for the movie?"

"I don't know. You have anything else going on we should know about?" Matt asked.

The kid thought for a minute. "No." He considered the question again. "What do you mean?"

"Don't pay any attention to him," Claire said. "He's a big city boy. They like to think they're clever. Two tickets, please."

The kid pulled two red tickets off a large roll and handed them to Matt, who handed over a twenty. The kid reached into a tin money box and handed back fourteen dollars in change. Matt looked at the money, surprised.

"Seriously? Three bucks a ticket?"

"A lot of movie theaters in other towns charge a lot more than that."

"No, that wasn't what I meant, it just surprised . . ."

"Yeah," Claire jumped in, smiling. "Don't be so cheap."

She grabbed hold of Matt's arm and turned him toward the door leading into the theater, looking back over her shoulder at the kid. "Like I said, ignore him. Seriously. I know I do."

Nothing in the theater appeared to have changed in the ten years since Matt last saw a movie there, except maybe a few more inches of popcorn butter acting as a type of impenetrable varnish on the floor. The place smelled like it hadn't encountered fresh air in decades, but the scent of popcorn still brought a sense of comfort, not to mention hunger.

It was a fairly good-sized theater, with twenty-five rows, each row with twenty seats. One aisle ran down the center of the room, splitting the rows in half. A heavy velvet fabric hung from ceiling to floor along the side walls to improve the sound, with the dark red felt-covered seats the same color as always, albeit slightly more worn. A few of the seats had holes in them, revealing rusted springs. Matt couldn't imagine the owner ever feeling compelled to replace them, since the theater would never be full. Patrons could simply sit elsewhere.

The cinema's screen had a brown splotch in the lower right-hand corner that looked like a small tumbleweed, most likely caused by a flying cup of Coke. Advertisements clicked across the screen every few seconds promoting the local swimming pool, the Dress Barn, and a realtor who appeared to be the happiest person ever. Matt wondered how anybody made a living in this town as a realtor.

They had the entire theater to themselves. Matt followed Claire two-thirds of the way down, where they claimed two seats on the aisle. Both cushions made a screeching cry when lowered, like a door hinge in a haunted house. Matt wondered how many times the two of them had sat in those same two seats.

"Popular place," he said, looking around at the empty theater.

"It's Tuesday. Hatchett doesn't go to the movies on Tuesday. That's just something you East Coast elites do."

Claire was in her seat no more than a few seconds before she stood back up and shuffled past Matt. He reached into his back pocket for his wallet, with no doubt about where she was going, but Claire held up her hand. "It's on me. Want a Coke?"

"Diet, I'm afraid."

She smiled and headed up the aisle.

"And would you mind not putting butter on the popcorn?"

Claire froze in her tracks, paused, then turned around and marched back down the aisle. She stood next to Matt's seat, looking down at him like a cop who had just pulled him over for going seventy-five in a school zone. "How about I just get you a bag of Styrofoam peanuts to munch on instead?" She shook her head in disbelief. "I'm fine getting you a Diet Coke. I'm actually with you on that one. But no butter on our popcorn? At this movie theater? Oh, I don't think so, mister. I don't think so." She turned and marched back up the aisle, hollering back at him as she went. "But if I see any bean sprouts or tofu bars, I'll pick some up for you."

Claire sashayed out of the theater, the door slowly closing behind her. Matt appreciated her effort to not keep things awkward between them, although who knows—maybe he was giving too much weight to what happened ten years ago. They were just kids back then. Claire had obviously grown up and become an adult, whereas he was probably the one who hadn't matured or moved on.

After Claire went to get the popcorn, Matt couldn't help but lean back and close his eyes. He was exhausted, and probably could have fallen asleep standing up. He hoped getting some caffeine in his system would help, but all he wanted to do was sleep, and he could feel himself slipping away.

The indignant cry of a seat cushion being lowered near the back of the theater brought him back, prompting him to sit up straight and force his eyes open. A few seconds later, he heard the creaky springs of another seat as it lowered. Thirty seconds later, two more seats made their presence known, one after the other. He found it strange he hadn't once heard the main door open or close.

He smiled, excited to report to Claire that apparently Hatchett does go to the movies on Tuesdays. When another seat creaked, he glanced behind him. The theater was still empty.

He looked around and tried to find the origin of the sounds. When he heard another drawn-out squeal, he stood and scanned the theater. Perhaps a door somewhere with unoiled hinges? As he narrowed his eyes, he saw a seat cushion in the back row lower on its own, then raise back up, as if lifted by an invisible hand.

Matt stepped into the aisle to get a better view when a seat in the second-to-last row lowered and raised. On the other side of the aisle, a couple of rows closer to him, another seat shifted into action, then four more, one by one, getting closer to Matt each time. He glanced up at the projection booth. No one there. Another seat lowered and raised. He stood still, moving only his eyes. What if Claire came back? Would she be safe?

The seats stopped moving three rows away. He waited, his muscles tightening, but nothing happened until—from his peripheral vision—he saw and heard Claire's seat being lowered. It did not raise back up.

The only sound in the darkened theater was the clicking of the advertisement slides, and Matt's own halting breath.

After an endless moment, when the seat cushion still hadn't returned to its original position, Matt cautiously stepped over to raise it back up. When his hand was only inches from the cushion, the seat flung back up on its own. He jerked his hand away, jumping back into the aisle. Then, suddenly, all the seats in the theater except for his started flapping up and down rapidly, their high-pitched squeals consuming the room, piercing his ears like a scream. The seats looked like the keys of an old player piano putting out a ragtime tune in double-time. He gripped his head, tried to suppress the spinning sensation that was hitting him, and pleaded internally for it to stop.

All at once, it did.

The silence disturbed him as much as the flapping seats. He started moving up the aisle, on his way to retrieve Claire, when he caught a movement near the back of the theater, behind the velvet curtain that covered the left wall. He froze. Someone was behind the curtain. Could this be a joke? That wasn't Claire's style. Besides, how could she have done that with the seats?

The human-shaped form behind the curtain moved again, creating a soft rustle, as if trying to escape the small, dark space between drape and wall. Then the bulge silently glided along the wall toward Matt's row like a huge, red velvet wave rippling forward, before returning to where he'd first spotted it. The same movement repeated itself on the other side of the theater, three times, back and forth. Soon the curtains on both sides were billowing up and down, as though multiple people were running the length of the theater behind the velvet.

The lights, which had been dimmed for the ads, splashed into darkness. Matt whipped around to the screen. It was illuminated with a strange light, backlit by a soft glow. A round, black circle the size of a dime appeared in its center, as if someone had taken a lit cigarette and pressed it on the other side.

It grew to the size of a quarter, and within seconds, it was as large as a dinner plate. It looked like it should be smoldering, but it didn't smell like anything was burning. The edges were ragged, and finally, as Matt's eyes adjusted to the glow, he saw the cause of the hole. Hundreds of humongous cockroaches were eating their way through from the back of the screen. The advertisements had frozen on an image showing a woman's beautiful, glistening smile. The roaches devoured her front teeth and seemed to fill her entire mouth. Matt gagged.

Within seconds, the swarm grew to thousands, with massive beetles eating through the woman's lips and pouring in from the other side. They fell like a torrent of rancid water flowing through the screen, scurrying across the stage, covering it like a living carpet, the mass of them heaving up and down like the gasping chest of a monstrous demon.

When the hole in the screen grew to four feet, Matt spied an animal peering out of the blackness from the other side of the screen, like something out of a post-nuclear war zoo. It had the head and body of a hyena standing upright. Not once did its hyper-focused pupils veer from Matt, who felt trapped in its hypnotic gaze. The creature didn't move or change its expression, but Matt felt as if it had already plunged through the screen and grabbed hold of his frantic heart. He froze, desperate to flee, but his legs felt like tree trunks and his feet were firmly locked in place.

Digging deep into his core, Matt focused on breathing deeply and visualizing his mental brick wall. He felt the force of the figure behind the screen trying to match his efforts, but finally, through sheer will, Matt managed to break eye contact. He pivoted to sprint up the aisle, nearly toppling Claire as she balanced their popcorn and sodas.

He gasped in surprise but somehow managed not to cry out, though he wanted to. Claire looked at him quizzically as he stood in the middle of the empty theater.

"Sorry it took so long," she said. "Had to wait for the kid to wrap up his phone call."

He shot a look over his shoulder at the screen. The smiling

woman's teeth sparkled at him with their whiteness. No seats moved. No curtains rippled. And thankfully, no hyena-demon glared at him from behind the dark beyond.

"Are you okay?" Claire asked.

No. Nowhere in the vicinity of being okay. Apparently, Rose wasn't the only person who needed to forgive Jake.

"You mind if we skip the movie? I'd rather just talk with you."

SIXTEEN

Matt and Claire drove silently past the city square on the way back to her house, as if on their way to a wake. Most of the kids who were out cruising looked carefully at Matt as they passed, trying to place the car, a couple of them with surprised looks on their faces, no doubt mistaking Matt for Jake.

One of Hatchett's two radio stations—the contemporary music station, not the country one—was in the middle of an endless series of locally produced commercials, most all of them voiced by the radio station's sole "talent," but that was preferable to filling the silence themselves.

Claire offered up a couple stabs at conversation after leaving the movie theater, but it was as if she had left with a completely different person. Matt couldn't focus on what she was saying. He felt an energy inside, his blood charged.

"You doing all right?" Claire finally asked, apparently deciding to just come out and ask, rather than take another shot at a monologue.

Matt nodded, remaining silent until he knew he couldn't delay the conversation any further.

"When I drove into town yesterday," he began, "a guy at the Gas and Go about took my head off with a wrench, mistaking me for Jake. I think his name was Teddy. Warned me to stay away from his sister. Do you happen to know who I'm talking about?"

"Sure. Teddy Peterson. His sister is Lorraine. They live together in their old family home off Eighth Street."

"Sounded like Jake did something to Lorraine."

Claire studied Matt for a moment, then sighed. "I'm not trying to be insensitive, Matt, but Jake was an asshole to a lot of people. Don't get me wrong, there were times when the old Jake would shine through: funny, informed, willing to do something for you, but most of the time, he was just a punk dealing meth and could be merciless when he didn't get what he wanted."

When Matt didn't respond with anything but a nod of

acknowledgment, Claire turned up the radio slightly as the music started back up. A young girl with a voice indistinguishable from all the other pop divas lamented losing her first love, and all the heartache that came with it. As cliché as the lyrics were, it surprised Matt how much of it rang true.

Claire looked over at him. "I get the feeling you thought tonight would be more fun than it was," she said. "You obviously forgot what a night in Hatchett is like. Sorry about that."

All this talk of forgiveness and righting old wrongs was one more reminder that Matt needed to take care of his own past wrongs while he could still do it himself, and it wasn't even a question whom he had hurt in his life. She was sitting next to him.

"No, that's not it at all. I just have something on my mind." He paused a moment, then forged ahead. "I don't know if you'll think I'm being ridiculous to even be saying anything after all these years," Matt started, "or if you'll think it's about damn time."

He paused, his pulse stuttering. Given how many years he had thought about this moment, he was surprised by how few words came to mind. He also wished he had a drink in front of him.

"But I wanted to tell you how sorry I am about how things ended with us. It's something that's bothered me all these years and for whatever reason, I never manned up enough to say I'm sorry. Actually, 'sorry' doesn't even begin to cover it. I recognize that."

He paused and glanced over at her, watching her stare out the passenger window, or, more accurately, watching his reflection in her window, as though she wanted to watch him talk but wasn't yet ready to face him directly.

"Thank you," she finally said. "And you're right: sorry doesn't even come close to covering it, but I appreciate you at least saying it. Finally."

"Maybe one day I can tell you what I was thinking," Matt said, "or can offer some sort of explanation that would make sense to you, but right now all I can say is I was young, and I reacted in a way that I can't justify."

"I was young, too. But it's okay. It's not a big deal."

"It was to me."

"It was to me, too," Claire said immediately, her sharp voice carrying a tone that fell somewhere between sorrow and fury. "I was seventeen, Matt, and it was my first time. A lot of my friends had had sex before me because they thought it was something they were supposed to do, but I waited until I was sure, because my mom's experience showed me what happened when you gave yourself to the first piece of shit who showed an interest."

She paused, then turned away from the window to face him head on.

"Don't get me wrong. Looking back at it now, I realize we're just talking about a first love. I'm grown up now. It's not like I think about it anymore, but I'd be lying if I said it didn't mess me up for a while. You just left, like what we had wasn't as special as I thought it was."

"It wasn't like that," Matt said. "I was scared. I know how stupid that sounds, but I was an immature jerk and instead of talking to you, I ran away."

"But I don't understand why. We'd always been able to talk about anything. What happened to our plan of me following you to college when I graduated? I never heard from you, other than a couple generic responses to emails I sent. It took me a long time to let myself trust a man again. I'm still not sure I do, although that's not all your fault. But I had always thought you were the exception to the rule, which made your running away hurt that much more. I just assumed you'd met some sorority girl and never looked back."

Matt pulled up in front of Claire's house and shut off his car. After a moment, he decided he needed to open up at least a little further.

"I never went to college."

Claire leaned back against her door, her jaw dropping open. She stared at him, stunned. "You what?"

"I didn't go to college."

"So how'd you get such a big job at an ad . . ."

"I don't work for an ad agency. That's just what I wanted to do. I never did anything about it."

"But your mom said . . ."

"I lied. It gave me an excuse not to come back home. You know, I could say I was busy. Crazy time at work."

Claire looked at him, her mouth open but no words coming out, as though she couldn't figure out what she could ask that would make any sense of all this.

"You really are an unbelievable piece of shit. I see now how lucky I am you left without me."

"You're right on both counts."

"Do you even live in New York?"

"I do. In Brooklyn. I moved straight there when I left Hatchett, but I've pretty much done shit with my life."

"I'm sorry to hear that," Claire said, no hint of sorrow in her voice. "But I'm guessing it's probably time for you to run away again. Let's be sure to do this again in another ten years."

"Claire, I'm sorry. Someday I hope to figure out a way to better explain it, but I don't expect you to ever fully forgive me because I've never forgiven myself."

"Well, that makes two of us," she said as she reached for the door handle.

"Please, wait . . ."

As she reached down to grab her purse, a cigarette bounced off Matt's window, sparks flying. He looked over and saw Bone push off from his Hummer and start walking toward them, his narrowed eyes focused on Matt's car.

"Does he come to your home?"

Claire looked out at Bone. She tried sounding confident, but Matt could tell she was uncomfortable with this development. "He hasn't come here before, but this doesn't involve you. Do what you do best and just go. Leave me the hell alone."

She got out of the car, and Matt followed.

SEVENTEEN

Despite the hot summer night, Bone wore a thin, black leather jacket, paired with ripped jeans and alligator boots that were crusted with dirt. He strode toward Claire, who remained outside the passenger door of the car. As he passed, he pointed his index finger at Matt but kept his eyes on Claire.

"Say goodnight, city boy, and get the hell out of here."

Claire kept her eyes on Bone, trying not to look intimidated, but Matt could see she was unsettled by his appearance at her house.

"I'll leave when you leave," Matt said, his face growing hot.

Bone stopped abruptly in front of the car, his figure illuminated by the headlights, and turned toward Matt.

"Why you act like everything I say is open to negotiation? You just don't seem to get it, so let me try explaining this one last time. I tell you what you're going to do, and then you do it. End of story. Now get out of here."

Bone turned to Claire.

"Aw, don't be looking like that, girl. I just want to talk some business. You're a businessman, aren't you? Businesswoman. Whatever. I got a proposition." Bone whipped his head back toward Matt and snarled. "I said git!"

"Go to hell," Matt said. It was an old Hatchett Pond strategy. Some kids crept in, letting their bodies acclimate to the cold water inch by inch, and others swung out on the rope and let go, submerging themselves all at once. Now, here with Bone, he had just let go of the rope and plunged into the deep water with one sentence.

Bone whipped out his switchblade, its razor-sharp edge glistening under the streetlight.

"Leave him out of this," Claire said. Her words bounced off Bone as he approached Matt, the heels of his boots kicking up gravel.

Matt's adrenaline surged. No way would he leave Claire alone with this thug. "You always need a knife, Bone?"

"Don't need one. Just found it's a lot quicker with one."

Bone grabbed Matt by the collar and whipped him around, slamming his back against the side of the car. Matt winced as the jolt against the car's metal vibrated up and down his spine. His feet slipped on the gravel, like he was standing on marbles, until he managed to gain traction and steady himself.

It was obvious Bone had been drinking. Even his leather jacket smelled like whiskey. He pressed the tip of the blade against Matt's cheek. "Let me make sure my blade hasn't gotten dull." He flicked it just enough to draw a thin trickle of blood. Matt flinched at what felt like a metal wasp sting, and yet felt strangely stimulated when Bone held up the knife and showed him the blood. "Still sharp enough, I suppose." He pressed his left forearm against Matt's neck, pressuring him in place against the car, then placed the blade next to Matt's right ear.

Matt's pulse slowed as he glared at Bone. For whatever reason, he didn't feel fear; instead, he looked increasingly pissed off. Matt thought he saw a flicker of surprise as Bone seemed to notice his prey didn't appear afraid enough.

"The number of souvenirs I take off your body depends on whether I heard you correctly a minute ago," Bone muttered as he pressed Matt's head back, exposing his neck while pushing him harder against the car. He leaned in close, lowering his voice as if sharing a secret, the whiskey on his breath as strong as cologne. "Now tell me again what it is you said?"

Bone's left arm crushed Matt's neck; the knife didn't leave the flesh of his ear for a second. Matt's feet once again shuffled on the gravel. He used one foot to push aside the small rocks in order to have solid footing. He tried to maintain his balance, even though the top of his spine felt like it might snap. Still, he remained unusually calm.

Matt lifted his head toward Bone as far as he could until he could see Bone's bloodshot eyes.

"I said, go to hell."

Matt slid his right foot forward, hooked it around Bone's left ankle and jerked hard. Bone's foot slid on the gravel, and he fell to one knee. Bone brought his free hand down on the ground to stop his fall, then cocked the knife back and started to roundhouse it toward Matt's right thigh.

Matt interlocked his fingers so that his hands formed a club. He bludgeoned the side of Bone's head with his hands, using the leverage upon the force of contact to leap to the side. The tip of the switchblade met the steel of the car, as did Bone's head.

"Guess your blade isn't so sharp anymore," Matt said.

Bone scrambled to get up, his feet spinning on the gravel, his balance already shaky from the booze. "It'll be sharp enough."

But before Bone could rise, Matt brought his foot up hard into his gut, almost lifting the wiry predator off the ground, before kicking him again in the ribs, even harder, causing Bone to drop to both knees. Bone tried to grunt in pain, but it seemed he had no breath in his lungs to make a sound.

Matt tasted blood, which fed his primal desire to hurt Bone, who crawled to the front of the car and grabbed the bumper as he tried pulling himself up. Matt followed him, taking hold of Bone's jacket collar with one hand and the back of his pants with the other, then flinging his head against the grille of the car like a battering ram. The force of the impact dazed Bone and cracked the aluminum grille—just one more thing to explain at the car rental place. He dropped face-down onto the ground.

"Leave her alone!" Matt shouted, now an unstoppable force. A porch light across the street flicked on.

Bone once again struggled to get to his hands and knees, his body practically waving a white flag, but Matt had no interest in accepting his surrender. He grasped the back of Bone's pants again and pulled him partially off the ground, but once the tips of Bone's shoes touched the ground, Matt swung him against the side of the car, his back smashing against the side mirror, causing Bone to bend backwards then crumple back down to the ground.

Matt stood over his rival, his breath hot. If he had a machete, he would have brought it down on Bone's neck. Instead, he stepped back and readied his leg for another shot at the wounded man's ribs.

"Matt, stop. You're going to kill him." Claire ran around to his side of the car and touched his arm.

Matt paused, panting, and stared down at Bone, not yet ready to call the fight. "You think he wasn't going to kill me?"

"And that's who you want to be like?"

"I just want him to leave you alone," Matt said.

"He doesn't know how."

An inner voice argued back in no uncertain terms that Matt

needed to kill Bone. The voice was firm, rational, demanding. And it was right. Only death would stop someone like Bone. It wasn't like anybody would miss him. It would be so easy. Stab him in the throat with his own knife. Watch his blood spurt from his jugular as his lungs and heart slowly expired. It would take next to no effort, and he could easily claim self-defense. No one would doubt his story, and he was certain Claire would back him.

His eyes shifted to the switchblade. Pick it up, he heard. Do it. He's going to go after Claire with no mercy. She needs you. You have to help her.

"Matt," Claire said. "Let's go inside and call the sheriff."

But Matt already felt the ecstasy that killing Bone would bring. Just the thought of feeling the blade cut into Bone's skin caused the hairs on his arms to rise, the payoff almost sexual in its intensity.

"Matt," Claire repeated more sternly. "I'm calling the sheriff."

Matt blinked, suddenly realizing the internal voice had not been his own. Wherever the voice came from, he hadn't completely rejected it, which scared him more than Bone had.

He watched Bone struggle to get to his hands and knees, but he kept collapsing back to the ground, blood pouring from his nose, his chest heaving.

"I just want to help you," Matt said to Claire, desperate for her to understand. "I need to be able to help you."

"You can help me by coming inside," she said.

He looked into her eyes and found a pathway out of the rage that filled his veins. His muscles slowly relaxed, and the voice in his head faded. He dropped the knife he didn't even remember picking up.

"Come on," Claire said. "We'll leave this trash for the sheriff to pick up."

Matt turned to follow her, but Bone swung his fist up between Matt's legs, quick as a shot, dropping him to the ground in pain. He rolled onto his back, the wind knocked out of him. Bone scrambled on top of him, his knee crushing Matt's stomach as the gravel from the road dug into Matt's back. This time Bone pressed the blade of his knife hard against Matt's throat.

"Bone, don't!" Claire screamed.

Bone's eyes emitted a psychotic glow as he glared at Matt. "Don't kid yourself, girl. I killed his brother, and now it's this one's turn. Up to you whether you're next." Bone turned his attention back to Matt, his yellow teeth snarling. "You shouldn't have crossed me. Don't nobody cross me."

Blue patrol lights from the sheriff's car filled the darkness like a flashbulb, and a single whoop of the siren quickly made Sheriff Wilson's presence known. Bone didn't look up, refusing to take his eyes off Matt. But he also didn't make any further moves as the sheriff stepped out of his car, gun in hand.

"Drop the knife, Bone," Sheriff Wilson's voice commanded, followed by the hard click of a revolver's hammer. "You may have the brain of a rabid dog, but you also know I'll shoot you like one without batting an eye. Now get off him."

With his blood saturating Matt's shirt, Bone held his death stare, then finally leaned down and whispered in Matt's ear, "Just a matter of time before I skin you alive, little rabbit. Just a matter of time."

He spit blood onto Matt's face as he stood, then folded his switchblade.

"Leave the knife," Wilson said.

Bone steadied himself against Matt's car for a moment, still dazed from his beating, then hobbled back toward his car. "Blow me," he muttered at the sheriff, sliding the knife back into his pocket as he passed by.

"Hey!" the sheriff yelled, but Bone obviously had no respect for whatever authority the sheriff should have had, and Wilson apparently didn't plan on pushing the matter.

Bone shuffled unsteadily across the street and slowly climbed into his Hummer, slamming the door once inside. He revved the engine, then peeled out, his tires screeching one last exclamation of contempt.

Claire helped Matt up as the sheriff joined them.

"Neighbor called in a disturbance," the sheriff explained.

"Why didn't you arrest him?" Claire asked, frustrated.

"Don't think I wouldn't love to," Sheriff Wilson said. "But he could have easily claimed self-defense."

"He pulled a knife on me!" Matt said.

"And once you got it away from him it was all good and kosher, but the second you kept on kicking him, you crossed the line. From down the block I could see you flinging his head into the side of the car. You could have simply picked up the knife and called me, but you

110

kept at it. So to answer your question, that's why I didn't arrest him. You went above and beyond self-defense."

"He admitted to killing Jake," Matt said, frustrated. "Claire heard him."

"Much as I wish it were that easy, he only said that to piss you off."

"Did you even look into him as a suspect?"

"Didn't need to," Wilson said. "He was in jail the night Jake was killed, sleeping off a DUI. Trust me, I'd love to lock him up for a long time, but it just didn't go down that way."

As Wilson headed back to his car, he shouted to Matt: "Come by my office tomorrow and let's talk. Bone's not going anywhere. There's plenty of time to press charges after we speak some more—if you want. It also looks like I need to remind you about messing with the wrong people in this town." He looked back over at Matt and Claire for a moment before getting in his car, turning off the squad car lights, and driving away.

Claire turned to Matt. "You need to be careful. Bone's not going to let this go."

"Yeah, I sensed that."

"And I doubt Wilson will be able to do much. Go on back to New York. There's nothing for you here."

"I have something I need to take care of first," Matt said, knowing Bone wasn't his biggest problem. "Besides, I'm more worried about you. I'm not leaving you."

She looked at him and rolled her eyes, her face saying, You did it before, but she didn't say it aloud. Perhaps because his efforts to protect her left him covered in blood.

"Go home," she said. "You can't do anything to help."

Matt pushed himself off the car, wincing with each step.

"That doesn't mean I'm not going to try."

Matt drove back to Jake's secluded house. Sometimes after working a long day in New York, he'd come home feeling like he'd been beaten up. But today reminded him that he'd severely underestimated the real thing.

When he reached the turnoff leading to Jake's driveway, he saw a patrol car parked down the road. The car flashed its lights once at Matt as he pulled into the driveway, probably some junior lawman letting him know he'd be keeping an eye on things in case Bone didn't believe vengeance was best served cold. Matt appreciated the patrolman's presence, and figured it was probably the highlight of the deputy's month, if not his career: a real live stakeout in Hatchett.

As Matt pulled into the driveway, he was relieved to see it wasn't covered with crows. The birds were starting to get on his nerves. If they had tried taking over the driveway that evening, he might have stepped on the accelerator.

He parked and dragged himself stiffly out of the car. As he started toward the house, he noticed a light was on in the barn. He wanted nothing more than to just crawl into bed and go to sleep, but since the objective was to not fall asleep, he walked down to the barn, hoping he had simply forgotten to shut off the light over the workbench the last time he was there.

He stepped cautiously into the barn, although he felt fairly certain no one was there, which turned out to be a correct assumption. There were three horse stalls with nothing but hay in them, and an assortment of broken household items along one side of the barn with tools scattered next to them. Matt figured Jake had been planning to repair the junk, either to use or perhaps to sell. A lawn mower had been torn apart but not reassembled, and a full-length mirror in a wooden frame leaned against one wall, a crack running the full length of the glass.

Matt checked himself in the cracked mirror. He, too, was in pretty bad shape. A crust of dried blood marked the cut Bone made on his cheek, and his hair was full of dirt, blood, and gravel. He decided his blood-soaked shirt and jeans were unsalvageable.

The sight of all the blood on his shirt reminded Matt how close he had come to killing Bone. The rage he felt, combined with the movie theater terror, left no doubt in his mind that Skiz's predictions were coming true.

As he examined himself more closely in the mirror, he saw the reflection of something moving behind him. He turned and saw a window on the opposite side of the barn. A bird flew past the window, the movement similar to what Matt had seen in the mirror. He exhaled a breath he had been holding far too long.

He continued staring out the window, sensing that something didn't feel quite right. He'd felt it as he turned away from the mirror and toward the window. A sound that didn't belong? Something else he'd caught in the mirror's reflection? It slowly dawned on him that as he'd turned his back to the mirror, his reflection hadn't followed suit.

He looked closer at the window. In the reflection of its glass, he saw the full-length mirror behind him. Although he had turned his back to it, his face continued watching him from the mirror, where he should have seen only his back. Matt made a small movement, but the reflection in the mirror didn't move.

He slowly turned around to face himself in the mirror, but this time his reflection didn't match his movements. It looked like his face, but now without a cut or any blood on it. The face in the mirror simply stared at him, looking him straight in the eyes, betraying nothing but a vacant expression.

"Jake?" Matt finally asked, even though he already knew the answer.

The face in the mirror broke out into a forced grin.

"How you doing, bro? Long time, no see."

EIGHTEEN

Matt could only nod at his brother's reflection in the mirror. He wasn't scared; maybe because he was too overwhelmed, or perhaps he had suffered a concussion during his fight with Bone and was simply imagining all of this. Most likely it was because this was his brother, and they used to be able to talk about anything, although things had definitely changed.

"Look, man, we need to talk," Jake said, a hint of desperation in his voice as his nonchalant facade faded away. "As you've already figured out, we've got us a real shitty situation here."

"Are you in . . . where are you? Are you okay?"

"You know where I am, and right now I'm okay, but let me tell you, the first couple days were a real son of a bitch."

"I might be able to get you out," Matt said. "You need to tell me the names of anybody you may have—"

"Yeah, yeah, I know what Skiz told you. Seriously, dude? You're taking advice from that fat psycho nutjob? You need to listen to me. Things here, they're not cool, okay? I know I wasn't the best human being, and I did a lot of shitty things, but nobody deserves this. The pain and the torture, it's unrelenting. Don't even try to imagine what it's like because you can't. It's . . . " Jake's voice cracked. "Let's just say it's not a positive experience."

"How are you connecting with me now?"

"Because of him. The prince who will be king. He knows about our connection."

Matt felt his body deflate. He'd already known what he was dealing with, but hearing it from his brother crushed him all the same.

"It's not as bad as it sounds," Jake said. "Or at least it doesn't need to be. All you have to do is let him in."

Matt looked at Jake like he'd started speaking in tongues. "You want me to let him in? Are you crazy?"

"The torture has stopped for me because of our connection, but you keep fighting when he tries to get through. If you open up and

114

reach back to me, he gains a portal to the living. He can return to Earth and in turn, you and I will have power beyond our wildest dreams."

Any doubt that this was Jake immediately disappeared. Jake's greatest desire in life always involved being powerful and feared. Even as a kid, he'd fantasized about getting a job where employees would start shaking every time he entered the room, doing as he commanded without question.

"I don't want power beyond my wildest dreams," Matt said.

Jake snapped back at him. "And I don't want to have my flesh peeled off and put back on, only to be ripped off again! Want to see what I looked like before he discovered our connection?"

Matt shook his head, but Jake's image had already begun melting. A flap of skin the size of a playing card dangled from his right cheek, twitching with each heartbeat. His other cheek displayed four long gashes, as if a jackal had ripped him open. His right eye socket revealed nothing but a black hole, although that didn't stop it from staring straight at Matt.

Jake's lower lip and chin had dissolved, as if from an acid attack, exposing his lower teeth, two of which had been broken off, leaving jagged edges. Only one ear was attached, and the remaining skin on the face once identical to Matt's was now covered in third-degree burns.

Matt looked away. "Stop, Jake. Jesus Christ."

"Hardly." Jake paused for a moment. "Okay, you can look again."

Matt felt like a kid and hoped Jake wasn't tricking him. He exhaled when he turned back and his brother appeared normal.

"Don't you get it, Matt? I'm of value to him. I have an important role I can play, and for that, I'll be rewarded. Even better, we'll be rewarded."

"How?" Matt asked.

"For one thing, I won't be going through what you just saw ever again. That happens nonstop. But if you let him in, I'll rejoin you. We'll be one, and whatever we want will become ours. Power. Money. Women. Don't you want a life that isn't covered in hamburger grease? All this time I thought you were some hotshot ad executive. I had to die to find out your life is shit, man. You've got no real relationships, no real job, no joy. I know brain-dead meth heads who have more going for them than you. But it doesn't have to be that way."

"Don't be talking to me about how my life turned out," Matt said in anger. His stomach kicked like a horse. He felt certain he was going to throw up, but managed to regain control. "At least tell me who killed you. Who did it? Let me get you some justice."

"Don't worry about that, bro. Justice will be dispensed soon enough, and it will be a hell of a lot more fun my way than anything the courts can dole out."

"I'm going to get you out of there, Jake."

"No! Don't you see? I don't want out, not the way you're thinking. I want to live forever. I want to walk down the street and see a car or a yacht or a beautiful woman, and it's mine for the taking."

"Jake, I'm not letting Satan in, or Lucifer, or whatever he calls himself, so he can destroy the world."

"Put away your fairy tale notions of him. He's not looking to rule Earth and enslave humans. He doesn't give a damn one way or the other about humans. He just wants to be released from Hell."

"He sounds like a great guy."

"If I were you, I wouldn't be so snide. He can knock that out of you fast, trust me on that. But he's not like you imagine him. He's just anti-establishment. He wants to throw off authoritarian figures that tell us what we can and can't do. Thou shalt not, and all that bullshit. He's the spirit of rebellion and wants people to be able to live the way they want to live. I can respect that. Hell, I support that."

"Of course you do. I'm sure that's how you justified selling meth. You were just letting people live the way they wanted to live. You weren't making them buy it, so it's not like you did anything wrong, right?"

"Get off your high horse. You want to lecture me about doing the right thing? You sure about that?"

"Jake, there has to be another way."

"There's not. Listen, he doesn't want to fight you. His power will be stronger if you work with him instead of against him. But don't kid yourself, Matt; he's taking you one way or another. Just stop fighting and I'll be able to join you. We'll be together again. Remember how it used to be growing up? You and me, always on the same team, always having each other's backs. It can be like that again."

"You know it can't be like that again. It can't."

"You're wrong. When you feel the connection coming on, stop resisting. It won't be painful. Not like before, when you felt what I was going through. That was before he knew of our connection. Now just open yourself up to it. It will be painless. Or simply go to sleep. How long do you think you can stay awake, anyway? You already look like the walking dead. I'm figuring the over–under for falling sleep is around an hour and a half."

"There has to—" Matt stopped, not even wanting to say it aloud, but suddenly another option was clear to him. "I could take my own life. End this now."

Jake looked at Matt incredulously, then shook his head. "Do you know what happens to souls that commit suicide? Do you know where they go?" Matt wouldn't look at Jake. "They come here, Matt."

"I don't believe that. I just don't."

"I don't care what you believe. And as unbelievable as the pain has been for me, think what it would be like for someone who really pissed him off. Remember what you went through last night in my bedroom? Imagine experiencing that for ten thousand years and then being told it was the equivalent of one day of your life. There's a reason they call it eternal damnation. I can't let that happen to you, man. Not to my brother."

Matt wiped the sweat from his forehead and turned his gaze to the ground. He didn't want to look at Jake, or have to deal with any of this anymore. All he wanted was to wake from this nightmare.

"Let him in, Matt," Jake said. "He's stronger than you. He's stronger than all of us. He will exploit our connection, and he will consume your soul—but if you let him in, you'll be rewarded. How is this even a question for you? You'd choose the life you currently lead over one of success and comfort and actual happiness? When did you become so stupid?"

Matt's ire rose, the resentments of childhood snowballing.

"I'll do whatever I can to get you released. Don't forget how well I know you, Jake. You lied when you said to ignore Skiz's advice, just like you lied about people who kill themselves. You've always lied, Jake. I'll make things right—"

"Damn it, Matt! You're such an idiot!"

"If I can't save you, I'll break this connection, but I am not holding the door open for Satan to enter this world."

Jake shook his head. "I can't believe you would abandon me to this fate, but fine. Do it your way, but I'm going to help him. Anything

I can do to strengthen the connection, I will. You can't keep this up forever. You have no idea what you're dealing with."

Matt closed his eyes and focused on his breathing. He heard Jake's voice yelling at him to grow up, warning him that soon he wouldn't be able to tune him out with his stupid mind exercises, but the vitriol eventually began to fade. Matt built a titanium wall around his brain and kept mentally reinforcing it until Jake's voice devolved into the buzzing of a horsefly, and then nothing at all, as he finally broke the connection.

He looked in the mirror and saw only himself. He was pale and beaten, but at least it was still him. For now.

Matt drove through town the next morning on autopilot, jittery after a night of coffee and sitting on Jake's front porch in an effort to stay awake. After his talk with Jake, every time he let his mind drift, he'd once again see his brother's flesh melting off his face. What could any soul on earth do to deserve that sort of eternal punishment after death? Was there nothing God could do to show a little bit of love and mercy?

He started the morning by slowly driving past the Gas and Go to make sure Teddy was on duty. To his relief, he saw him sitting behind the counter, his eyes glued to the station's TV, so Matt continued down the main road before turning onto Walnut Avenue, where Teddy's sister, Lorraine, lived. He eventually pulled up to a tiny brick home with a well-manicured yard and a Cornhusker football flag hanging from a pole near the front door. A Ford Escort that had to be at least twenty years old sat in the driveway, so he took that as a good sign that Lorraine could be home. He hoped she didn't have another brother like Teddy answering the door.

He checked the cut Bone's knife had left on his cheek, and decided it was small enough that Lorraine wouldn't be frightened. If she experienced any anxiety, it would most likely come from him being a dead ringer of the person who hurt her. He knocked on the front door. A moment later, a woman in her mid-twenties opened the door cautiously, peering out with the chain still on the latch. She didn't seem frightened, but she also made no move to open the door wider.

"I'm Matt Davis. Jake was my brother, as you probably already guessed. I was hoping I could talk with you for a minute."

She continued staring, without speaking or displaying any sort of expression.

"If you'd feel more comfortable," he continued, "we could sit on the front step. It shouldn't take long."

Lorraine tilted her head slightly to the side, so at least Matt knew she wasn't catatonic.

"Please?"

Upon hearing what must have been the magic word, Lorraine offered up a slightly crooked Mona Lisa smile. She unlatched the door and gestured for him to enter, apparently preferring the air conditioning inside over the cauldron that was the morning sun. Matt followed her to the living room where she sat on the floor with her back against the sofa. The smell of baking bread wafted through the house.

Matt sat in an overstuffed cloth armchair that faced the television, probably Teddy's chair of choice, given the small motor oil stains visible on one of its arms. The furniture and assorted knick-knacks scattered around the room looked like they had been there for fifty years, indicating that neither Lorraine nor her brother saw any need to change the décor decisions made long ago by their mother.

Lorraine still hadn't said a word, and Matt wondered if perhaps she was mute. For a second, he imagined Jake somehow being responsible for her inability to speak, but he banished that thought quickly. Claire would surely have mentioned that.

"I understand my brother wasn't nice to you. If that's true, I'd like to apologize on his behalf."

Lorraine stared at the beige carpet, picking at stray pieces of lint. "Okay," she finally said, glancing up again. Her voice was soft, not in a shy sort of way, but like someone vulnerable who had never been rewarded for speaking up.

"I'm hearing a lot of stories about how Jake wasn't a good person. If it's not too personal, can you tell me what he did to—"

"He got me hooked on meth," she said matter-of-factly, as if answering a question about her favorite color. "I know ultimately it was my own doing. I'm not trying to avoid taking responsibility, and I don't want to come across like a victim or anything. Teddy says the best way to get back on track is to take ownership of my decisions."

"I understand how that—"

"But it wouldn't have happened without Jake. He pretended to be interested in me, you know, like boyfriend and girlfriend. I'd never had a boyfriend before. After a while he had me try some meth. Just a try, he said. Said if I was interested in him, I should at least see what he was into. Didn't take long before I was more interested in the high than in him, which is what he wanted in the first place. He didn't want a girlfriend. He wanted another customer."

Matt wondered what sort of life she had led up to this point. He pegged her as being one of those kind-hearted people who always got taken advantage of. Always. A nice person who went through school and life wondering what the secret was, why others seemed happy and well adjusted, while she sat at the receiving end of everyone's cruelty.

Matt silently cursed Jake. "I'm sorry he did that to you."

"I got to a point where I stole from my dad to buy more meth. It had taken so much control over me that I was no longer myself. Mom passed away a couple years ago, and I had always taken care of my dad and Teddy, and suddenly here I was, sneaking into my dad's bedroom at night to take money from his wallet. One time I could tell he was awake, and he knew what I was doing. He wanted to help me but didn't know how, so he just laid there pretending to be asleep, and listening to me, his daughter, stealing from him."

Her voice revealed no emotion as she spoke, as if she were reading a police report. It had to hurt her deeply, but her tone never betrayed the pain.

"Teddy told me I either needed to get clean or get out. Threatened to kick me out of the house. And he would have, too. Teddy's a good brother and I know he loves me, but he didn't know any other way to handle the situation. So I went to see Father Pearman—"

"Andy?" Matt asked, still not used to his friend's new title.

"He worked with me and helped me through the withdrawal. Helped me break the grip it had on my soul until I could take back control. He also helped me see what Jake was doing and talked to me about the evil in the world, how I shouldn't let it in. How meth was evil."

The words struck Matt. Could it have been more than a coincidence that she'd used the same phrase as Jake about letting evil in?

"Lord knows Jake tried wheedling his way back into my life, doing whatever he could to get me to lower my resistance. He was only interested in getting his money. Ruining my life didn't appear to be any concern of his. But Father Pearman helped me keep Jake out for good."

Matt was impressed, and more than a little envious, of the difference Andy was making in the community.

"Did you by chance write a letter expressing your disappointment to Jake?"

"A letter?"

"Yes, a note saying how he'd hurt you."

"No. I didn't need to. He knew how he hurt me. He just didn't care."

"I wish there was something I could say that could explain why Jake did what he did, but I don't know what to say. I'm not sure what happened to him over time, but I'm glad you were able to get help."

"Thank you."

"I can understand why you would harbor hateful feelings for him. I absolutely understand. I actually came here today hoping to see if I could get you to forgive him, but I don't know that I have the words, given what he did to you."

"I have forgiven him," she said plainly.

"You have? Oh. I'm pleased to hear that," Matt said. "But I have to admit I'm a little surprised."

He wondered if the meth had affected her mentally, or if her monotone way of talking about this helped her cope with the traumas she'd experienced. At first, he wondered if she was being truthful about her forgiveness, but as he watched her, he could sense an air of peace within her.

"It's part of the Lord's Prayer. 'Forgive us our trespasses, as we forgive those who trespass against us,' so that's what I've done," she said quietly, as if in prayer. "Father Pearman helped me see we are all sinners. We've all done things we're not proud of—like me stealing from my father—and it's not my place to judge others. I don't know Jake's story. I don't know what made him the way he was, but Father Pearman told me we all have our own bag of rocks that we carry, so I'll leave the ultimate judgment to God." She stood. "As for me, I don't hold any anger toward him, especially now that he's dead. Blessed are those who forgive. That's me. Blessed."

Matt believed her. She was obviously much more forgiving than he could ever be.

She didn't tell Matt it was time for him to leave, but he could tell there was nothing more to say. He thanked her for her time and apologized again for stopping by unannounced. As he started toward the door, he paused.

"You're very special," he said.

"I stole from my father. I'm not special."

"I think you're wrong about that."

"You look just like him," she said.

"We were identical."

"No, you're not identical. Jake told me you and he were very similar, yet not at all alike. He was right."

"But we were brothers. That's supposed to count for something, isn't it?" Matt turned and walked back out into the heat, not waiting for an answer.

NINETEEN

Matt sat on his mother's front porch for ten minutes before finally trying the front door and finding it unlocked. He had forgotten that hardly anyone in Hatchett locked their doors, especially if they only planned to be out for a few hours. It almost felt inappropriate to enter while his mother was out, like he was a stranger in his childhood home.

In the kitchen, he found a pitcher resembling the Kool-Aid Man, likely the same one from his youth. He poured himself a glass of lemonade and went back into the living room so he could see when his mother pulled into the driveway.

A Barbara Cartland novel sat on a side table next to his mother's reading chair, an expired coupon for orange juice torn from the newspaper serving as a bookmark. Matt found it hard to picture her ever sitting on the sofa, and especially not the plaid, overstuffed La-Z-Boy, which had been the domain of his father. She had never cared much for TV, but didn't have any trouble reading when the rest of the family had it blaring. She easily retreated into her novels, and he bet she still resided there most every night. What else was there for her to do? Then again, how would he know what her life was like nowadays? He didn't even know she'd started going to church again. For all he knew, she was very active in church-related events. He didn't really know much about her anymore.

The oven-sized TV box still consumed one corner of the living room. He remembered how he and Jake would lie on the floor every night when they were young, watching one show after another. When his father was in the room, he, of course, was the final arbiter of what they would watch, but his taste wasn't much different from that of the two boys.

More often than not, however, their dad could be found either out working in the field or puttering around the barn. In the bitterest of cold winter nights, he might sit at the kitchen table under the bare lightbulb, staring at an old notebook he used for tracking his expenses and making plans for planting season. Matt used to think the notebook was just an excuse for his dad to sit alone in the kitchen. It made him look busy.

The round, faded rug in front of the TV served as Matt and Jake's turf, just as the recliner had been their father's. He could tell his mother had tried removing as many of the rug's stains as possible, but a long run of use by twin boys had rendered her efforts futile. It probably cost no more than twenty dollars new, and that was many years ago, but apparently it hadn't yet outlived its usefulness.

He and Jake used to lie on their stomachs, chins cupped in their hands, staring at whatever the screen offered. Commercial breaks meant wrestling or trying to guess the identity of the killer in that week's police drama, both activities easily escalating into punches and pinches, not out of anger but because they were brothers.

It didn't take them long, however, to figure out that a solid punch landed by one would hurt them both. They couldn't even hold the other down for tickle fights because that made them both squirm. So, they'd settled for wrestling. It was just one more way to be close.

Matt felt flushed. Beads of sweat surfaced on his forehead. He hoped it was the heat, since the window air conditioner was turned off. He held the glass of lemonade to his cheek, welcoming its coolness, but just to be safe he closed his eyes and focused on his breathing as he visualized a brick wall flying up around his brain, with a thick iron band lining the outside of it. It wasn't always effective, but it gave him a fighting chance to hold off connections.

The period right before a connection began could be compared to an oncoming panic attack: a sudden wave of heat, his body tightening, every nerve tingling like he was strapped to an electric chair that was powering up. Right now, though, he only felt hot, so that was a good sign, and one that could easily be explained by the summer heat.

Matt turned away from the TV; he shouldn't have lost himself in the past. If anything, he needed to avoid thinking about Jake and their relationship at all. If there was going to be a connection, the attack would have hit him by now. He took a long drink of the lemonade and headed back outside where a breeze offered at least a bit of a respite.

As he stepped back onto the front porch, he heard tires on gravel and saw his mother's car pulling in. The car slowed for a moment, as if she was trying to figure out who was on her porch, then she pulled on up the driveway.

"I didn't know you were coming over," she said, as she got out of the car. "You should have called and let me know."

"I just stopped by to see how you're doing," Matt said.

"Good thing I forgot to lock the door. Hard getting into the habit after all these years, but crime is at such a point nowadays around here." She pointed toward the back seat. "Would you do me a favor and grab one of those sacks?"

Matt walked over to the car and scooped up both paper bags filled with groceries.

"You don't need to get both," his mother said, sounding offended.

"It's fine. They're not heavy."

His mother sighed as she walked ahead and pulled the door open for him. In the kitchen, he started unloading the groceries, but she shooed him to the side, once more reminding him he didn't know where things went.

"You getting along all right at Jake's?" she asked.

"It's fine."

"I can't imagine he has much in the way of food over there. If you see anything you need, feel free to take it. Or maybe you're already getting ready to leave. You never said how long you're staying."

"I don't know. I'll probably be here at least a couple more days."

"And your boss is fine with that?"

"It's not a problem." He leaned against the counter and watched as she put several ears of corn in the refrigerator. "So, Mom, did Jake talk with you much about things going on in his life?"

She glanced over at him, partly suspicious, partly put out. "No, he was a twenty-eight-year-old man. He had his own life. Do you tell me much about what's going on in your life? I just know Jake did the best he could to get by, like everyone else around here."

"Was he dating anyone?"

Her expression transitioned to one of impatience. "What is it you want to know, Matthew? Don't poke around like you're just making small talk. Say what's on your mind."

Matt looked down at the floor, feeling both reprimanded and exposed. "I'm trying to understand what was going on with him. How things got to the point that someone wanted to kill him. If I can help figure out what happened, I don't think that's a bad thing."

"Sheriff Wilson will find whoever did this. And he certainly doesn't need your help. You just stay out of it. What could you possibly know about your brother that could help him?"

"I already talked with the sheriff," he said.

She stopped putting the groceries away but didn't look up at him. She waited to hear what else Matt had to say.

"The sheriff said Jake was caught up in the drug scene. That he ran with a bad group that dealt meth. I'm also hearing he wasn't exactly a great—"

"Stop it! I told you there'd be rumors."

"These aren't rumors. They're things the sheriff himself—"

"I don't care who told you. You can't believe everything you hear. When's the last time you even spoke to Jake?"

He couldn't tell her it was just the previous night. Before then, though, it had been years since he and Jake had had any sort of meaningful conversation, and six years since they'd even said hello on the phone, and that was only because his mother handed Jake the phone when Matt had called her on Mother's Day.

"That's what I thought," his mother said in response to Matt's silence. "Jake had his faults, as do we all. He didn't go off to college and get a good job; he stuck around. He did what he could to help me after your father passed away. He stayed in Hatchett when he didn't have to."

"Jake stayed because he didn't have any interest in going anywhere else. He didn't stay here out of some sacrifice of his own happiness. It was easy staying in Hatchett, and that's what Jake liked."

"I'm not going to listen to you talk about your brother like that. Not now. And not from you, who totally shut him out of your life. Maybe he was involved in some things I didn't approve of, but I don't know that for a fact. But here's what I do know: he helped me stay in this house. He helped me pay for groceries whenever things got tight. He was around. That's what I know about your brother."

"Mom, I didn't know you were having money problems. I would have been more than willing to have helped if you'd asked."

His mother slapped her palm down on the kitchen counter like a gavel. She took a deep breath and shoved the paper bags into the bottom cupboard to join an already impressive stack.

"I didn't ask Jake," she yelled. "He just helped. I wouldn't still be in this house if it weren't for him. The only reason you're able to visit your family home is because of Jake."

"I'm not trying to make Jake look bad. I'm trying to figure out what happened. I need to help set right anything he may have done, whether intentionally or unintentionally. For him. That's all."

"For him. Right. Because you've always been there for him."

Matt struggled to refrain from describing Jake's dangling skin or his chemically dissolved chin and lip. "Goddammit, it is for him, Mom! Can you quit protecting him just once and tell me what you know?" He couldn't remember ever having sworn at his mother, but a serious lack of sleep didn't help when it came to holding back his temper.

His mother started to respond, then halted. Her knees buckled slightly, as though she was about to collapse, then she steadied herself by leaning on the kitchen counter.

"Mom, are you all right?"

She paused, collecting her breath, then stood more erect than he'd ever seen her, throwing her shoulders back and displaying an entirely new presence, one of command. She no longer looked tired or beaten down. Her voice remained calm but strong, with the confident timbre of a prosecuting attorney. She had changed.

"You want to know about Jake? He did his best. He didn't abandon me like a goddamn traitor."

His mother wielded the line like a crowbar. He couldn't believe she said that. He'd only heard her swear once, when he was twelve and she thought her husband had been trampled by a steer. He felt like he was dealing with a totally different person.

"What's the matter, son?" she asked in a condescending tone. "I thought you wanted to hear what I knew, so I'm laying it out for you. Jake had the backbone to do what needed to be done. He took care of me. He didn't take shit from anyone, and he didn't hesitate to fight anyone who crossed him. He was a hell of a lot stronger than you could ever dream of being, you self-centered asshole."

She glared at him defiantly, one end of her lip curling upward to reveal yellowing teeth.

"Do you know what I had to deal with raising you? Always worried someone would find out that you and your brother were some sort of supernatural freaks? The entire time I raised you, I wished you'd never been born. If it had just been Jake, I wouldn't have had to deal with all the bullshit that came with your connection, and he wouldn't have ended up in this horrible situation."

"What's going on, Mom? This isn't you. Who's talking for you?"

He stepped closer to her but stopped when she bent over and screamed with a deep howling voice that sounded half-human and half-animal. Saliva spewed from her mouth as she assaulted him with a torrent of abuse.

"What makes you think I'm not speaking for myself, you pathetic worm? You do nothing but lie to me. Who the hell do you think you are? Stop trying to save your brother. Let him in or when he takes you over, he'll rip out your soul by the roots and feed it to the jackals. Let him in. Let him in. LET HIM IN!"

She snarled, looking ready to charge at him with bared teeth, then she pulled a nine-inch, serrated butcher knife from a cabinet drawer and pointed the tip at him before placing the blade firmly against her own throat.

"You have no idea what you're up against! NO IDEA!" she screamed.

Matt was too far away to stop her if she wanted to hurt herself. She continued looking at him with nothing but contempt until her face contorted into a manic smile, like she'd just thought of something hilarious. Raising her elbow higher, the blade poised to slice open her jugular vein with one clean stroke, she teased the motion with light pressure and a quick jerking of her arm, as if ready to cut herself.

"No!" Matt screamed.

She cackled, then set the knife down on the counter. "You shouldn't lose your temper, son. Bad things may start happening to those you love when you lose control."

She then sighed, her posture folding back to normal as if she were deflating. Wiping her hands on her dress, she turned and started walking out of the kitchen. When she spoke, her voice was tired once again. She was back. "I've told you everything I know about Jake. He wasn't perfect, but he was there for me. Now if you'll excuse me, I need to lie down for a minute. It's been a long day."

She walked down the hall, letting him know their conversation had ended. Or at least the conversation with his mother had ended.

The other one was likely just getting started.

TWENTY

Matt arrived at St. Luke's Catholic Church an hour before the noon service. He'd called Andy and said he needed to speak with him about something that was best explained in person, then ended up telling him everything over the phone anyway. Andy had that kind of sway over people. When Matt finished his story, an understandable silence stretched on for a long moment until Andy told him he'd be waiting for him at the church.

As he got out of his car, Matt glanced at the cemetery. The two large sprays of flowers that had been laid at Jake's burial had withered and died, likely from the heat. He was tempted to walk over to the gravesite, then decided that was just tempting fate. He didn't see how any good could come from such a visit.

Matt walked into the empty nave. Impressive thirty-foot stained-glass windows flanked the room, doing their best to illuminate the dark interior. It was a good-sized room, with pews extending in both directions from the center aisle. It probably seated three hundred, which seemed optimistic for a town of Hatchett's size, but perhaps that's where faith came in.

On the front wall behind the altar, a fifteen-foot statue of Jesus on the cross was fixed ten feet from the ceiling. Matt remembered once seeing a coffee-table book that showed pictures of various churches in Italy. The variety of expressions on the different Jesuses had struck him: some were in peaceful repose with eyes closed, others bloody, the crown of thorns having cut deep. Hatchett's Jesus appeared to be at the pinnacle of suffering, with lips closed tight and eyes open wide, gazing upward in pain as blood trickled down his forehead from the thorns. Definitely not subtle in its message: *See what I did for you?*

"Sort of creepy, isn't it?"

Andy stood in a side entrance wearing a Nirvana T-shirt, jeans, and an old pair of Vans, looking more like the friend Matt remembered. "I'd like to replace it with a slightly less masochistic Jesus, but the old-school parishioners are more comfortable with maximum guilt. Plus, it makes it easier to scare the young children into being good."

"At least you don't have to face it when you speak."

"There is that." He waved Matt closer. "Come to my office and tell me you were bullshitting me earlier on the phone."

Matt told Andy everything that happened, in greater detail this time, from the bar in New York City, Skiz's advice, the encounter with Jake in the barn, the theater screen getting eaten, and his mother threatening to spray him with her blood. All of it. Andy listened intently, never taking his eyes from Matt. He leaned back as Matt finished.

"I'm not surprised to hear the movie theater has cockroaches, although eating the screen sounds extreme. But your mom . . . is she okay?"

"Like it never happened," Matt said. "But I can feel him—it—working its way into my soul. I don't know what to do."

"As surprising as this may sound, I've never encountered anything quite like this before." He chugged from a can of Dr. Pepper sitting on his desk. "I suppose it's more than an understatement to say all of this is pretty incredible."

"I swear to you, everything I've said . . ."

"No, no," Andy said, putting up his hand. "I believe you. I've read a lot of crazy shit about spirits and demons. Plus, the big book is full of some pretty messed-up stories. Miracles. Possessions. Exorcisms. After all, the foundation of the entire church rests on someone rising from the dead. Things impossible to believe, but which happened nonetheless. I wish I knew what to do, but I'll be the first to admit I'm out of my league here."

"The thing is, I don't think I've got much time left. I can only keep fighting it for so long, and I haven't slept for over two days. I'm lost here and I don't know what to do," Matt said, defeated.

"You should come to communion. You need to break the connection with Jake, then you can focus on trying to get him out of Hell. If what Skiz told you is correct, you don't need to have the connection with Jake to release him, so we need to get you more time to help him."

"I'm open to that, but I don't know how to break the connection. There are things I can do that slow it down, but not always, and not for long."

"I take it you're still not a religious man?"

Matt smiled with a trace of despair. "Recently I've become a lot more open to the idea."

"So come worship with us. Ask God to help. Matty, you're trying to take on something you're not equipped to fight, and you're going to lose unless you have somebody on your side who's bigger and badder than what it is you're battling. God is your best chance. We will ask Him to help you. And when communion is offered, come to the front and accept it. Let's not do this half-assed."

"I'm not Catholic."

"I'm not a priest."

"Perfect. How could this not work?"

"Act as if ye had faith, and faith shall be given to you," Andy said solemnly.

"You know your Bible."

"Actually, it's a line from the movie The Verdict. Paul Newman's character implied it was Biblical, but David Mamet wrote it. See? Everybody is making this shit up as they go, but it's the spirit of what's being said that's important. You need to have faith. Let's start there and build on that."

"Peter tells us, 'Be self-controlled and alert. Your enemy the devil prowls around like a roaring lion looking for someone to devour.' So what the heck are you supposed to do about a prowling devil? What chance do we as mere mortals have against something like a devil prowling like a lion?"

Andy stood in front of his congregation, speaking solemnly. Even though Matt knew Andy was talking directly to him, everyone who was listening probably felt the same way. At least a couple of the people in attendance looked like they either had dealt with—or were still dealing with—drug addiction, so wrestling with the devil likely rang true to them as well. Matt thought Andy delivered his lines like a true professional. He wasn't acting. It was from the heart.

"I'm not here to tell you that taking on the devil is easy. Let me tell you about a couple of men who learned that firsthand. First there was

131

Solomon. Nobody was considered wiser than old Solomon. And then there was Samson. Nobody was stronger than Samson. And yet both of these men fell, unable to rise above the schemes of the devil. So if these two gifted men were brought down by the devil, what chance do we have?"

What chance, indeed, thought Matt.

"But in James 4:7, we are told, 'Submit yourselves, then, to God. Resist the devil, and he will flee from you.' And how we do that can be found in Ephesians: 'Put on the armor of God so that you can take a stand against the devil's schemes. For our struggle is not against flesh and blood, but against the rulers, against authorities, against the powers of this dark world and against the spiritual forces of evil in the heavenly realms. Therefore, put on the full armor of God, so that when the day of evil comes, you may be able to stand your ground, and after you have done everything, to stand.' That's how we do it."

Matt gazed up at the crucifix. The expression on Jesus's alabaster face seemed to empathize with him: the torment, the pain, the distress. When Matt had understood what he was up against, why hadn't his immediate reaction been to turn to God? Would his hesitation make his prayers seem less sincere, since they came from a place of desperation? Did God even work that way? He hoped God wasn't petty like that.

He glanced up and saw Andy looking directly at him.

"So as you put on God's armor, remember Luke 10:19 which says, 'Behold I give unto you power to tread on serpents and scorpions, and over all the power of the enemy, and nothing shall by any means hurt you.' With the support of God, you will prevail. My friend, I know you will prevail."

Matt felt strengthened, ready to finally have faith and put on the armor he needed to fight this evil. The armor metaphor didn't seem all that much different from the mental walls he built around his mind to keep the connection from overpowering him—except this armor hopefully came with a powerful wingman.

He watched as Andy prepared the wafers and the wine for communion, moving through the ceremony with the same gravity as if it were the first time he'd ever done it. It made Matt think of actors who played the same role on Broadway for years, yet each night had the ability to make it feel fresh and original.

"May the receiving of your body and blood, Lord Jesus Christ, not bring me to judgment and condemnation, but through your loving mercy be for me protection in mind and body and a healing remedy. Amen. Please come forth and take communion."

Most of the congregation rose and formed a line in front of Andy. Matt stayed seated and watched as a middle-aged woman in a gray dress kneeled in front of Andy.

"This is My body," Andy said quietly as he placed the wafer on her tongue. "This is My blood." She sipped from the silver chalice he offered.

Matt self-consciously rose and took a place at the end of the line. A man who appeared to be in his late seventies and wearing overalls that looked even older shuffled up behind him.

As Matt drew closer to the front, he started to understand what Andy said about former classmates seeing him not as the theater geek they knew in high school, but instead as a surrogate of their faith: the robe, the accoutrements, the stage on which he performed these acts of ritual. As Matt came closer, he began to feel spiritual too.

Two women stood ahead of Matt. The younger helped the older to her knees to take part in the Eucharist sacrament. Matt looked at Andy, hoping to make eye contact before his turn, but Andy remained focused on the old woman. Sweat beaded on Andy's forehead and his cheeks looked paler than when they had talked in his office.

When Matt's turn came, he kneeled and looked up at Andy, who wavered a moment before steadying himself, as if struggling to continue with the sacrament. Andy's breathing grew shallow and quick, but he still reached for the wafer and, after pausing a moment to compose himself, managed to croak, "The Body of Christ."

"Amen," Matt said, opening his mouth.

Andy flinched before setting the wafer on Matt's tongue, as if someone had jabbed him in the side with a nail, but he sucked in a deep breath and put the wafer in Matt's mouth. Once again, Andy paused, as if each step in the sacrament was suddenly taxing. He placed a hand on the table next to him and leaned on it, trying to steady himself.

After catching his breath, Andy picked up the chalice and lowered it to Matt. His hands shook noticeably, and he almost spilled the wine. Matt put his hands on Andy's to steady them. When Andy said, "The

Blood of Christ," Matt leaned forward to take a sip, but saw a drop of something red fall into the chalice. And then another drop. Matt looked up to see a trickle of blood worming its way out of Andy's right nostril, quickly followed by a trail from the left side.

Andy seemed unaware of his bleeding nose until some of the blood fell onto his robe and trickled down the fabric's white trim. He set the chalice on the table, grabbed a cloth, and held it to his nose. Now blood began pooling in his ears until it ran down both sides of his neck, staining his collar a deep crimson.

Matt looked on in horror as small tendrils of blood began streaming from both of Andy's eyes, trickling down his cheek, and mixing with the blood from his nose. Andy staggered to the pulpit and blindly felt around until he managed to grab a box of Kleenex. He pressed a handful of tissues to his eyes.

The congregants gasped, and one woman screamed. The murmuring amongst the group turned into shouting, although nobody seemed to know what to do. Andy raised a hand, trying to calm them and let them know he was all right, but it was obvious to everyone he was far from okay. Partially blinded, he almost fell after walking directly into the table that held the wafers, but was able to catch himself at the last minute.

Matt ran to the altar to steady his friend. "Oh my God. Andy!" He pulled a couple more tissues from the box and began wiping the blood from Andy's eyes, but the tissues became saturated too quickly to be of any use. He put an arm under one of Andy's armpits to help steady his friend but wasn't sure where to lead him.

The blood refused to stop. Andy began choking, blood spraying from his mouth and onto Matt's shirt as he coughed and tried to clear his airway. Matt could sense the panic Andy struggled to hold at bay.

"Leave," Andy finally managed to choke out when he could breathe again. "Matty ... please ... get outside ... call 911 ... you need to leave the church. Right now."

Matt froze, then turned and stumbled down the steps. A couple of parishioners stepped up to take hold of Andy, as if they had been hesitant to get too close to Matt.

Matt pulled his phone from his pocket as he staggered down the aisle before breaking into a run. He felt the eyes of others on his back, blaming him, even though they couldn't be sure why. But he knew.

He crashed through the front doors and out into the blinding sunlight.

"Nine-one-one. What's your emergency?"

"It's Andy. St. Luke's priest. He's been . . ." Matt's voice caught as he found himself wanting to cry.

"He's been what, sir?"

"You have to help him. Please. God knows I can't."

TWENTY-ONE

Matt sat at Jake's kitchen table, despondent, with two empty cans of Red Bull and most of a pizza still in its box in front of him. He had managed to finish part of one slice, but couldn't force himself to eat any more, despite the fact he hadn't eaten for nine hours. He had picked up the sixteen-inch thin crust pepperoni and black olive from Pizza Hut, Hatchett's only chain restaurant, thinking it wise to eat something other than peanut butter and potato chips, but by the time he sat down, his appetite had abandoned him.

Earlier, he had finally gotten hold of Andy after he'd been treated at the Hatchett Medical Center, a fancy name for a three-room clinic staffed by the local physician who was at least 150 years old and a nurse practitioner in her twenties. Dr. Foster could not find anything wrong with Andy. Nosebleeds, of course, weren't uncommon, although they were for Andy. Blood coming from the eyes and ears, on the other hand, remained a mystery, and not one the doctor could solve.

The bleeding had stopped as soon as Matt left the church, and other than being shaken, Andy hadn't experienced any negative repercussions from the attack. He told Matt he wanted to help him, but at the present time had no idea what he could do. He would pray on it and read some literature about demonic possession, to see if that offered any direction, but he also felt that if they did get together again, the church didn't appear to be the best setting. He made sure Matt understood he wasn't abandoning him; he just needed a better sense of how he might be able to help.

In the church, surrounded by the trappings of ceremony and faithful believers, Matt had felt a sense of hope. For a short time, he didn't feel alone in his battle, and thought that perhaps he had a power on his side that would give him a fighting chance. Then the bleeding started. When the initial drops of blood fell into the cup Matt held, he looked up, and the first thing he saw was the statue of Christ. He thought the blood was coming from Him, that perhaps He again had taken on Matt's sins. Then he saw Andy, and the feelings of hope that had been building in his chest shot away from him like a startled covey of quail.

He tossed the mostly uneaten slice of pizza back into the box. As he rose, he grabbed hold of the table to regain his balance as a sudden dizziness ricocheted throughout his head, as though he'd had one drink too many.

What he really needed, even more than food, was sleep. Trying to figure out how to break the psychic connection, how to find the person Jake had wronged, and how he would get that person to forgive Jake— all of those questions consumed him and were challenging enough with a clear head, but none weighed on him more than the question of when Satan would take him over. His despair bloomed when he realized he had just phrased his question as "when" he lost his battle, not "if." He knew he was running out of time.

The sun eased itself on down to the horizon, although it wouldn't be totally dark for a couple more hours. As he washed his glass in the kitchen sink, knocking and scraping sounds once again started coming from the attic.

He walked over to the stairwell and listened. The clawing sounded as ominous as the first time he'd heard it, but he felt no need to check the attic a second time. He knew nothing good would come of it.

As he turned to go back into the kitchen, he saw the living room curtains in front of three windows blowing, as though a strong breeze had developed outside. He didn't think a storm was brewing, but this time of year, one never knew.

Matt went into the living room and parted the curtains to shut the window closest to the front door, but it was already closed. There weren't any air vents near the windows, but even if there had been, they would only be for heat: the house didn't have central air.

The curtains danced on the invisible breeze. He finally reached over and pushed one of the curtains down, but it immediately rose again, resuming its dance. He put his hand next to the window to check for a breeze that might be coming through a crack in the seal but couldn't feel anything. He looked outside, but the trees and shrubs betrayed no movement.

He did, however, see that the black crows that had crowded the driveway a few evenings ago had again overtaken the front porch.

The football-sized bird had also returned, perched on the railing that displayed Jake's blood stain. The size difference from the other birds was striking, along with the fact that while most of the other birds shifted from one foot to the other, jerking their heads back and forth, the larger bird stared straight at Matt with its black eyes. It began to peck hard at the crimson-stained wood, leaving its mark.

As Matt studied the humongous bird, a smaller crow crashed into the window, cracking it. Matt leaped back, now wide awake. Angry, he ripped one of the fluttering curtains off its rod, wadded it up, and threw it across the room, at which point the knocking upstairs resumed, but this time louder. Once again, he stood at the bottom of the steps and listened for a minute. Whatever was up there could knock all it wanted.

He strode over and locked the heavy oak front door, then turned around and leaned against it, trying to decide what he should do.

A loud knock from the other side of the door startled Matt, causing him to jump away from it. He watched the doorknob turn slowly, but the dead bolt kept it secured. He froze until the second knock on the door, at which point he raced to the back door that led into the kitchen and locked it as well.

The knock at the front door became louder, more urgent. Matt cautiously ventured back to see if the knob turned anymore, but it remained still. He thought about grabbing a butcher knife from the kitchen, even though he didn't believe it would do him any good.

"Matt?" he heard from the other side. "It's Claire. Are you there?"

Claire's voice surprised him. He reached for the dead bolt, pausing for a moment, suddenly uncertain whether this could be a trick. What if something out there was using Claire's voice to get him to unlock the door?

Had it really come to this? Doubting everything, suspicious of all his senses? Besides, if he was facing something able to perfectly mimic Claire's voice, could a locked, decades-old farm door stop that type of entity?

He opened the door and saw Claire holding a large box from Pizza Hut.

"Sorry I didn't call. I didn't have your cell."

He stepped to the side and waved Claire in. Outside, all the birds had vanished.

"Not a problem," he said. "I'm glad you stopped by."

She held up the box. "Have you eaten?"

"No," he said, noticing that the remaining curtains no longer fluttered in the air.

"Everything all right?" she asked, concerned.

"Not even close."

Matt and Claire sat on the living room sofa, balancing plates on their laps. Matt had eaten half the pizza; it was as though Claire had provided him with the security he needed to take care of himself for a moment. She asked if he'd heard about what happened to Andy; the Hatchett grapevine was high-speed. Matt said he was there when it happened, then proceeded to tell her about it, which led him to talk about his psychic connection with Jake still being intact, how he needed to get Jake out of Hell, and some of the things he'd dealt with along the way. He didn't share as much as he had with Andy, but he told her enough for her to understand the gravity of his situation.

She asked a few questions but seemed to accept everything as fact. "Now I understand why you've been asking who Jake wronged."

"Problem is, if Jake is in Hell because of an accumulation of smaller wrongs he did to a wide range of people, I'm screwed."

"Maybe, but I agree with Andy. The first effort should be finding a way to break the connection, and then figure out how Jake earned his place in Hell. Didn't anything work in the past?"

"I learned some mental imaging tricks that sometimes helped."

Claire put her hand on the side of Matt's head and stroked his hair. "I am so sorry, Matt. You never talked a lot about your connection with Jake. I knew the two of you sometimes felt each other's strong emotions, but I thought that was something that rarely happened. I had no idea how much you were struggling with it. No wonder you moved away. It had to be a relief to finally break the connection. Did you feel free?"

"In a way, yes. I wasn't just living on my own, I was literally on my own. Jake tried his best to reconnect, but I overpowered it. At the same time, I felt so incredibly alone. I never realized that part of my self-confidence came from the connection. We had always been a team, and even though we fought, he was still part of me, far more than I realized. And then that disappeared. And you were gone. And I felt so overwhelmed."

Claire pulled Matt's head toward her and kissed his forehead. "I wish you had told me."

"I tried starting over, but all I did was quit on myself. I didn't feel like I deserved anything good, especially after what I did to you."

He dropped his chin to his chest. Claire put an arm around his shoulders, pulled him closer and continued stroking and lightly kissing his head. If he could hold on to any single moment in his life, he wanted it to be this one.

"I'm so sorry I left you," he said. "I'm so sorry. These past ten years, my life has been nothing but an open wound that just won't heal."

He lifted his head and turned to face her. They stared at each other for a long moment, their past reconnecting them. He wanted another chance to make things right. He wanted to feel again.

So, he kissed her.

Matt thought being ten years older and a little more experienced would give him confidence as they cascaded toward intimacy, but he felt as nervous and uncertain with Claire as he'd ever been. He had not allowed himself to imagine holding her in his arms again and kissing her passionately and ending up in bed together. At best he had hoped when he returned to Hatchett that she would speak to him, perhaps without disdain, but now they fell back into an easy and natural rhythm.

They laid in each other's arms on top of Jake's bedspread, naked, Claire's head resting on Matt's chest. He stared up at the ceiling as he caressed her hair.

"I can't tell you how much I missed you," Matt said.

"I missed you too. There was nothing keeping you from coming back, though."

Claire started to say more, then stopped. She raised her head until she could see the pained look on Matt's face.

"What say we not relive the past?" she said. "What's done is done. And you also don't need to worry about me looking to go steady or waiting for a ring. We're adults now. We can have sex and go our separate ways. In fact, I think that's how it's mostly supposed to work when you become an adult."

"We don't have to relive the past, but let's not try to figure out the future just yet, either. I'm pretty happy in this moment."

Claire rolled onto her back, taking his hand in hers. "I can do that, but we need to cut your cord to Hell. If you want, we can talk through the different things I know Jake did to others. And I can ask around and hear what's being said. If you want to know anything going on in Hatchett, all gossip goes through the Creek."

"I appreciate it, but we can talk about it in the morning." Matt rolled onto his side and put his arm around Claire, who turned and nestled next to him. "Stay with me tonight. You can help keep me awake."

"I've been trying my best to do just that," she said.

"And I truly do appreciate the effort," he responded, laughing.

As he lay there, Matt imagined staying in Hatchett with Claire. After New York, the thought of living in a small, rural town with nothing to do seemed beyond comprehension, but now he found himself easily imagining softball games with her, volunteering at fundraisers, and lying on the grass in the backyard, gazing up at the never-ending sky that twinkled like a Christmas tree.

More than anything, he saw himself happy. Maybe that's why so many of his classmates had stayed. It had eluded him all those years, but he was finally experiencing it here, in Hatchett, with Claire.

As he sat up in bed, Matt heard the soft caw of a crow outside, but he ignored it. Despite everything, at that moment he knew what he wanted. Who he wanted. It didn't matter to him right then that his happiness likely would not last.

TWENTY-TWO

Matt felt himself being nudged.

"Hey, wake up. You fell asleep," Claire said gently.

With much effort, he opened his heavy eyes. He was sitting up in bed against a couple of pillows, but apparently that hadn't been enough to keep him awake. He nodded to Claire and half-raised his hand to let her know he was awake, then sat up straighter against the pillows.

Claire got out of bed and threw on an oversized T-shirt as she headed down the hall toward the bathroom. Matt looked around the room and smiled when he saw their clothes strewn across the floor, as if a summer storm had torn through the room, but his smile disappeared when he saw his suitcase in the corner, a reminder that this was temporary. He wasn't going to worry about that right now, though.

He looked down the hallway to the closed bathroom door. Moonlight spilled through the adjacent bedroom's windows, creating shadows of tree branches that lined one wall of the hallway like a gauntlet of arms and arthritic fingers waving back and forth as a gentle breeze blew outside. The shadow fingers looked like they were ready to grab whoever walked past them.

He closed his eyes again, knowing it was a mistake to do so, but fooling himself that he would just rest them a moment longer. He heard the toilet flush, then Claire's footsteps as she made her way back to the bedroom. When she entered the room, she called out to him again.

"Hey. Being awake means eyes opened. That's how it works."

"Mmm-hmmm," Matt said, unconvincingly.

"I'll bet I know what might wake you up."

Matt opened one eye halfway and smiled sleepily as Claire headed toward the bed, then saw her stop in front of the open walk-in closet, leaning down as if she thought she saw something.

"Don't tell me you have mice in here."

She stopped and looked in the closet, then bent over to look under some of the hanging clothes.

"Did you know there's a lock box in here?"

Matt barely mustered the energy to nod his head as his eyes hung like half-closed shades.

Claire stepped into the closet and picked up a metal box from the back corner. Holding the box, she stood between two rows of clothes that ran the length of the closet. She did a quick survey of what Jake owned.

"I have to be honest," she said, "I'm a little surprised to see Jake even owns a suit, although it probably makes sense that it's the color of cow manure. And how fitting that the only tie matching it has skulls and crossbones. Very classy. He was probably saving it for his wedding day."

"Come on back to bed. I thought you were going to wake me up."

"Hey, don't be greedy. I'm doing detective work here. Maybe there are other letters or something else in the box that might help."

Matt watched her shake the box.

"There's no padlock on it." After a moment, she gave him another update. "Just his car registration and some bank statements. Shoot. This detective work is harder than you'd think."

Matt closed his eyes again and patted the side of the bed, a call for her to come back to him. He slid down further on the pillows so that he was now lying flat on the bed, waiting for Claire to return, but instead he heard her giggle.

"Are you trying to seduce me in a closet? Kinky."

Matt opened one sleepy eye, confused, and looked at Claire. She was still standing in the middle of the closet with her back to him as one of Jake's long-sleeve shirts hanging behind her had reached out and was caressing her hair. A shirt sleeve from the other side of the closet also reached out to touch her, but she obviously thought it was Matt.

She slowly turned her head to kiss what she would have thought to have been Matt's hand.

"Why are you wearing clothes? Don't you understand how seduction works?"

She turned and found a shirtsleeve with no hand, just as Matt could finally process the bizarre scene he was witnessing. Immediately three other shirts extended their sleeves as well. Claire screamed and turned to run, but the numerous shirts held her in place, gripping her tightly, holding her fast. The sleeve closest to her face wrapped itself across her mouth, stifling her scream.

"Claire!" Matt shouted.

He grabbed the corner of the sheet to throw it back, but the sheet suddenly pulled taut, pinning him to the bed. It compressed across his chest and stretched so tight over his body that not a wrinkle was visible on its surface. He struggled to free himself, but everything from his neck down remained immobilized, like he was in restraints in an insane asylum, which is what the entire scene felt like.

"Claire, hold on! Try to get the clothes off the rod!"

He watched her pull at the garments, but they wouldn't come off their hangers. She wrenched her neck to the left and right, but the shirt sleeve on her mouth only tightened.

All the clothing seemed to launch into motion at once, groping for her blindly, but sensing she was nearby. Sleeves and pant legs stroked her hair and body. A belt wrapped around her right bicep and tugged her closer to one of the clothes bars, allowing more pieces of clothing to latch on to her. A pair of gray pants reached out, fastening themselves around her left leg.

Matt continued to struggle against the sheet, but to no avail. He thrashed under it and tried rising, but it was as though the sheet was bolted all around the bed.

"Let her go!" Matt shouted.

As Claire continued fighting, a pair of work pants dropped to the floor, lurched over, and trussed her legs like she was a steer at a rodeo. She kept her balance, mostly because the shirts forcefully held her up. More sleeves and pant legs joined in, wrapping around her wrists, arms, and shoulders like vines, pulling her tight from one side of the closet to the other, eventually lifting her a couple of inches off the floor so that she dangled in the air.

Matt stopped resisting for a moment. He closed his eyes and took long, deep breaths. At the end of his third inhalation, he managed to jerk one of his arms free, but that was as much as he could move. He saw Claire watching him desperately as he tried using his free hand to pull off the sheet, but all sides of it slid further under the bed. He continued struggling, now gasping for breath under the tightening sheet.

Matt saw Claire's look of horror as several neckties dropped off their nails and slithered toward her like multi-colored snakes. When the ties reached her, they slid up her legs, two wrapping around each thigh, while a dark red tie wrapped one end of itself around her upper arm like a tourniquet as the other end flicked at her like a cobra's tongue. Her muffled cry was of no use.

The skull and crossbones tie worked its way up her body, gliding up her arm until it reached her neck. It wrapped itself around her throat and incrementally constricted. Her eyes widened in terror as it choked off her oxygen.

By now, several shirts and pairs of pants had wrapped themselves around her arms, legs, and waist. A couple of shirtsleeves continued petting her hair, while another squeezed her around the waist. The shirts on each side of the closet then started pulling at her in a tug-of-war, gently at first, almost good-natured, then rougher. She resisted with all her might, jerking at the clothes, but the hangers wouldn't come off the closet rod.

The tie around her neck continued to slowly tighten. She thrashed her head back and forth, but that didn't bring her any air. One of the shirtsleeves reached out, wrapped itself around the end of her hair, and savagely jerked her head back, apparently punishing her for trying to get away.

"Hold on!" Matt shouted.

Matt continued struggling but couldn't free himself from the sheet. He tried unsuccessfully turning over onto his stomach, hoping he'd be able to push himself up onto his hands and knees, then saw a Budweiser bottle on the nightstand. As he leaned over and tried grabbing it, the sheet tightened more, but he remained close enough that even though his back was being pressed hard onto the bed, he could still reach the nightstand.

He had to stretch for it without looking directly at it, unable to turn his head to the side. His hand fumbled over the lamp and the clock until he accidentally knocked the bottle over, but instead of falling off the nightstand, it only spilled its remaining contents onto the wood surface.

Matt again reached blindly until he finally grabbed hold of the beer bottle. He brought it down hard against the nightstand repeatedly. The first couple of times the bottle only made the nightstand rattle, but the third time the bottle broke.

Using the jagged edge of the bottle, he stabbed at the sheet until finally slicing it. He then began ripping the sheet apart. The long, thin strips of cotton struck wildly at him like a nest of angry vipers, but he managed to tear a large enough slice in the sheet to escape from the bed.

The pieces of sheet continued reaching for him and tried wrapping themselves around his leg, but he pulled himself loose. He ran to the closet and pulled at the tie around Claire's neck, but he couldn't get a grip on it because of how tightly it had wrapped itself around her throat. She was turning blue from lack of oxygen, on the brink of passing out.

Some shirtsleeves and pant legs started reaching out for Matt, but he never let them get a good grip on him. He tried loosening the shirts' grip on Claire, but they kept constricting tighter and tighter. He tried pulling the clothes off the hangers, but the clothing only tightened around the hangers to secure leverage. The clothes pulled on Claire so that the hangers couldn't be lifted.

Matt pulled and pulled, but there were too many pieces of clothing. Whenever he prised a shirt or tie from Claire, within a few seconds, it reattached itself while he focused on another shirt. He finally managed to get a grip on the end of the tie choking Claire and unwrapped it from her throat, allowing her to take a gasping breath of air, but then the shirtsleeve around her mouth and nose began suffocating her. He worked his fingers under the sleeve until he could unwind it from her face, finally enabling her to take another gulp of air.

"Matt! Make it stop!"

He grabbed one of the clothes rods and pulled down on it as hard as he could. Nothing happened at first, but then he felt the brackets loosen. A couple more solid pulls and the rod crashed to the floor, removing the clothing's leverage and enabling him to slide the hangers off the end of the clothes rod. Then he pulled them off Claire, flinging them into the bedroom piece by piece.

Every once in a while, he had to stop and turn his attention to a tie or belt or shirt sleeve that moved again toward Claire's throat, but he slowly gained control.

He pulled down the rod on the other side of the closet. Again, without their solid base from which they could pull at her, Matt could now toss the pieces of clothing out of the closet. One of the belts snapped at him like a whip, leaving a welt on his ankle.

As soon as Matt pulled Claire from the closet, the clothes became inanimate. She stumbled into the bedroom, accidentally stepping on a couple of shirts on the floor and scrambling away from them as if they were electrified. She ran from the bedroom, still gasping for air.

After calming himself with a few deep breaths, Matt gathered up the clothes they had been wearing earlier. He paused when he heard the knocking from the attic, then froze when the sound was replaced by Claire's scream. A high-pitched crescendo of terror that sounded like she was being gutted filled the attic.

He raced out of the bedroom and found her standing beneath the closed trapdoor in the ceiling. She stared at it wide-eyed, listening to the deafening screams. Her screams—but they weren't coming from her.

As the screams echoed throughout the house, Matt grabbed hold of Claire's arm and led her down the hall, then down the stairs, away from the bedroom and the attic door.

She would not be coming back to Jake's house.

TWENTY-THREE

The city square was quiet, but Hatchett was always a ghost town at 2:30 in the morning. Matt and Claire hadn't seen a single car for forty-five minutes as they sat in the gazebo killing time. Even the local meth-heads had disappeared into their burrows.

Claire sat with both hands wrapped tightly around a can of Budweiser, as if concerned Matt might abandon his second can of Red Bull and try to claim the beer for himself.

"I believed you when you told me what you'd been going through," Claire said, "but now I believe-believe you." She shuddered and shook her head. Her neck bore a long, narrow bruise from the tie that had choked her.

"I'm sorry I got you involved," he said. "You probably shouldn't even be with me right now."

"Well, I'm not spending the night at Jake's again, and if you need me to get you anything from a closet, you're on your own. But other than that, I want to be with you."

"I just don't know what to do. How do I keep the wall up and block the connection?"

"Have you ever tried hypnosis?"

"No, I never got to that point. I'd always been able to block the connection on my own."

"There's a guy in town—Ivan Binet—who does hypnosis. Works across from the bakery. He's a bit of a pompous ass, but he's into all sorts of alternative medicine and has helped a few people I know. You know that bartender I was telling you about who smoked? Ivan helped him stop through hypnosis. Maybe there's a way he can enable your subconscious to keep your mental wall up even if you fall asleep."

"Sure, why not? Hypnotism. Exorcism. At this point, I'm open to any of the 'isms'."

"I'll go with you. He opens at ten."

Matt had planned to get a room at the Hatchett Hotel, but the sign on the front desk said no one came on duty until 5:00 a.m., and he didn't want to risk bringing evil into Claire's home, so they had a few more hours to kill. Sitting in the gazebo with Claire didn't seem like a bad way to pass the time.

"I remember Jake and me, when we were probably in junior high, riding our bikes downtown on Thursday nights in the summer when the Hatchett City Band played here in the gazebo. A lot of people drove down here and parked all around the square, although of course my dad never wanted to do that, so Jake and I came here on our own. The band was probably awful, but to us it sounded like a Philharmonic Orchestra. After each song, everyone honked their horns in applause."

"You don't do that in New York?"

"Well, we do have a lot of cars honking, so I guess there's that."

"Just out of curiosity," Claire said, "since you're not a big-shot marketing executive, what do you do for a living?"

"I'm a cook at a diner."

Claire burst out laughing. "You used to be an awful cook!"

Matt smiled and shrugged. "I still am."

They leaned back, taking in the quiet of the early morning darkness. Red, yellow, and green circles of light from the town's sole stoplight took turns reflecting in the window of the farm supply store they were facing, while cicadas provided the soundtrack to the summer night. The temperature hovered around eighty degrees, refusing to give up the good fight, but compared to the daytime highs it almost felt refreshing.

There was a simplicity in Hatchett that Matt hadn't appreciated when he left his hometown behind. Sometimes, when he was leaving work at two or three in the morning, Matt would think about how there were probably fifty times more people out and about on one block in New York than were even awake in all of Hatchett, and yet he had felt so much more isolated in the city. But now, sitting there, in the middle of the night, he had never felt less alone. For the first time in years, if not forever, he could see why people stayed here. It wasn't flashy, but it seemed genuine. He felt like his real self, although he recognized that a lot of that was likely thanks to the person sitting next to him.

149

A little before 10:00 a.m., Matt and Claire sat on the hood of his rental car outside Ivan Binet's office. They both looked like they felt: two people on the wrong side of a hard night. Wearing the same clothes as the day before didn't help them look any less disheveled. Every ligament and muscle in Matt's body felt scalded, growing weaker as exhaustion settled in.

What they did have going for them, however, were a couple of hot sugar donuts and cups of coffee from the Hatchett Bakery across the street. Walking through the entrance of the bakery was like stepping into a warm, welcoming place from a childhood story. The enveloping aroma of baked goods sprinkled with sugar caused them both to smile at the same time. Now, outside on his car, Matt could still detect the smell of the delicious treats wafting down the street, tempting him to pick up a couple more donuts for later.

They waited about ten minutes before a man in his early forties came around the corner and walked toward them. Claire nudged Matt and nodded in Ivan's direction.

Ivan Binet was a cannonball of a man, a little over five and a half feet tall with a body that looked like it had been sculpted in part by a case or two of steroids. He carried a clear thermos containing a green liquid that resembled toxic moss, along with a stuffed gym bag. He strode down the sidewalk like a former jock, albeit one with a gray fedora on his head, which struck Matt as a little too hipster for Hatchett. Matt guessed the man always somehow managed to resist the sugary donuts.

"Ms. Chamberlain," Ivan said as he saw Claire. "What a pleasure. Are you by chance waiting for me?"

"Matter of fact, we are."

Claire hopped off the car. Matt waited a minute, then slowly pushed himself from the hood as well, already not liking this man. He stood next to Claire as Ivan walked up and extended his hand.

"Ivan Binet." He looked at Matt closer. "I've seen you around, but of course in this town that's not saying much. I don't believe we've met, though."

Matt shook Ivan's hand, matching his alpha-male grasp. In New York, every young man seemed to think the goal of a handshake was to break at least one bone. Compared to the East Coast alphas, Ivan was on the junior varsity team.

"You probably saw my brother. I live in New York."

"Matt's interested in being hypnotized," Claire offered. "This morning, if at all possible. I told him you did a pretty good job with Chet and his smoking."

Ivan walked over to his office door and unlocked it. He flipped on the lights, then held the door open and motioned for Matt and Claire to come in, nodding at Claire's napkin from the bakery as she walked past.

"Those things will kill you, you know," he said,

"Well, something has to, so it might as well be delicious," she responded, using her tongue to check her lips for any residual sugar.

They walked into a wood-paneled waiting room large enough for five plastic chairs. An unmanned receptionist's counter overlooked the tiny room. A scarred coffee table the size of a TV tray in one corner held a stack of magazines that looked as though no one had disturbed them in years. Matt could make out a few issues of GQ and several issues of Men's Health, each announcing a guaranteed way to achieve six-pack abs. He guessed Ivan had read them all, and took copious notes.

Ivan directed Matt and Claire to take a seat, then hopped up on the counter and leaned forward, his feet dangling. He took off his fedora, placing it on the counter next to him. His hair had thinned dramatically in the front, which likely explained the hat. Matt figured the quickly retreating hairline had to be the bane of someone like Ivan's existence, given how much time he apparently spent working on his physique.

"So, how can I help you today? Are you trying to quit smoking too?" Ivan asked. "Or something more addictive?"

"Like what?"

Ivan shook his head. "Sorry. That was probably unprofessional. It's just that we've got a small addiction problem making its way through our town, and I've been getting a number of people coming to me for that. Guess I'll just let you tell me what's up."

"You have time to see me now?" Matt asked.

Ivan chuckled. "As luck would have it, my first appointment isn't until 3:30 this afternoon. I'm not sure why I thought an alternative medicine practice would flourish in such a podunk place. Welcome to Hatchett, Nebraska: please set your watches back seventy-five years."

Matt glared at Ivan. "If you haven't learned to see the things this town offers, maybe you're in the wrong place."

"Says the man who moved to the big city."

"No, says the man who recently has learned to come down off his pedestal."

Claire looked at Matt like he'd been drinking. She couldn't help but smile.

"Sorry if I touched a nerve," Ivan said. "Not my intention. Let's start over. Tell me what I can do for you, sir."

"I'm trying to break a connection I have with someone," he started.

"You're trying to get over a break-up?" Ivan asked.

"No. The person is already dead."

"And you're struggling with depression."

"You should probably just let me tell you. I'm guessing you haven't heard this one before."

Matt didn't go into all the details. He thought it better not to, since he wanted help, not a one-way ticket to a mental hospital. Instead, he talked about the psychic connection he had shared with his brother, and the desire to block out whatever residual waves remained in the atmosphere. That sounded bizarre enough, and he knew it didn't make a lot of sense, but he also figured Ivan's business plan didn't include turning away any paying customers, regardless of their story.

Ivan put a sign on the receptionist counter that optimistically said, "With Client, Please Wait Quietly," and the three of them went to Ivan's office at the back of the building, a space of about two hundred square feet that held a cheap laminate desk, an army-green file cabinet, a love seat, a ratty padded chair, and Ivan's desk chair. Three floor lamps, each with a blue-tinted, low wattage lightbulb, gave the room a calming ambiance.

Matt sat in the padded chair which, though stained on the back, was surprisingly comfortable. Claire sat on the love seat off to the side, and Ivan rolled his desk chair and positioned himself directly in front of Matt.

"Okay then, let's take this out for a spin and see what happens, shall we?"

Ivan picked up a small device that looked like a garage door opener and pushed a button. Gentle, nondescript music played from the remote control-operated CD player, a new-age hodgepodge of soft flutes, piano, and guitar. He reached over to flip a switch, which turned on a small desk fountain that looked like it had cost thirty dollars, although Matt had to admit the gentle, flowing water added to the overall relaxing environment.

Ivan sat in his chair for a long minute, staring at Matt before finally speaking in a low, soothing voice.

"I want you to relax, but don't close your eyes. Instead, watch my eyes, but at the same time feel the rest of your body calm, as your muscles unclench. Take a deep breath in and hold it . . . and now let it out."

Ivan instructed Matt to keep focusing on his breath as he gave instructions. Before long, Matt's eyes looked heavy.

"Matt, can you hear me?"

Matt nodded slowly, his head barely moving.

"Good. I want you to focus on what I say. Listen to my words; allow them to flow into your mind and heart like a stream of warm water. Do you understand?"

Matt didn't respond.

"Matt, are you understanding what I'm asking you to do?"

Again, Matt didn't answer. Ivan nodded as if answering his own question.

"Okay then, here's what I want you to do. I need you to visualize the wall you mentioned. It's made of bricks, but it's not a physical wall. It's the wall you are building around your mind at this moment. A wall you said can keep out all others. Can you see this wall now?"

"Yes," Matt answered softly.

"Your wall is keeping me out. I need you to visualize it being lowered, brick by brick so that you can let me in more fully. I sense resistance from your subconscious. I want you to visualize each row of the wall being lowered as you let me in."

Claire leaned forward. "Are you sure that's safe, Matt? You don't want . . ."

Ivan scowled at Claire, raising a finger to silence her, but she kept her attention on Matt, who offered a subtle nod of his head, letting her know it was all right. Matt could see Claire's right foot bouncing up and down in apprehension as she leaned forward on her seat, but if this was going to work, he needed to truly try.

He closed his eyes.

"Now then, the wall is coming down. You are hearing my voice. You are feeling my words wash over you. You are floating in a warm river, totally relaxed, opening your mind."

Matt began to relax, but after a moment he furrowed his eyebrows, his eyelids closing tighter as if a piece of dirt had gotten into them. His facial muscles tightened, then relaxed again. He felt like someone else had suddenly seized the controls. He knew immediately that he had made a grave mistake. He wanted to speak out, but something else spoke for him.

"Is this the point where you touch me?" Matt said to Ivan, softly.

Ivan paused for a moment, confused. "No, I am not going to touch you. We're just going to talk. I am going to help you to . . ."

"Is it because I'm not a young girl? Is that why you're not touching me?"

Ivan glanced uncomfortably at Claire for a quick moment before Matt continued.

"Do you think I don't know what you do to young girls? Once you've hypnotized them, Ned?"

Upon hearing the name Ned, Ivan shoved his chair back and jumped to his feet, his quiet tone replaced with one that sounded threatened. "What the hell is going on?" He spun on Claire. "Who sent you here?"

Claire stood, keeping her focus on Matt, who continued gazing at Ivan, his head cocked, a smile revealing itself on his lips.

"Don't be angry, Ned," Matt said. "Why should you be angry? Shelly Mahone should be angry, but instead she's just sad. She knew as soon as her session with you ended that something was wrong. You told her she wouldn't remember, but deep down, she knew."

"Get out," Ivan said. "Get the hell out of my office!"

"Maybe she just had a bad taste in her mouth. Maybe that's how she knew. And you think I'm going to put my trust in you, Ned? You?" Matt chortled, glaring at Ivan with frozen eyes.

Claire put her hand on Matt's shoulder. "Matt, wake up."

Matt shook his head. "I'm sorry, Claire, but Matt can't take your call right now. He's busy." He stood and slowly stretched his arms over his head. "Ahhhh, movement. I have movement! This is what it shall be like."

154

"Wake him up, Ivan! Get him back! You've let it in!"

"What are you—"

"Bring him back now or I'm calling the sheriff!"

Ivan got in Matt's face, but then he froze, and his tense body seemed to soften and go weak, as though he were the one being hypnotized.

"Ivan, goddammit, wake him up!"

Ivan's face rotated toward Claire as if on a spit, his expression glazed over. She slapped Ivan—hard—and he appeared to rejoin the normal world once again. Ivan turned back to Matt, his voice as strong and determined as he could make it.

"At the count of three, you will return Matt to us. One. Two. Three."

Matt's head quavered, and he acted shaken. A soft expression on his face seemed to give Ivan and Claire tremendous relief. Then a sly smile slithered across his face, and he cocked his head to the left.

"Easy as one-two-three, eh, Ned?" He placed his index finger on his chin, as if trying to solve a riddle. "And why are you calling yourself Ivan now, by the way? Did we not register with the Violent Sex Offenders registry? Tsk-tsk, Ned." He flicked his brows. "Though I suppose it does make it easier for mommies and daddies to leave their children alone with you if they can't search your real name. Always one step ahead, aren't you, Ned?"

"I command you to wake," Ivan stammered.

"You command me? You command me?" Matt's voice rose in indignation. "I do not believe you understand what is happening here, Ned. No one commands me. There are only those commanded by me."

Ivan started to speak but Matt raised his hand, immediately muting him as he tried to respond, as though the words had jammed in Ivan's throat.

"And what about your time as a junior high school nurse practitioner? Ah, talk about a sweet gig, right, Ned? All those young girls you said had some sort of chest cold. You were simply doing your job checking them out, weren't you?

"But the coup de grace, Ned, had to have been the sleepover you had with your eight-year-old niece, Ashley, the little girl who thought it would be fun to be hypnotized. Do you think she had fun, Ned? You would have told her to remember having fun except your 'session' was interrupted by her mother. Is it safe to assume you haven't received any Christmas cards lately from your brother and sister-in-law? I have to tell you, Ned, even I flinched at that one, and that's saying something."

Ivan's eyes widened. Nothing but garbled vowels and consonants made their way out.

"Wake him up!" Claire yelled, even though she knew it was no use. Ivan could only clutch at his throat, as though that might shake his words loose. She spun around to face Matt and grasped him by the shoulders. "Matt, please. Come back to me. Come back." Matt stepped to the side of her, continuing to focus on Ivan.

"On the off-chance you didn't know, Ned," Matt said, "I have a special place saved for you in Hell, although there won't be any children there. Whatever shall you do?" He laughed. "I'm sure we'll think of something."

Matt pulled Ivan close to him, their chests practically touching. He whispered, as if in confession, "Did you know I was an angel before I was so rudely cast aside? And the small angelic side that still exists inside me knows children are sacred. They should be sacred to everyone. Even I know that."

Matt reached out and rested his hand gently on Ivan's crotch.

Ivan looked surprised, as if he'd expected Matt to squeeze and torment him, but suddenly his eyes shot open. He parted his lips to scream but only muffled agony came out, filling the room as surely as a cry for someone to help him. Matt slowly brought his hand back to his side and looked at Ivan as if they'd just shared a secret.

"You shall not be rising again, Ned."

Ivan grabbed his crotch and doubled over, gasping for air. Matt watched for a moment, then slowly turned to Claire, a soft but menacing growl sliding from his throat.

Claire punched him in the gut. The blow startled him but didn't hurt. He raised his head, anger blossoming across his face. She slapped him as hard as she could. As she brought her hand back to hit him again, Matt held out his hand as if signaling for her to stop.

"Claire, my dear, you have been a spot of bother to me. That's never a good idea."

Claire's hand froze in place, despite her obvious struggle to resist. She began to choke, her eyes watering as she stared into Matt's. He continued to hold his hand up in front of her, clearly unfazed by her suffering.

"Matt," she rasped. "Please help me. I know you can hear me. You said you wanted to be able to help me."

Matt gave her a small smile and shook his head. She was about to pass out, her face turning red, but she refused to break eye contact with Matt.

"I need you now," she choked out. "Baby, I need you now."

Through sheer willpower, she managed to reach out and gently intertwine her fingers with Matt's, never breaking eye contact, even though she was only able to choke out three more words.

"Matt. Help me."

She tightened her fingers, looking desperately into his eyes, beseeching, no oxygen left.

Matt looked into her gray eyes and fought to regain control of his body. He didn't break eye contact until he finally managed to release her from her torment and she was able to gulp in sweet oxygen. Dazed, he dropped to his knees, then fell to all fours, staying in that position for a moment, heaving. He then scrambled like an animal to a nearby trash can where he threw up.

He finally looked up at Claire.

"What did I do?" he asked.

"You saved me."

She walked over and kneeled next to him, stroking his hair until he could finally stand, albeit unsteadily.

"Who are you?" Ivan managed to say, his voice raw but finally working once again.

"Come on," Claire said as she turned Matt toward the door and shot a disgusted look at Ivan. "We're getting out of here."

She put her arm in Matt's and led him out of the room.

"But I've got to tell you, I'm really getting tired of being choked. It's starting to piss me off."

TWENTY-FOUR

Matt sat in the rear booth at the Dirty Creek, with his back against the wall so he could keep an eye on anyone coming into the bar. He'd remained vigilant since his encounter with Bone the other night, although he recognized that the drug dealer was far from being his biggest problem, which said something about his main concern.

The lunchtime business was modest, but steady. No matter what time of day, the place always smelled like beer. Matt hunched over a greasy cheeseburger and a pile of french fries that required their own plate. He had dined at some well-reviewed restaurants in New York, acclaimed for their incredible cuisine, but nothing tasted as good as a Midwest cheeseburger that was dripping grease. If this ended up being his last supper—and he figured there was a good chance it would—he couldn't have asked for anything better.

A super-sized glass of Coke and a shot of whiskey, flanked by two spent shot glasses, sat next to his food. His ears picked up the distinctive snap of cowboy boots approaching. He glanced up to see Andy hovering over his booth in a decidedly unpriestly manner, wearing a black T-shirt and faded jeans, his consummate high school uniform.

"Mind if I join you?" Andy asked.

"Did you bring a bag of O-positive?"

Andy slid into the booth and pulled a crucifix on a chain out from under his shirt. "Just in case."

"If a fifteen-foot statue of Jesus wasn't enough to keep you safe, then good luck with that."

"Point taken."

"You doing okay?" Matt asked. "You scared the hell out of me."

"No, apparently I didn't, although that was the goal, wasn't it? But I'm fine now." Andy looked out the window, as if trying to distance himself from his thoughts. "I felt the evil, though. It was unlike anything I've ever experienced."

"I'm sorry I brought that into your church."

"Don't apologize. It made me decide to become a real priest."

"Seriously?"

"It's what I want to do. No more acting. But it's going to take some time before I'm ready to do an exorcism," he said, smiling, "so you'll have to hang tough a while longer."

Claire appeared with another burger and fries and set it in front of Andy, along with a bottle of beer.

"Bless you, my sister."

"Enjoy, gentlemen," she said as she turned and walked back to the bar.

"She tell you I was here?"

"Yeah. She also told me the two of you have had a bumpy twenty-four hours."

"Yeah, that's exactly the term I would use. A little bumpy."

Andy nodded toward the empty shot glasses. "I thought the goal was to stay awake."

"That's what the Coke's for."

"And the whiskey?"

"It's an acknowledgment that it's hopeless." Matt finished off the third shot of whiskey, then stuffed a few french fries in his mouth. "Do you think people who kill themselves truly end up in Hell?" he asked reluctantly.

Andy looked at Matt with a pained look on his face. "To be honest, I never thought Hell literally existed until recently, but I have always believed our God is an understanding God, so no, I don't believe people who kill themselves end up in Hell."

"Mom raised us to believe suicide was an ultimate sin."

"Well then, Matty, I guess that means you don't need to be thinking about suicide, do you?"

"Even if it keeps Satan from being on Earth? People have sacrificed themselves for far, far less."

Andy shook his head but didn't seem to have a response to that argument. "You can't give up. The women you spoke with about Jake—Lorraine and Rose—you got them to forgive him and nothing changed?"

"Nothing."

"To be honest, I can't see either of them being able to kill anyone. They both had a rough go of it, but neither of them are killers."

"I need to figure out who wrote that letter, but everything so far has been a dead end."

Andy took a bite of his burger and closed his eyes. "How could anybody eat something like this and not believe in God?" He followed it with beer. "Tell me more about the letter. What did it say exactly?"

Matt leaned back in his booth and put his hands on the table, as if to brace himself. He told Andy everything he could remember about the letter. About its author telling Jake he had hurt her badly, and Jake saying he was truly sorry, and that he knew the woman thought he should eat a bullet for breakfast, but that that wasn't going to happen.

He started reciting more of what he remembered when Andy put his hand up for Matt to stop. Andy didn't speak at first when Matt paused; he just sat there staring at his food, hand in the air, as if deep in thought.

"What?" Matt said. "Does any of that sound familiar?"

Andy still didn't speak for a long moment, then nodded slowly, more to himself than to Matt's question. "A couple of weeks ago, someone from my church came to confession and said Jake had tried taking something from her, and she used that exact phrase: 'I told him to eat a bullet for breakfast.' But I felt she was saying it more from a place of sorrow than anger. Like she felt lost."

"Andy, I know the confessional is sacrosanct. I don't know what happens if you violate that, but I—"

"Did you not notice blood pouring out of my eyes and ears earlier? After what that thing did to me, hell yes, I'm going to tell you who it was. Besides, she told me she'd yelled it pretty loud at Jake, right here at the Creek, so that makes it public, right?"

Matt leaned forward and spoke as if in a confessional booth himself. "So who was it?"

"You might want to get one more shot of whiskey first," Andy said, glancing back toward Claire as she disappeared down the hallway toward her office.

Matt knocked on Claire's half-opened office door and leaned in. The room served as part-office, part-storeroom, with pallets of dry goods piled against one wall and empty beer kegs on the other. Her metal desk laid claim to the center of the room, leaving just enough space for a file cabinet and chair. On top of the file cabinet was a four-by-six-inch framed photograph of Claire with her mother. There were no pictures of her father. A folding chair leaned against the other side of the desk for the rare guest.

"Can I interrupt you for a minute?"

"Sort of crazy busy right now," Claire said. "One of my bartenders called in sick. If you don't mind me working while we talk, I'm all yours, but I will have to get back up front in just a minute."

Matt opened the folding chair and sat in front of her desk. "You told me Jake did some things to you that you didn't appreciate. Would you tell me more about that?"

Claire paused from her work without looking up, then went back to sorting through invoices.

"Jake strongly suggested I let Bone and him deal drugs out of here. I told him no, and he said that wasn't an option. Said I didn't know what I was up against and that he could personally guarantee things wouldn't get out of hand."

"What'd he mean by that?"

"He meant I didn't need to worry about tweakers getting high here. It'd be more like a convenience store where meth-heads would be required to buy a drink or two before they could get their fix and go on their way. Jake saw it as a win-win proposition. Anybody who caused trouble would be taken care of."

"But you still said no."

She looked up at Matt. "And he told me I didn't have a choice."

"And then you told him you hoped he ate a bullet for breakfast."

She stopped her paperwork and sighed. "What do you need, Matt?"

He leaned forward. "You remember that letter I found at Jake's? The one where he wrote what appeared to be an apology?"

She nodded.

"In his response on the back, he mentioned that the person who wrote the note had suggested he eat a bullet for breakfast."

Claire stayed silent and stared, as if trying to regain her composure before speaking—something she'd never mastered even when they were younger.

"So now you're here in my office wondering if I killed your

brother?" she said, her voice razor-sharp. "Is that it, Matt? Is that what you need to ask me?"

"Of course not," Matt said too fast. "I'm not saying the person who wrote the note killed Jake, but I do think the person who wrote it needs to forgive him."

The tension in Claire's face lessened. "Okay, I can understand why you'd think it was me. The bullet-for-breakfast line is probably not the most common among the hundreds of insults hurled at Jake, but no. I didn't write the letter."

"The letter wasn't signed. Maybe he thought you wrote it."

She shrugged. "I have no idea. I can't answer that. Look, I want to help you, Matt. I really do. But I don't know anything about the letter."

"But do you think you're the one who needs to forgive him?"

Claire pushed back her chair, putting distance between them. "I've dealt with a lot of shit trying to keep the Creek open after Dad died. It hasn't been easy. Jake was just one more thing. Yeah, he pissed me off, but honestly, I got the feeling he was only doing what he was told."

"So you didn't hate him?"

Claire sighed. "You know, in a funny way, I felt sorry for him, and more than a little empathy."

"Why?"

"Because you left both of us. You hurt both of us."

Matt glanced at the floor. He couldn't apologize again.

"So in answer to your question . . . did I like your brother? No. Did I feel like I had some common ground with him? Yeah, a little. And if things had turned out—if things do turn out—where I have to sell the Creek to avoid drugs being distributed here, to be honest, I'll be fine. Maybe I'll finally leave Hatchett, too. That was our plan, wasn't it? To go see what else is going on in this big ol' country?"

Matt could only nod, thinking about their long-ago conversations of escaping their little town.

"If you think it would help for me to say I forgive Jake, then I forgive Jake. He may have been a jerk, but he was your brother, so I could only hate him so much."

"Which of us did you hate more?" Matt asked before thinking.

Claire walked around the desk and took his hand. "I never hated you, Matt. I grieved for you, and I was hurt by you, but I never hated you. And I'm glad you came back, even under these circumstances, but you can't leave again. Not without saying goodbye. You owe me that."

He lifted her hand to his lips. "I'm so tired," he said. "And I'm out of options."

"No, you're not. We'll keep looking."

"What else can I do?" With no answer, Matt stood and kissed Claire tenderly. "I might have no choice."

"No," she whispered, her voice shaking as she pulled Matt closer.

As he tried to summon the willpower to loosen himself from her embrace, he kissed her lips one more time.

"You said you didn't want me to leave without saying goodbye. I know what I need to do now, so I'm afraid this is me saying goodbye."

"Matt, don't go. Wait until I can leave with you. Earl should be here any minute and he can cover for me."

"Please know I've always loved you, Claire. Even with everything that's been going on these past couple of days, this is the first time in years that I've felt happy."

"Matt, don't do this. Don't go. Please don't."

He turned and walked away from her one last time.

TWENTY-FIVE

Matt sat in his car, staring at his childhood home. His mother's home. Nothing about it was his anymore. Memories flashed like black-and-white snapshots, a collage of scenes from when he was a kid, a totally different person—back when there was movement, noise, and life in and around the house.

He saw his brother and himself racing around the house, each armed with a water gun, shooting tiny streams at each other from a distance until Jake got smart and turned on the hose full blast, waiting until Matt turned the corner before thoroughly drenching him.

Matt remembered the two of them walking out into the cornfield as eighth graders with their .410 shotguns pointed down to the ground, hoping to scare a pheasant or two, and sometimes actually bringing one home, much to the surprise of their father.

After a few more minutes of reminiscing, he got out of his car. His mother had to know he was out here; cars couldn't help but announce themselves on the gravel driveway.

Exhaustion rippled through his body. Just walking toward the porch was a struggle. If Satan commandeered his soul, would he feel more powerful? More virile? Would he—Matt—still even exist at his core? It didn't matter. He wouldn't let it come to that. He still had one trump card to play.

Jake said Matt would join him in Hell if he killed himself. If that were true, Matt knew Satan would make things unbearable for him, but he didn't see any viable alternatives. Let Satan take over his body and rule the Earth? What would happen to his mother? What would happen to Claire? The dark force at play here had already tried to kill Claire twice.

He knew he wasn't going to find the person who needed to forgive Jake in time. Maybe the whole thing was a quixotic effort anyway. It was now just a matter of hours before Satan would overpower him. He had to hope God wouldn't punish him for doing what he felt he had to do. God had to understand why he was doing it.

His mother's words came back to him. I wish you had never been born. Intellectually he knew it wasn't her speaking, but emotionally, it still hit him hard. He had always wondered if it was true, if his and Jake's connection was the cause of the unspoken chasm that existed with his mother. Had she ever wished that Matt had never been born?

He made it to the front porch before turning to take in the yard he and Jake had taken turns mowing, although now it was mostly dirt and weeds. He gazed out across the cornfield, thinking he could still smell the soil. His East Coast acquaintances would call it dirt, but for whatever reason, he took it as a matter of Midwestern pride to call it soil. He lowered himself onto the top step, relieved to be sitting again, and looked out to the horizon.

He remembered sitting on that same step years ago, making plans to leave Hatchett in the fall for college. He'd been accepted at the University of Nebraska—had even been offered a partial academic scholarship—and had wondered what it would be like living in a big city on his own for a year, until Claire could join him. He had also been more than a little nervous about being apart from Jake, although by that time there was already a noticeable distance between them.

Earlier that year, Jake often talked as though he was going to the university as well, and spoke excitedly about rooming with Matt and how great it was going to be having blowout parties at their place with college girls. Matt remembered the crushed expression on Jake's face when he told him he was going to stay faithful to Claire, and that he and Jake could only share a place their first year, after which he planned to live with Claire.

But Jake never went to college. He didn't study very hard in school, even though he was probably brighter than Matt, who got straight As. The last few months of their senior year, he and Jake drifted further apart, as Matt started spending more and more time with Claire. Jake even tried moving out of their bedroom and into the barn, but the lack of insulation, combined with the critters at night, eventually brought him back into the house. Their nighttime conversations, however, came to a halt. Claire changed their relationship in a fundamental way.

Matt recognized that much of this was his fault, although he didn't think "fault" was a fair way to phrase it. He simply wanted to spend his free time with Claire. Wasn't that a part of growing up? If Jake had a problem with that, he needed to say something, but his brother was far too stubborn to do that.

The screen door squeaked open, and his mother now stood next to him, also looking into the distance, perhaps trying to see if Matt was staring at anything in particular. He looked up at her.

"Hey," he said.

"You feeling all right?" she asked. "You look beat."

"I am, but I'll be okay."

"You getting ready to head on back?" she asked.

He tried answering, but choked on his words before managing to calm himself. "Yes, I have to go. I'm sorry."

"Don't apologize. You stayed longer than I thought you would."

"I don't just mean I'm sorry for leaving. I'm sorry for everything. I wish things could have been different."

There was silence, then she sat down next to him on the step. She didn't speak at first, nor did he expect her to, but then she surprised him by saying, "I know. I do, too."

"I haven't been much good to you these past few years, and I wish I could change that."

Another long period of silence enveloped them until his mother emitted something that sounded like a small laugh.

"Do you remember that time when you boys were eight and we went to the county fair?" she asked. "A part of you wanted to ride the roller coaster so badly but you were scared, so Jake went on it so you could have the experience." She laughed softly at the memory. "You stood there watching him with a big ol' smile on your face, squealing and holding your stomach whenever Jake went down a big drop or whipped around a corner. That was something special."

Matt remembered. He remembered putting his arm around Jake's shoulder when he got off the roller coaster as they walked down the carnival midway together, reliving the ride. Every summer, the fair was in town for three days, and Matt and Jake were out at the fairgrounds every one of those days and nights. It was a rinky-dink operation, in large part because Hatchett's population didn't make it financially viable to pay for anything larger, but for the two brothers the county fair was, without a doubt, one of the most special times of the year. They squeezed every drop of fun they could from it.

"I don't know if you realize how important you were to Jake," she continued. "He really missed you when you left. Some kids are closer to their mother, some are closer to their father, but Jake was always closest to you. You were always the most important thing to him."

"I felt the same way about him growing up."

"I know you did, but maybe not to the same degree though, in part because you had other friends. And you had Claire." She paused, then smiled again, shaking her head. "You probably don't even remember this, but when you were around five years old, for whatever spiteful reason, you told Jake he was adopted. Said that it used to be just your dad and me and you, and then we adopted Jake, which meant you weren't really brothers. Jake got so upset it took me forever and a day to get him to stop bawling his eyes out. The two of you were mirror images of each other, for crying out loud, and yet he was convinced you weren't related because that's what you told him. It shattered him to think you weren't his brother."

Matt laughed. "I don't remember that. I'll bet you wondered what was going on in that brain of his not to see we were brothers."

"Tell me about it!" she laughed out loud. "I wondered about him for believing it, and I wondered about you for saying it." She paused, then grew serious again. "What happened between you two?"

"We grew up, Mom. Went in different directions, but mostly we just grew up—and apart."

"Always brothers, though," she said.

"Always brothers. But sometimes, I guess, that's what brothers do. They grow apart."

She glanced at him, then looked back toward the horizon. "There's something you're not telling me, but that's your choice. I'm not going to pry."

The way she smiled when talking about his and Jake's childhood struck him. It was the second time a story about their childhood caused her to express amusement.

"Do you know why Dad always felt uncomfortable with Jake's and my connection? He always made us feel like we were broken in some way."

She nodded sadly. "I know, and I always told him he was being unfair, but I couldn't get him to see it differently. He did love you though, in his own way. He just never was comfortable around something he couldn't understand."

"But didn't it also affect how you felt about us? You hardly ever spoke about it, but it almost had to, didn't it?"

She spoke without having to think. "Of course not. It's just who you boys were, and I didn't talk much about it because I didn't want you to feel it merited a special conversation. You have to love people for who they are, not for who you think they should be. Besides, you weren't special because of that, you were special because you were my sons, and that was enough."

It surprised him to hear her say that he and Jake were special to her. Maybe the loss of Jake was getting her to open up.

But when he thought about it further, he realized his mom never treated them as though they were unusual or broken. That was probably the greatest gift she could have given them, but instead of appreciating that, he had chosen to interpret it as a lack of affection.

He noticed that their conversation had stopped, and he knew it wouldn't be long before she thought of an excuse to go back inside. Some chore that needed tending to, but for now he enjoyed this quiet time, sitting next to her.

He didn't know what one should say to a parent they'd never see again—didn't know how to sum up everything he felt, everything he wanted her to know, understanding that he wouldn't have another chance. He didn't know how to get past the wall that had risen between them. Had he built this wall, this one separating him from his mother? He didn't know how to tell her what she meant to him, how much he loved her. It was, unfortunately, too late for all of that.

"Guess I better head back on over to Jake's and start packing." He stood, and she slowly joined him. "You should probably get back inside and out of the heat."

As he turned to her, she stepped forward and gave him a formal hug.

"Thank you for coming back, Matthew," she said softly in his ear. "I hope I didn't do something to keep you away for so long. If so, I didn't mean to."

She let go, but Matt wouldn't release her. After another long moment, he finally loosened his hold, but she surprised him with another tight squeeze and a kiss on the cheek.

"You didn't do anything," he said. "It was all me, and I'm sorry about that. I'm so sorry. I understand if you're angry at me."

"I've never been angry with you. I was just afraid you didn't like me, and that hurt. If I acted standoff-ish, it's just because I was a little sad." She took his hand and squeezed it. "If you think about it," she said wistfully, "give me a call when you get back and let me know you got there safely."

"I love you, Mom," he said.

"I love you, too. It'd be nice to see you more often. I've missed you."

"I missed you, too. It's been too long. I hope you can forgive me."

Matt sat quietly at Jake's kitchen table, writing notes to his mother, Claire, and Andy. He sat for quite a while, trying to figure out what to say. In the end, to each, he mainly said he was sorry, for everything. He said he loved all of them and knew he had let everyone down. There was a reason he had run away ten years ago, but looking back now over the years, it wasn't a good enough reason, which only left him with the need to apologize. He also wrote that as much as he didn't want to kill himself, he felt he had no other choice. He hoped Andy would be able to explain it to his mother.

He wrote one additional, brief note and put it in the mailbox, although not in an envelope. He had written instructions for the mailman, explaining what he had done and where his body could be found, and asking for the sheriff to be called. That way his mother wouldn't have to be the one to find him.

He pulled from the kitchen drawer the revolver he'd found his first night at Jake's, checked that it was loaded, then made his way toward the barn. Perched on a nearby tree branch, he once again saw the monstrously large crow watching him, its head occasionally cocking to one side, then the other. He lifted the gun and aimed it at the bird but didn't fire, tempting though it was. He didn't feel it would do any good even if he hit it.

Matt walked into the barn, the dirt floor lit up by the light that poured through the large side windows. He took in the scent of straw that filled the empty horse stalls. It smelled like sunshine and childhood.

He gazed at the gun for a long minute, then switched off the safety. He knew what he needed to do, but that didn't mean he was in a hurry to do it, even though he knew there wasn't a lot of time left.

He felt scared to finish the fight, but even more scared not to. He had resigned himself to this fate.

He entered the stall that contained the most straw, shutting the door behind him. The sunshine ricocheted off the straw and warmed Matt's face. If someone had asked him to describe the word "yellow" to a blind person, he would describe this space where he now stood. It was a comforting place to die.

After taking in the moment, he knew he couldn't put it off any longer. He watched the shadow of his arm lifting and the gun pointing at his temple, watching it as if it were a separate person standing in the stall with him, hoping it would put down the gun on its own, but knowing it was all up to him now.

He said a quiet prayer, aloud, asking not only for forgiveness but also for understanding. He hoped God appreciated the reason for him undertaking this mortal sin, and asked Him to absolve him of its inherent punishment. He also asked God to watch out for his mother, and Claire, and to be with Andy as he made a difference in the lives of others.

Matt closed his eyes and put pressure on the trigger, pulling it slowly, the cold barrel against his right temple, his teeth clenched as the trigger moved. A noise consumed his head, a blast so loud that at first, he thought he had actually heard the gun fire, but he quickly realized it came from inside his own mind. He dropped to his knees and bent over, placing his forehead on the ground as he pressed his hands over his ears, the gun now pointing up at the ceiling.

"What the hell do you think you're doing?" Jake's voice echoed as the roar filling his mind started to subside. "You have no idea what death will be like for you here, and trust me, you'll be coming here, despite your petty little pleas to your worthless god. A god, I might add, you don't even believe in."

The pain lessened as Matt lifted his head. He slowly rose, and as he did so, he saw his shadow moving on its own, pacing back and forth along the wooden wall in front of him as Jake's voice filled the stall.

"You have a chance at immortality!" The shadow's arms flung in the air while pacing, as if incredulous. "You will still be conscious once Satan gains access to your body and soul. You will benefit from having whatever, whoever it is you want, in whatever way you want them. Infinite power. And I will be with you, free of this place. My body may be gone, but I will be a part of you, and we will be together, like old times. Matt, I've missed you. I've missed you so much."

Matt closed his eyes and took a deep breath. He opened them again and saw the shadow now appearing to lean against the stall door, watching him.

"I can't be a part of this," Matt said. "I just want this to all be over."

"Well, it's a little too late for that now, isn't it? How did you turn out to be so weak? What are you afraid of? This is your chance to have it all. Take it and revel in it, or resist it and be consumed anyway, with your mind and soul silenced as I live your life for you. I don't understand why you are fighting this. You don't have a choice."

"Yes, I do," Matt said as he quickly raised the gun to his head and tried pulling the trigger, but his fingers were paralyzed. Try as he might, he couldn't put any pressure to fire the gun.

The shadow glided across the horse stall and reached out to Matt. "It's too late for that. You could have done it earlier, but you thought you could defeat Satan. Such arrogance."

Matt lowered the gun and shot three times at the shadow, his fingers now functioning and the wood splintering with each shot, but Jake only laughed.

"Ow, you got me, Sheriff," Jake said in mock pain as the shadow doubled over.

Matt pressed the gun to his own stomach, but again the trigger froze. He sat down in the straw. The sunlight faded as a cloud passed by, but the shadow remained as distinct as ever.

"Why are you doing this to me?" Matt asked.

"Let's not be confused about who has the power here. I'm not calling the shots, but I'm also not fighting it. Second, although I'm sure you won't believe me, I am doing you a great favor. All you have to do is let him in, but instead you continue fighting him, to no avail. But it's better for everyone if you let him in willingly, so don't act as if I have forsaken you, because I haven't."

Matt threw the handgun across the stall at the shadow.

"That's a good boy," Jake said as the shadow slowly got absorbed by the sunlight. "See you real soon, bro."

TWENTY-SIX

Matt heard the sharp clapping of flip-flops across the yard coming toward the barn as he sat crumpled on the floor of the horse stall. The sun had begun to retreat behind the house, as if exhausted from having worked particularly hard that day.

Claire called out Matt's name as she neared the barn, desperation carrying her voice. She stopped at the barn entrance and paused, likely afraid of what she might see.

"Matt?" she called. "Matt!"

"Over here," he said quietly.

"Oh thank God," she exclaimed as she ran across the barn and into the stall, kneeling next to him, holding his head against her chest. "I was so scared," she said. "I found your note and then heard the shots."

"My note?"

"I was worried about how you left, so I came over to check on you. Jake's mailbox was open, and I saw your note to the mailman. What were you thinking?"

"I was thinking it's the only way I can stop this from happening. But I couldn't do it."

"You made the right decision."

"No, I mean I physically couldn't. He stopped me from pulling the trigger." Matt shook his head, at a loss as to what he could do now, before having an idea. He looked pleadingly at her. "But you could do it, Claire. Maybe he can't stop you." He nodded toward the handgun across the stall.

She leaned away from him to get a better look at his face. "Do what? Shoot you? Are you serious?"

"It would end it. My only fear is you would end up going to Hell for killing me."

"I'm not doing that, Matt."

"But if I don't do something soon—"

"I'm not shooting you! You're talking crazy. Look, we can keep trying to find out who wrote that letter. I'll go door-to-door if need be.

It's not a big town, Matt."

"Baby, there isn't any time left."

"Tell me again what the letter said. You mentioned the line about eating a bullet for breakfast. What else did it say?"

Matt reclined until he was looking up at the roof of the barn and thought once again about the letter.

"It said Jake had hurt the person so badly, she could never forgive him. Said he never cared what he did to anybody else. Said the scars he left would never heal."

"Do you think she meant literal scars?" Claire asked, grasping for any possible lead.

"That wasn't my impression. I sensed it was more like emotional scars. She said she would carry them inside of her . . ." Matt stopped as he stared intensely at the ceiling. He then sat up quickly, suddenly alert, focusing straight ahead as if working out a math problem in his head.

"What is it?" Claire asked.

He didn't answer for a moment, then turned toward her. "I think Sheriff Wilson knows who it is." He thought for a moment more. "I'm sure he knows. We have to go find him."

"What does he have to do with any of this?"

"I'm betting he's protecting someone. I need to find out who."

It was after 8:00 p.m. when Matt and Claire arrived at the sheriff's office, the summer evening's sunlight reluctant to surrender. They were relieved to see a light on inside. They had tried calling before they left Jake's, but no one picked up. They also tried 911, but no one answered that, either. Claire told him that wasn't unusual with recent budget cuts. They tried his house and got hold of the sheriff's wife, who said he was still at the office and had probably been in the bathroom when they called earlier.

Sheriff Wilson looked up over his *Field and Stream* magazine as the bell over the door announced Matt and Claire's arrival.

"Evening," he said, curiosity tagging alongside his greeting. "What can I do for you two?"

Matt and Claire sat across from him.

"You all right, son?" Wilson said to Matt. "You're looking sort of pale."

"Just haven't slept for a while. Sheriff, when I was here before, I told you about a letter I found that somebody wrote to Jake. Somebody he hurt."

"I remember. I also remember you were gonna bring it in to me, but you never did."

Matt looked Wilson straight in the eye, hoping the big man would see Matt wasn't trying to con him. "It's important I find the person who wrote that letter. Extremely important. I'm not looking to stir up trouble. I just need to talk with her."

Wilson seemed to contemplate his words carefully. "What makes you think I know who wrote it?"

"The person who wrote the letter talked about having been scarred. When I mentioned the letter to you, your immediate response was that internal scars cause more murders than physical ones, but I didn't tell you about that being in the letter. About the scars."

"You ever think I was just talking generally?"

"You couldn't have been. It was such an unusual thing for you to have said on your own, talking about internal scars. I think you know who wrote it. Lives depend on me finding that person."

"You mind telling me what's so almighty important about it?" Wilson asked.

"I don't have time to explain, but I need to make things right by her."

"He's right, Sheriff," said Claire. "If you don't tell us, I'll call Judge Taylor and see if there's anything he can do. It's really important. I realize you don't know Matt, but you need to trust me on this one."

The sheriff leaned forward, put his elbows on the desk, and interlocked his fingers, resting his chin on them as he stared at Matt.

"I *may* know who wrote the letter. At least I think I do. I haven't asked her about it directly, but your asshole brother did something bad to her. I don't think it was something that merited killing him, though, if that's what you're thinking, and I'm damn sure she's not the type of person who would murder anyone regardless of how badly they hurt her."

"I'm not necessarily saying the person who wrote the letter killed Jake. I just really need to speak with her."

Wilson glanced at Claire. "You vouching for all this, Claire?"

"I'd put my life on it, Sheriff."

Wilson appeared to think about it, then nodded. "Let me call her. You two wait in the front office. I ain't promising anything, but I'll let her know you're asking."

"Please tell her—"

"I'll tell her you feel it's incredibly important," he said, a skeptical tone in his voice. "I get it."

Matt and Claire waited as the sheriff made his call. After he hung up, he grabbed his hat off a hook and joined them again.

"Okay, so she said she did write a letter to Jake. I obviously can't say if it's the letter you're referring to, but I'm guessing it's the same one. So here's how it's gonna go down, and this is non-negotiable, got it? I'm coming with you and I'm going to be with her when you're talking with her. I don't care if it's something personal or secret-squirrel information that you need to know, she wants me there, so I'm going to be there. If at *any* point she wants us to go, then the three of us get up and we're out of there, no argument. Understood?"

Matt nodded. "Agreed," he said. Claire followed suit.

"I'm serious. She's the one calling the shots, and she's the one who decides how long this conversation goes, and if I feel like you're starting to badger her or she says stop, then I'll arrest you right there on the spot if you don't leave her alone."

"I understand, Sheriff," Matt said. "I appreciate you helping us with this."

"All right then, let's get going. Y'all better not make me regret doing this."

They headed out to his car. When they reached it, the sheriff looked in through the front window. "I forgot I have four boxes of files in the passenger seat. I can either move them to the trunk, or you both can just sit in the back. Your call."

"Just leave them," Matt said, desperate to move things along. "We'll sit in the back."

"Suit yourself."

Claire slid across the back seat, and Matt got in after her. A metal cage separated the front seat from the back seat with a locked pass-through in the middle of it.

The sun had completed its rounds. Before long, it would be dark.

If Matt didn't make this meeting count, he wouldn't live to see another sunset, at least not as Matt Davis.

When the sheriff started the car, a country-western song blasted from the radio, startling Claire. Wilson quickly turned it down. "Sorry 'bout that. I suppose that might be part of why I'm a little hard of hearing."

They drove through town to some song about drinking too much, the volume now low but still audible. Claire reached over and took hold of Matt's hand while looking out the window on her side of the car. The stores around the city square had closed up shop for the day, and the town was settling in for another quiet evening. Matt watched where they were going, trying to guess their destination. Once Wilson turned onto one of the country roads, Matt gave up trying to figure it out.

"Sheriff, can you give me a sense of what Jake did to this woman, so I'm better prepared to speak with her?"

Wilson didn't answer. Matt didn't know if the sheriff hadn't heard or if the music was louder in the front.

"Sheriff? I'm wondering how it is—"

"I heard you, son. Best you hear it from her. It's too complicated to explain in the short amount of time we're going to be in the car, but soon as you meet her, you'll understand."

TWENTY-SEVEN

Wilson hooked a left onto a dirt path and put the car in park. Five feet in front of them, a barbed wire gate gave access through the fence that ran alongside the road.

"Want me to get that, Sheriff?" Matt asked, reaching for the door handle but not finding one.

"I got it. Those doors don't open from the inside. Give me a sec."

He got out, the headlights illuminating his path. Like most pasture gates, it wasn't locked, but needed to be unhooked and swung open. Wilson got back in the car, drove through the gate, then got out again and shut it closed behind them.

Wilson continued driving at a slow pace along the tire tracks that extended before them, the sound of prairie grass brushing the undercarriage of his vehicle like a car wash. The car bounced softly along the uneven path, making the ride feel more like they were in a boat on a lake. A small key hanging from a chain on the rearview mirror clanged against the metal frame as it swung back and forth while the car made its way down the bumpy path.

Matt peered out the front window as they drove further into a cow pasture. It wasn't unusual for ranches to be located in a field, but they were typically built closer to the road, and everything was dark up ahead. Matt glanced over at Claire, who had the same questioning expression.

"Sheriff," Claire said. "Who lives out here?"

"Nobody. It's just a cow pasture. Part of Roland Jenkins's acreage, but since he landed in the nursing home after his stroke, nobody grazes cattle here."

"I don't understand," Matt said.

"Then let me explain it to you in plain language, boy. You should have minded your own business and left the rest of us the hell alone. Instead, you drag Claire into this with your questions about that letter and your asshole brother and her threats about dragging the judge into it. That's what pisses me off more than anything. Goddammit!"

Wilson whacked the steering wheel in anger. He glared at Claire in the rearview mirror.

"And you, little miss, you shouldn't have been so stubborn about letting Bone deal at the Creek. We never would have let it get out of control."

"We?" Claire asked, her fingers turning white as she gripped the cage.

Wilson sighed. "I don't expect you to understand, but meth was bound to steamroll through Hatchett one way or the other. There wasn't a thing anyone could do to keep it out, so I inserted myself into the equation early to keep it under control."

"Keep it under control, my ass," Matt said. "You're in it for the money like everybody else. You even told me you were the only person I should trust since there was so much money involved. You're nothing but a scumbag meth dealer."

"Watch your mouth, boy! I doubt you would know this, but it's stayed clear of the schools. I've got rules. If there's meth in my town, it's going to be controlled. And just to set the record straight, I didn't say I was the only person you should trust. What I told you was not to trust anybody, which I think you'd now agree was some pretty sound advice."

They came up over a small hill and saw Bone's Hummer parked about thirty yards from a pond, its owner leaning against it, smoking a cigarette. Matt realized who the sheriff had really called back in his office.

The full moon illuminated a large cluster of trees several hundred feet from the pond. Wilson parked his car closer to the lake than Bone's and shut off the engine.

"The letter," Matt said. "I'm assuming you wrote it, given you knew the part about the scars."

"I did. I figured if anyone from the state came in to investigate, it'd throw 'em off the scent."

"You purposely used what I said to Jake," Claire said. "You were trying to set me up! What else were you gonna do, Sheriff? Plant the murder weapon behind my bar?"

"Depended on whether or not you changed your mind about letting Bone deal there."

"So who shot Jake?" Matt said. "You or Bone?"

"Shit, I wouldn't trust that bag of wingnuts to pick up my laundry.

I did it because it needed to be done, and it was also a message to Bone letting him know I wasn't screwing around. But Jake brought it on himself. Acting like he was some sort of partner of mine. Shit. Sometimes bad things happen to bad people."

Wilson reached under his seat and pulled out a holster and revolver. He got out of the car, then opened Claire's door. At first, she didn't move, but Wilson gestured with the gun for her to get a move on. He told her to stand in front of the car, then turned back to Matt.

"You slide on over here, but you best do what I tell you or Claire's going to be feeling some pain."

Matt got out and stood next to Claire.

"Head on over to Bone. Let's make this quick."

Instinctively, Matt and Claire held hands, then walked toward Bone, Wilson following close behind. Bone's face lit up in a big shit-eating grin upon seeing Matt and Claire headed his way.

"Well, well, well. If it isn't Mr. Big City and his bitch girlfriend."

"Shut up, Bone," Wilson said. "If you'd done your job, we wouldn't be in this mess."

The smile fell from Bone's face, but he continued eyeballing Matt, letting him know who controlled this dance now.

Wilson directed them to the edge of the pond, then he and Bone stepped back, Wilson still holding the revolver by his side.

"So what's the story going to be on this one, Sheriff?" Claire asked. "Hunting accident? Murder-suicide? Whatever it is, you're not smart enough to pull it off."

"Hard to say what story we'll come up with, Claire, since y'all caught me off guard, but given Matt's history of disappearing, and seeing as how you've been sniffing around him like a cat in heat, people will probably assume the two of you simply up and ran off together. Maybe a letter will even appear to that effect on your refrigerator. But I'll tell you one thing: it's a hell of a lot easier getting away with something when you're the one investigating it."

"If you go with writing another letter, try to spell the words right, otherwise people will figure you wrote it," she said.

The sheriff chuckled. "Fightin' till the end. I admire that. It's a shame it had to come to this, but business is business, and unfortunately for you, this is an unforgiving business." Wilson gazed up at the full moon and all but sighed. "Either of you have anything you want to say before we call it a night?"

Matt turned to Claire. "I never wanted you to be hurt."

"I know, but if it has to happen, I'd rather be next to you."

Bone turned and spit. "Christ, Sheriff, if you don't shoot 'em soon, I might get sick."

Matt wished they'd get it over with. If Claire weren't beside him, he'd not only be ready to die, he'd put his mouth over the barrel of the gun to make sure Wilson didn't miss. But she was now a part of this, and it especially grieved him that she was going to be killed because of him. He wanted more than anything to keep her from being hurt—he just didn't know how.

Static suddenly deafened Matt and made him dizzy. It grew louder by the second, like a fast-moving thunderstorm. At first, he instinctively tried blocking it, but Claire's presence—and her safety—made him change course. He had fears of what this could mean in the long term, but the only question he had right then was whether or not he could protect Claire, so he took a bulldozer to his mental wall, letting the connection grow from analog to digital to high-speed fiber optic as he mentally screamed for Jake to take the reins. As he felt the connection getting stronger, it made him suddenly fold in half in gut-wrenching pain.

Wilson flinched, then relaxed as he watched Matt grimace.

"Doesn't surprise me you're a user," Wilson said, "but I didn't realize you was so bad off. Guess I'll be putting you out of your misery."

Wilson raised his pistol and pointed it at Matt. Claire took hold of his hand and closed her eyes tight, her face clenched in anticipation of the shot.

Wilson pulled the trigger, but as the bullet soared through the chamber, a crow dive-bombed the space between Matt and the bullet. Upon the bullet's impact, feathers and small organ parts flew through the air, some of them hitting Wilson in the face. The crow's body dropped to the ground like a wet sandbag between Wilson and Matt.

Bone's eyes shot open wide as quarters as he let out a whoop. "Oh my god, are you kidding me? That weren't like no crow I ever seen!" He pointed at the bird to clarify, as if somehow maybe no one else had noticed.

The sheriff shook his head as we wiped his face with his sleeve.

"Well I'll be. Wish I could tell this story when we leave, but of course, that ain't going to happen." He turned toward his lackey. "Is it, Bone?"

"Nope. Not gonna tell no one, but still, you gotta admit. Whoa!"

Wilson returned his attention to the two people about to be assassinated, but seemed surprised to see Matt standing straight, his chest puffed out, his eyes like lasers, glaring at his killers with complete confidence.

"If it isn't the fat coward, Wee Willy," Matt said, his voice harsher and more hostile than usual. Claire looked over at Matt, uncertain as to what was happening.

"Wha . . . What'd you call me?" Wilson demanded.

"Acting like you're some sort of businessman doing right by the town, but you're nothing but a thug. Why don't you tell them about that fifteen-year-old girl you snuffed out because she made a joke about you being the ringleader of the meth trade? She was only kidding, but you were too scared to take a chance. Were you protecting the youth then, too?"

Bone looked at Wilson, confused.

Wilson stared at Matt, appearing to vacillate between anger and fear. "How . . . how do you . . . your brother write you a note or something?"

"A note? A note! How about a video on my phone of you shooting her?" Matt said with a laugh that could only emanate from the underground. "Besides, why send a note when you can say it in person?" Matt's body went rigid, as if he were experiencing a seizure.

As Wilson once again extended his pistol, a second form began pulling itself away from Matt. Everyone watched, stunned, as Matt appeared to split in half, one organism dividing into two, like some sort of macabre magic trick. The second body emerged slowly, making a sucking sound like boots walking in deep mud as it pulled itself away from Matt's side.

Jake finally freed himself and stood next to Matt, a little unsteady at first. Now there were two of them, exact copies of each other, standing side by side.

Twin brothers, together again.

TWENTY-EIGHT

Jake's body was significantly decomposed when he first pulled himself free, but within seconds he became more solid, though a section of the back of his head remained missing, having been blown away by Wilson's gun during his murder.

His T-shirt and jeans, stained with blood, clung to him so tightly they looked like part of his skin. He wiped a sticky substance from his hair, stumbled a step or two to the side as he continued working to find his balance, then eventually straightened up and grinned at Sheriff Wilson.

"What up, Willy? Miss me?"

Wilson and Bone could only stare.

"What's the matter?" Jake asked. "Something behind me?"

Without moving the rest of his body, Jake rotated his head until he faced the complete opposite direction. Then he continued rotating it until it had turned 360 degrees. "Don't see anything back there, so you must be looking at me. Good to see you again, boys!"

Bone spewed the contents of his stomach onto the ground.

"Hey, show a little class, man." Jake said before spitting a small puddle of blood from his own mouth that struck the ground with a spark.

Jake's stench filled the pasture, and Matt could feel heat radiating from him like a wood stove. The grass beneath Jake's feet shriveled and died every time he took a step.

Sheriff Wilson looked dumbstruck at what stood before him, but he quickly snapped back to reality, questionable though it was. He raised his gun, gripping it firmly with both hands. He fired a bullet into Jake's chest, but it passed through as if Jake were vapor. The sheriff gaped in disbelief, then let loose with two more shots aimed at Jake's head, the first bullet whizzing through his forehead, the second penetrating his right eyeball. He might as well have been firing at a cloud.

"Oh, come on, Willy. You can do better than that, can't you? Or do you need to be standing right behind me to do any real damage?"

The sheriff, panicked, took aim once again, but as Jake held up his hand, the sheriff lost control of his arm.

"Hold up there, Wee Willy," Jake said as he looked at the crow that had been shot. "I can't remember whether you've shot four or five times, but you need to save at least one bullet. I wouldn't dream of having all the fun and not sharing it with you."

Jake stared intently at Wilson. The gun in Wilson's hand started turning toward his own head. Wilson grunted as he resisted, sweat quickly appearing on his forehead partly from his effort to resist whatever was controlling him, and partly out of fear. He fought his own arm, tried straightening it, lowering it, rotating it in the opposite direction, but his elbow kept bending and his wrist remained resolute and firm until the barrel pointed directly at his mouth. His fingers trembled as he tried opening his grip to drop the gun, but to no avail.

"No," Wilson pleaded. "Jake, please, don't. I'm begging you."

"Now, Sheriff, I didn't cry and plead with you when you shot my brains all to hell. Course you never gave me a chance, did you? At least I've got the balls to look you right in the eye."

"Bone! Help me, goddammit! Push the gun away!" But Bone couldn't move. Whether Jake was keeping him from moving or he remained frozen out of sheer fright, Matt couldn't tell, but the piss running down Bone's leg argued for the latter.

Wilson inserted the barrel into his mouth, a millimeter at a time, until he gagged. Claire turned her head.

Jake's grin evaporated. "See you in Hell, Sheriff. And I do mean that literally."

Wide-eyed, Wilson pulled the trigger, blowing a sizable hole out the back of his head. He remained standing for a couple of seconds like a cartoon character, smoke slithering out the back of his head, then he crumbled toward Bone, who finally found his legs and jumped out of the way. A pool of blood quickly formed from the gaping hole in Wilson's skull.

Claire put her hand over her mouth, muffling a sob, then pressed her face against Matt's shoulder.

Jake glanced at Matt.

"See what we can do with ultimate power, bro? And if you think that was cool, wait'll you see what I got in store for my good buddy Bone." He slowly turned his attention to Bone, who panted like an abused dog about to be kicked.

"Jake," Bone said, "I didn't have nothing to do with you getting killed. You know I'd never be a part of that. Like you just said, we're friends."

"Friends? You told Willy it was either you or me. Fortunately for you, I was the smarter one, so the good sheriff decided to keep the braindead dumbass around 'cause he knew you'd never pose a threat to him. Friends? Shit. If you had even one ball, you'd have taken me out yourself. And correct me if I'm wrong, Bonehead, but you were getting ready to watch Willy gun down my brother." Jake's voice grew violent as he spoke until he shouted so loud it sounded like twelve voices screeching at once. "My brother!"

The rustle of hundreds of crows filled the air, so numerous they blocked out the moon that shone through the trees. The chorus of their caws drowned out all other sounds. Matt saw the already dark treetops all but disappear as more and more birds flew to the branches, the trees undulating with movement and sound.

"You shouldn't have hit my brother, Bone."

"I'm sorry, Jake," Bone cried.

"Yeah, well, 'sorry' just won't cut it. But hey, Bone, you always enjoyed a good laugh. You know what they call a bunch of crows?"

Bone looked at Jake with a barely detectable trace of optimism, trying to force a smile as though they were just shooting shit again at the bar.

"No, what?"

"A murder. A murder of crows. Pretty ironic, don't you think?"

Jake lifted his hand and a sudden thunder of wings filled the air. Bone whirled around and saw an enormous black cloud of crows flying directly at him, a wave of darkness sweeping across the night sky. He turned and ran, but before he could get to his Hummer, the birds descended upon his body, dive-bombing again and again until he collapsed onto the ground. He thrashed at them, trying to fend them off, but they pecked relentlessly at his arms, hands, neck, and torso. One beak finally broke through to Bone's jugular. As he reached up in a futile attempt to stanch the bleeding, four birds attacked his face with razor-sharp beaks. His eyes, nose, and tongue all fell under assault.

Bone continued rolling over and over on the ground, trying to shake the birds loose, but they refused to relent. Whenever he moved his arms and hands to fight off the birds, others would focus on the newly exposed area. Before long, his T-shirt looked like a combine had shredded it.

He tried scrambling to his feet one last time to run, but the birds had blinded him. They flew into him at high speeds, knocking him to the ground once again. More birds focused on his throat, and soon Bone's screams turned into a garbled cry for help.

"What's the matter, Bone? Crow got your tongue?" Jake said.

Bone turned silent before long, the birds' frenzy slowing until they pecked calmly at bits of skin from all over his body. Then, as quickly as they came, the birds flew off and gathered again in the cluster of trees in the distance. All other sounds of nature had been silenced.

Matt and Claire turned toward Jake, who shook his head as he looked at Bone's body. He finally spit toward the corpse, although what came out of his mouth was something more gelatinous than liquid. He turned toward Matt and smiled with a "what-do-you-think-about-that" look.

"You saved our lives," Claire said.

"No," Jake said coldly. "I saved my brother's life. You're of no consequence to me whatsoever."

"Still, I appreciate it."

"Well, let's see if you still feel that way in a minute," Jake said with a malevolent chuckle.

TWENTY-NINE

Matt stepped closer to Jake. "What do you mean by that? Leave Claire alone," he demanded. He wanted to reach out and touch his brother, but something kept him from doing so. "How are you able to be here like this?"

"The connection is almost complete."

"But I don't want this."

"Trust me, you won't look back. You'll be a god. We will be gods."

"You act as if you're doing this for your brother," Claire said, "but like always, you're only interested in what it gets you."

Jake whipped around toward Claire, who reflexively took a quick step back.

"If you'd been through what I have, you'd know that that's not a small motivation. I have had every bone in my body twisted and snapped, then mended so I could experience it again, over and over. My flesh melts before my eyes, but the burning doesn't stop, like I'm some sort of damn human Duraflame log that never burns out, and those are the good days. So if you're asking if I'm happy to become part of my brother and get the hell out of Hell, then yes, Claire, yes I am."

"What happens to everyone else?" Matt asked.

"If they do as he bids, they continue living their shallow, meaningless lives. But be ruled or be slaughtered." Jake looked at Claire. "And speaking of being slaughtered . . ."

Matt stepped between Jake and Claire. "No! Why?"

"There are reasons for everything, Matt. It's time to say goodbye to your best gal. If she doesn't fight, it will be a less gruesome death than Bone's. The crows know to go for the jugular, but if she resists, they'll pick her apart until she exposes it to them."

"Jake, please. I'm asking you to spare her. I'll do whatever you need. Anything you want."

"It's a little late for that, bro. You have nothing to offer me now. The possession takes place with or without your consent. But what are you so upset about? You got what you always wanted from her, didn't you? You got to have sex with the wonderful Claire. Finally."

Jake laughed as Matt's face flushed with anger. He wanted nothing more than to pummel his brother, and if Claire's safety wasn't at risk, he would have lunged at Jake regardless of whether his brother was already dead.

"Oh yeah, even in Hell, I could experience your ecstasy at finally being inside of her," Jake said. "So very exciting. Tell me, brother: is that what you felt all those years ago?"

Matt's fists tightened as his blood grew hot, his hatred all but blinding him. Jake stared at him innocently, as if truly curious, then spoke in a mock stage whisper. "She's a good lay, isn't she? Definitely one of the best we've had."

Matt moved toward Jake, but Claire grabbed his shoulder, stopping him. He saw the realization wash over her.

"It wasn't you, was it? All those years ago. It was Jake. He made me think he was you."

She started to tremble as she looked first at Matt, then down at the ground as she tried to absorb it all. She looked back up at Matt and put her hand on his cheek.

"That's why you left suddenly. Why you cut off communication."

Matt looked away from her, ashamed to make eye contact. He nodded.

"I knew you didn't know. I wasn't trying to punish you. It's just that it shattered me. I loved you so much, but I thought it was better if you didn't know. But I also didn't know how to go forward, knowing what Jake had done."

Claire took hold of Matt's hand and held it tight. "I'm so sorry. I'm sorry you had to go through that. I'm sorry you had a brother who would do that to you." She then turned to Jake. "You disgust me, but I'm used to dealing with men who are hateful. Hell, I was raised by a man who didn't have a compassionate bone in his body, so I will not be broken by a coward like you. But you had a brother who loved you, and you did this to him."

Matt turned back to Jake. "Tell me why you want to kill Claire. Haven't you already done enough to me? What can you possibly gain from it?"

"I don't answer to you, Matt. Never have, never will. I do what I want, and this is what I want."

The crows began rustling again in the trees, their wings flapping restlessly, awaiting the signal for take-off.

"You can have my body, my soul, whatever you need, but leave Claire out of it. Why should she have to die?"

Claire was the one who answered.

"Because you're the one who needs to forgive him. What he did to me was beyond vile, but I didn't know it was him. You did. You're the one who has been living with that hatred for all these years. Your own brother. He did something so heinous to you, and now he needs to kill me to make sure you never forgive—"

"Shut up!" Jake roared in a voice that echoed to the heavens and back. He glowered at Claire then raised his arms, swirling them madly. At his signal, crows rocketed out of the trees like winged black missiles. Matt screamed at Jake to make them stop, but his brother's focus remained solely on the birds.

Matt scanned the area for a place of safety for Claire. He grabbed her hand and spun her around violently. "Run for the sheriff's car!"

She shot off toward the car as the birds closed in. When she got within ten yards of it, Jake pointed his hand at her. Her legs froze in place. She turned and saw the birds closing in.

Matt wheeled Jake towards him and wrapped his hands around Jake's throat. Claire regained control of her body and continued racing toward the car, the distance between her and the birds fading with every step.

One of the lead birds careened off her head as she grasped for the front door. The bird drew blood, but Claire managed to fall inside and slam the door as scores of crows began crashing into the windshield and side windows.

Birds started pecking at the windshield, chipping away at the glass, while others continued bombarding the car at full speed, their bodies breaking as they pummeled the steel more forcefully than baseball bats.

Matt sprinted toward the car, but Jake's words stopped him. "You can't stop it, Matt. There's nothing you can do."

Matt turned back. "What happened to you, Jake? How did you get to this point?"

"I didn't think you would leave me. It was a joke. Sure, maybe a really sick joke, but to just up and leave? Abandon Mom and me? I wanted what you had. I wanted to experience it."

Matt realized Claire was right. His life had been torn apart by what Jake did, and when he thought back to the act of betrayal, he couldn't help but feel immense anger. Seeing what Jake was trying to do to Claire brought out of him the same primal rage he experienced when fighting Bone.

Then he remembered the warning from Skiz. The man who could communicate with the dead told him the evil he would be battling fed on hate. It needed hate. That's why Jake needed to kill Claire. To ensure Matt's hatred. And if Jake was successful in killing her, then he would have it.

Matt suddenly saw something in Jake he'd never seen before: vulnerability. He realized now that Jake regretted what he had done, but stubbornly remained too proud to admit it.

The birds pecked larger and larger holes in the windshield, the largest crow using its beak like a jackhammer. Matt saw that several dozen crows had now managed to squeeze their heads partway through the holes in the windshield, their beaks snapping at Claire maniacally. He saw her punch and fight back, but he knew she wouldn't be able to hold them off much longer. The glass was already starting to cave.

He saw her look at the backseat, but the steel barrier blocked her from it. She tried opening the passage in the middle of the cage, but it was locked. She looked frozen, as if she'd run out of options.

"The rearview mirror," Matt shouted. "I saw a key hanging from it."

He saw her look and find the key on a chain. As she reached for it, one of the birds reached far enough through one of the holes in the windshield to peck at her hand. She finally managed to grab the key, losing small pieces of flesh in the process. Matt wanted to run to the car to help her, but he knew there was nothing he could do there to stop the attack.

Matt held his breath as larger pieces of glass started falling onto the dashboard. He silently cheered her on as she inserted the key and unlocked the cage door. As she turned and began squeezing herself through the narrow opening, one of the crows had pecked a hole in the windshield large enough to get through. It started pecking at her feet as she was almost all the way through the metal wall.

She kicked at the bird, knocking it back against the windshield, but the force of her foot accelerated the collapse of the glass.

"Hurry!" Matt cried out.

Claire got all the way through to the back seat and slammed the metal door shut right as the windshield collapsed. Crows poured into the front seat like a black flood of water. They pecked and screeched and flung themselves against the metal cage, but since it was built to withstand a large man kicking at it, Matt knew the birds had no chance. He could hear the car filling with deafening bird cries, like some sort of macabre fire alarm.

Crows started flying to the back windshield and the back side windows, once again chipping away at the glass. Matt knew it wouldn't take them long to breach the back window, at which point Claire would have nowhere else to go.

Matt again started toward the car but stopped. He turned to Jake, who had a forced smile on his face. It looked like this wasn't something Jake wanted to do; it was something he felt he had to do. He wanted to make sure Matt could never forgive him, and he knew this would do it.

Matt realized he had let Jake down, having behaved like the eighteen-year-old he was. He had grown older, matured, yet never reached out to his brother, abandoning him instead to life as a meth dealer in Hatchett, Nebraska. He had cut himself off from the person with whom he had always been so close.

Matt took hold of Jake's wrist. The skin peeled beneath his hand, making it slippery, but he maintained his grip. Jake flinched as if ready to fight Matt, then tried pulling his hand back, but Matt wouldn't let go. Matt put his other hand on top of Jake's and squeezed it.

"I'm sorry, Jake," Matt said softly. "I'm sorry for what I did to you. For abandoning you."

Jake jerked his hand back, layers of his skin fluttering to the ground, then kicked out at Matt.

"Why the hell are you sorry? I'm the one who screwed your girlfriend. And she liked it, Matt. She liked it."

Matt saw the desperation in Jake. He was like a scared little boy striking out because he'd never learned any other way to behave.

"And now I'm going to kill her. I'm going to have these crows pick apart her flesh." He raised both hands and even more crows flew from the trees. They shot across the field and began dive-bombing the back windshield like a never-ending squadron of kamikaze pilots.

The back windshield started caving in under the birds' unrelenting attack. Matt saw Claire turn around and press her hands against the glass, as if she could maintain its protection, even though she had to know it was only a matter of seconds before it broke apart.

"I understand why you did it, Jake, all those years ago. You were lonely. You felt like I had abandoned you to spend time with Claire. Did you think it was her idea for us to leave Hatchett?"

"I just thought she'd be good in bed, Matt. That's all. And she was."

"I'm sorry, Jake. I really am. I've held on to all of this for far too long."

"No!" Jake screamed. "You're only doing it to save her. You don't mean it. You can't."

"I do mean it. We should have talked about this years ago. I'm responsible for that. I can't even begin to describe what your betrayal felt like to me, how completely devastated I was, but I need to let this anger go, as much for my sake as yours. It's been destroying me, Jake. It has been for years, and I've been unable to move on from it, but it's time that I do."

Jake grabbed Matt's arm.

"Stop it! This won't get me out of Hell, Matt. It won't! All you'll do is break our connection. Don't send me back there! Please! I'll let Claire live. I promise! Just don't condemn me. It said your forgiveness wouldn't release me."

"What if it lied to you, Jake? I can only pray it did. Its entire existence is built on lies. But it's time our connection was broken. You died. I'll pray for your soul. I hope you can forgive me."

Jake stepped back, his eyes staring at Matt in disbelief, crimson tears of blood pouring from his eyes. He began sobbing.

"You don't know what it's like!" Jake cried. "I'm begging you, please don't send me back there. I'm sorry for what I did to Claire. To you. I'm sorry. I just wanted things back the way they were. I didn't want anyone coming between us. I didn't think you'd leave me like you did. I love you, Matt. Please don't abandon me again. Please don't leave me."

Matt stepped forward and wrapped his brother tightly in his arms. Jake tried pushing him away, but Matt held him close.

"I'm sorry, Jake. I'm so sorry for hanging on to my anger. I'm sorry for everything. You're my brother. I love you. I've missed you." Matt pulled Jake even closer. "And I forgive you."

The birds abruptly stopped flying into the windshield, and those that had been pecking suddenly stopped, like they'd awakened from a trance. They departed simultaneously, as if a shotgun had fired, fleeing in different directions.

Jake slowly vaporized until Matt was left with his arms wrapped around himself. Silence replaced the soft, white noise that had previously filled his head. He chose to fill it with prayers that Jake had been released from Hell.

Matt turned to the sheriff's car. Claire's face was pressed against the side window, looking at him, a small trickle of blood running down her right cheek. She tried getting out of the car but couldn't open the back door, so she leaned back in the seat and wiped the blood off her face with her shirtsleeve.

Wilson's revolver lay on the ground next to the pool of his blood. Matt picked it up, weighing it in his hand, studying it. He opened the chamber and saw that one live bullet remained. He closed the chamber, then slowly walked over to the car, finger on the trigger.

The enormous crow remained, still perched atop the car by itself, staring at Matt. It shifted its weight from claw to claw, as if ready to take flight. Matt stopped three feet from the car and watched the bird. Its eyes occasionally took on a red tint, but otherwise remained lifeless. The handgun hung against Matt's side.

The crow let out a manic, ear-piercing shriek and took off. As it lifted into the air, Matt raised the revolver and fired at the crow, hitting it square. Feathers sprayed into the air, but instead of falling, the bird continued flying ten more yards before exploding into a ball of fire.

Matt let the gun drop from his hand, then opened the car door. Claire remained still until he held out his hand. She took it and slid out. Dead crows covered the roof, hood, and trunk of the car, as well as the ground. She stepped over the carcasses, then kicked one of them as hard as she could, releasing a quick outburst of anger.

Matt drew her close. She wrapped her arms around his waist and rested her head on his shoulder. Matt continued holding her tight, feeling the warmth from her body, never wanting to let her go.

Jake was right about one thing: if he had killed Claire, Matt would never have forgiven him, regardless of what it meant for anyone else. His hatred would have known no bounds. But he now also knew he had held on to his anger long enough. All of what had happened in his life had stemmed from that.

As the remaining crows flew away from the trees, no longer acting as one collective, the Nebraska night sounds resurfaced. The frogs and crickets made their presence known, while the neon glow of fireflies reflected off the dark water like tiny spirits. The only silence was in Matt's head. Their connection had been severed.

For good.

He gazed toward the heavens at the infinite Midwest night sky with its thousands of stars. There were no clouds to hide the glittering lights shining down on them from one horizon to the other, as if someone had placed a star-filled bowl over the pasture. He imagined one of the stars being Jake's soul.

Matt thought back to his childhood, when he and Jake would lie on their backs in their yard and gaze up at the night sky as the tree frogs and the occasional cow lowing in the distance filled the air with the soundtrack of a Nebraska summer night. On those evenings, while Jake talked about whatever had happened to him that day, Matt pondered the thousands of galaxies and the billions of miles between him and all the stars above, making him feel insignificant, and lost.

But tonight, gazing up at the tiny points of light, he was overwhelmed by their beauty. And in the arms of the woman he loved, he no longer felt lost. He knew he finally had a place in the world.

He had a new connection.

ACKNOWLEDGMENTS

I greatly appreciate the support and kind words from my family (whether by blood . . . the Cordells . . . or through marriage . . . the Sallwassers), and from my friends who reached out in one way or another to offer enthusiastic encouragement following my first novel, Contempt. It's partially your fault that another novel now exists.

A sincere note of thanks to the early readers of Our Trespasses, who provided me with thoughts, suggestions, questions, and reactions. They include Holly Auten, Donna Spearman, Richard Thomas, Randall Klein, Melinda Lee, and Carrie Brownhill. You all contributed to this story.

A special call-out to another early reader, Don Davis, teacher extraordinaire, friend extraordinaire-ier, and human being extraordinaire-iest. You've touched so many lives with your kindness and your enthusiasm.

An extra-bright spotlight continues to shine on Anne McAneny who is always generous with her extraordinarily detailed line edits, ideas, encouragement, experience, random acts of support, and sarcasm (but in a helpful way—usually). She is most often my go-to fellow writer to whom I turn when I hit a writing wall.

Thanks to my weekly Zoom author group (David, Rochelle, Shai, Don, and Angelina). You all have been a welcomed lifeline of human connection and friendship, especially during a year of self-quarantining.

I also want to acknowledge the small Nebraska town where I grew up, which shares some similarities of the town in this novel. I'm hopeful that the good parts of my hometown come through in this story. The darker parts (the drug issues, the violence, the dying town, etc.) are completely made up . . . at least as far as I'm aware . . . since a story must have conflict, you know. I have a lot of love for my childhood town.

And finally, as always, a special thank you to my wife, Kate, who belongs in all of the above categories (except for being part of my hometown): she's encouraging, an early reader, extraordinarily supportive, and a treasured lifeline. You are the stars in my night sky.

ABOUT THE AUTHOR

Michael Cordell is a novelist, playwright, and produced screenwriter. His first novel, *Contempt*, was a Top 10 Amazon Kindle legal thriller. He has sold three screenplays to Hollywood, including *Beeper*, an action-thriller starring Harvey Keitel. Michael currently lives in Charlottesville, Virginia, where he has taught screenwriting for over fifteen years.

CONNECT WITH MICHAEL CORDELL

Sign up for Michael's newsletter at
www.michaelcordell.com/newsletter

To find out more information visit his website:
www.michaelcordell.com

Facebook:
www.facebook.com/michaeljcordell

BOOK DISCOUNTS AND SPECIAL DEALS

Sign up for free to get discounts and special deals
on our bestselling books at
www.TCKpublishing.com/bookdeals

CPSIA information can be obtained
at www.ICGtesting.com
Printed in the USA
LVHW112024111021
700111LV00001BA/11